MW00326004

Kudos for Clutch

"This book is absolutely hilarious!"

"LOVED. The perfect blend of sassy, smart and stylish!"

"I thought the comparison to men and handbags was so genius! Becker really knows how to write to her audience, and this clever novel had me giggling throughout."

"I adored everything about this book – the plot, characters, humor, and witty banter. The writing style was crisp, engaging, highly enjoyable, consistently entertaining, and lushly descriptive. I think I have a girl crush..."

"Clutch: a novel is a bit like Sex and the City meets Fifty Shades of Grey sprinkled with a bit of Bridget Jones' Diary. It is a fun and light hearted read and highly enjoyable."

"The writing is simple yet smart and detailed...If you are looking for a sweet and sexy romance, then Clutch is for you."

"Clutch is a quick and entertaining read about a woman looking for her one true love. I had so much fun reading Caroline's love adventure. Never a dull moment."

"Clutch: a novel is a light, fluffy read which is a must-read if you're on the lookout for a cute, short chick-lit to devour in one sitting!"

"Clutch is a wonderful, entertaining look at the dating world and I can guarantee that you will start thinking about what category of bag the guys you meet would fall into after reading this book. What fun!"

"Grab a bottle of Caroline's favorite wine, Chardonnay, and sit back and enjoy this fun dating tale!"

"As with the Click series, Becker writes good characters, with great, witty dialogue."

Also by Lisa Becker

The Click Trilogy
Click: An Online Love Story
Double Click
Right Click

Links

Clutch

a novel

Lisa Becker

For SJB – my clutch
With gratitude to KP

Table of Contents

"Woman should have a purse of her own."

Susan B. Anthony

Getting Purse-onal

*m*imi Johnson was casually dressed in a brightly-colored blouse with enormous turquoise jewelry and equally-oversized glasses. Despite that largesse, the only thing truly bigger than her personality (and her bosom) was her handbag. Always perfectly matched to her clothing, shoes, and jewelry, she was like a walking Chico's advertisement, if you added forty years, forty pounds, and a Virginia Slims cigarette. From her Mary Poppins-like bag, she pulled out a box, impeccably-wrapped in glossy pink paper with a white grosgrain ribbon bow. A cigarette teetered between her two fingers while she produced a lung-hacking cough.

"Open it… *<cough, cough>* …sweetie. Open it," she said to her seven-year-old great niece, Caroline, a beautiful and vibrant girl with long blonde hair and oversized blue eyes.

Alive with anticipation, sweet young Caroline eagerly took the box and smiled up at Mimi. She gingerly removed the ribbon, planning to save it for later. The glossy paper was of less interest and she ripped through it quickly. She opened the box and gently lifted out a hot pink purse, adorned with pale pink flowers and rhinestones. An enormous smile overcame her. Caroline nearly set her own hair on fire from Mimi's cigarette as she bounded into her aunt's arms.

"Oh, thank you, Aunt Mimi. It's lovely."

And that was when Caroline's love of handbags began. From big and loud ones that would make Mimi proud to unimposing wristlets, from bowler bags to satchels; it didn't matter if they were made of canvas or calf-skin leather, were distressed or embellished with metal studs. Hell, she didn't care if you called them pocketbooks or purses. She just loved them all – almost as much as she loved Mimi.

By the time she was a junior in high school and well on her way to being class valedictorian, it was the hundreds of bags Caroline owned that helped her conceptualize her ticket out of her suffocating small Georgian town. She would design handbags. And it was Mimi who was her steadfast cheerleader.

"Caroline, sweetie… *<cough, cough>* …you find something you love and you just hold onto it." It had never mattered if Caroline was asking Mimi's advice about a friend, lover, or career. The advice was always the same: "Find something you love and hold onto it."

Mimi's words ever-present in her mind, Caroline headed to the Fashion Institute of Design and Merchandising and spent four years in Los Angeles learning everything there was to know to pursue her passion. Then, right out of college, she spent three years working in the design and marketing departments of two of the world's leading, high-end handbag designers.

She was schooled in beauty and how to accessorize the perfectly-coiffed women on the way to their Botox appointments. But Caroline was pulled by the nagging feeling that the very person who had inspired her career, Mimi, could never afford the bags she designed, even if Caroline used her generous employee discount on Mimi's behalf. And God forbid Mimi would ever accept one as a gift, always preferring to give rather than receive. But Caroline believed there was no reason for anyone to be denied the ultimate in accessories. She saw an untapped market of designing beautiful and affordable bags, but she just wasn't sure she was start-up potential. Again, it was Mimi who nudged her to learn the business side of things and apply to MBA programs. When Caroline was accepted to Harvard Business School, Mimi, of course, encouraged her.

"You've got this, sweetie. *<cough, cough>*," she said. "It's in the bag."

•　　•　　•

Caroline was sitting in Financial Reporting and Control on her first day of Harvard classes (and yes, the class turned out to be as boring as it sounded). That's when she first eyed Mike, who was wearing a faded pair of Levi jeans, a washed-out vintage Rolling Stones T-shirt, and Converse sneakers. He oozed charisma. Turning her head away from him and back toward the front of the lecture hall, Caroline thought that if he were a handbag, he would be a grey leather tote – confident and dependable, but not trying too hard.

Mike surveyed the large lecture hall as he walked in, a Starbucks coffee cup in each hand. After descending the steps slowly, he took a seat next to Caroline and planted one of the white and green cups on her desk.

Flashing a wide, dimpled smile, which she mused he reserved for getting girls to drop their panties, he said, "Here. You look like you're going to need this."

"Thanks," she replied in a suspicious tone, turning her head sideways to look at him and raising an eyebrow.

"I'm Mike," he said, again flashing a smile and reaching out for a handshake.

"I'm Caroline. Thanks for the…"

"Latte."

"Latte," she confirmed. "Thanks. But just so you know, I'm not gonna sleep with you," she said in an apparent attempt to establish up front she wasn't taken in by his obvious charm.

"I know," he replied matter-of-fact.

Before she could respond, Professor Beauregard, a stout man with excessive eyebrows, spoke up. "Please take note of where you are seated. I will send around a seating chart for you to mark your spot. This will be your seat for the remainder of the semester."

"Looks like we'll be seatmates," Mike said, grinning at her.

"Looks like it."

•   •   •

About three months into the first semester, Caroline learned that her fun-loving, easy-going, new best buddy Mike wasn't exactly who he appeared to be.

A blanket of white snow dusted the Harvard grounds and it was a particularly slow day in another mutual class, LEAD – Leadership and Organizational Behavior. Professor Moss, a frail man who weighed less than his years, was droning on and on about establishing productive relationships with subordinates or something to that effect. He initiated a discussion about what works better – the carrot or stick approach.

"Mr. Barnsworth," he called, referring to his seating chart and scanning the room until he found Mike in the fifth row. "What are your thoughts?"

"Well, it seems to me that good management is all about empathy and being able to enthuse and inspire your staff. You know, appreciating them and respecting them. Showing you care," he said, placing his hand over his heart in a gesture of true compassion and concern. "And if they can't get that through their thick skulls, you fire 'em," he continued, drawing his finger across his throat.

Several students sitting around them started to chuckle while Caroline stifled a laugh. Mike looked around the room and nodded his head, soaking in the appreciation of his sense of humor.

"Mr. Barnsworth," said Professor Moss in a menacing tone, "I would have expected a better answer from you, considering your family history."

Confused by the conversation unfolding before her, Caroline leaned over and whispered to Mike, "What is he talkin' about?" Mike put up a hand to quiet her.

"Later," he hissed.

Twenty minutes later, the two shared a bench outside Baker Library, the chill of winter causing Caroline to pull her scarf closer around her neck.

"What was that all about?" she asked, scrunching up her nose in confusion.

Reluctantly, Mike began to speak. "My full name is Michael Frederick Barnsworth the Third. My family owns a large brokerage firm in New York," he confessed, unsure of how Caroline would react.

Caroline listened as she took in just how old money his family really was. Mike's great, great, great, great – actually it was hard to keep track of how many "greats" it went back – grandfather ran the first Bank of the United States, which Congress chartered in the early 1800s. His family had advised presidents, dined with royalty, and amassed a fortune that continued today through the Barnsworth Brokerage Firm.

"I'm the seventh person in my family to attend Harvard including my father, uncle, three cousins, and grandfather, who was a classmate of Professor Moss," he continued.

Surprised by this unexpected news, she joked, "So you're just slummin' with a simple Southern girl like me – and makin' me pay for drinks, mind you – until you go join the family business and marry someone named Muffy…"

"That's my family's plan," Mike laughed. "There's even an office in the Woolworth Building owned by my family, sitting empty, until I finish business school," he said reluctantly.

"But…" she pressed, touching his hand gently, sensing the family plan may not actually be Mike's plan – though they had never discussed his plans before.

"I want to open a bar," he said, matter of fact and looking her square in the eye.

Caroline's head leaned back as she let out a raucous laugh. "You want to own a bar?" she questioned, her shoulders shaking from laughter. "Now I get your goal to drink at every one of the six hundred bars in Boston before you graduate."

"Yup, it's research," he said emphatically.

"Research?"

"Yeah. Every time my parents call, which isn't very often – they are usually off with their snobby society friends or at Met Balls – I tell them I'm working hard and doing research."

"Gotta give you credit. That's pretty clever," she replied, nodding her head.

"And true. If I'm going to open the best bar ever, I need to know what works and what doesn't."

"Okay. I get why you don't want to be a wizard of Wall Street. But why a bar?" she asked, not understanding his desire for the life of a bar back.

"My parents weren't around a lot growing up. My father spent more time in the office than my mother spent jetting between boutiques in Paris and ski chalets in Switzerland. And believe me, that was a lot," he confessed. Caroline looked down in her lap, her heart sinking at the thought of the small boy with the winning smile being ignored by his family.

"I was pretty much raised by a series of *au pairs*. My favorite was Linnea who was nineteen when she came from Sweden to live with our family. She was obsessed with Tom Cruise movies and we would watch them all the time," he explained, a wistful look on his face as he recalled fond memories.

"*Cocktail!*" Caroline exclaimed.

"Yup, I want to be the sole proprietor of a place where you can shake margaritas bare-chested," Mike laughed. "It's going to be called *The Last Drop*," he stated, not looking for her approval.

"Great name," she admitted, nodding her head. "Especially when your folks drop kick you out of the family."

"I know. I'm preparing to be disowned, which is why I'm getting *you* used to buying the drinks," he said, flashing her a smile.

"Well with any luck my business will allow me to continue payin' for drinks."

"The purse thing?"

"Yes. The purse thing," she said, mocking him. "I aim to start a line called Clutch, because it's one of my favorite handbag styles, and in honor of my Aunt Mimi. She always says 'Find somethin' you love and just hold onto it.'"

"Sounds like a smart lady."

•   •   •

Weeks later, the two sat in TOM – Technology and Operations Management – with Professor Lakin. He was a gruff man in his mid-fifties whose receding hairline only exaggerated the five long hairs protruding from his perpetually flared nostrils. With a reputation for being harsh, within the first few weeks of class he typically honed in on the weaker students and punished them with his confrontational style, acid tongue, and relentless antagonism. "Nice typing. Horrible writing," was a favorite expression he scrawled on top of papers that looked bloody with red ink from his ferocious comments and corrections.

Legend had it that a graduate student was once daring enough to take him on by defending her use of the word irregardless. The brave – or as some may say, foolhardy – student pulled out a copy of the Webster's dictionary, walked briskly down the lecture hall stairs, and slammed it on the table, informing Professor Lakin and the entire class that the word was indeed in the dictionary. Not missing a beat, Professor Lakin opened the thick tome and read the definition aloud: "Illiterate use of the word regardless."

Aware of his reputation, Caroline routinely took a seat toward the top of the lecture hall, hoping not to draw attention to herself. However, it was no surprise that Professor Lakin saw an easy mark in her. While she excelled in her written assignments, she never raised her hand in class, engaged in discussions, or volunteered to be a team leader on group projects. After trying to get her to explain her rationale for advocating less cross-firm integration when working through language barriers, he took aim and fired.

"Ms. Johnson," he started, his voice calm and deliberate, "let me put this in terms a blonde Southern debutante like you will understand. Continuing that line of argument would be like perfuming a pig." The classroom erupted in laughter. Mike glared at the classmates sitting around him. He took a deep breath and looked at Caroline, who unsuccessfully fought back the tears welling in her eyes.

A heated flush crept across her face as she stammered and spluttered to get any words out. Her breathing accelerated and a thin sheen of sweat beaded on her forhead as she glanced around and saw her classmates sharing grins and whispers at her expense. Mustering all of her courage, she did the most uncourageous thing of all, but the only thing she could think of – she stood up and took the stairs two at a time before pushing the door open and feeling the cold Boston air on her warm, perspiring brow.

A moment later, the door pushed open again and Mike sprang forward, turning his head left and right in a panic until he found Caroline seated nearby on a small iron bench, her head laying in her trembling hands as she sobbed. He approached her slowly and placed a gentle hand on her shaking shoulder. Seeing her like this nearly undid him, and he had to take a deep breath himself to control his anger.

"Hey," he said in a quiet tone, easing himself down next to her on the bench. "Hey," he repeated, gently lifting her head up from her hands and turning her face to his. He looked into her swollen eyes as tears continued to stream down her cheeks. "Don't let him get to you. Professor Lakin's known for being an asshole," he said, imploring her to stop crying.

Caroline pushed her tongue out of her mouth and let it rest on her lips as she shook her head and looked upward. She pulled her tongue back in and opened her mouth, about to speak, when the tears started rolling again and she dipped her head back into her hands.

"Hey. Talk to me," he said quietly, rubbing her back.

"I shouldn't be here," she sobbed.

"What do you mean, you shouldn't be here?"

"Clearly, I don't belong at Harvard," she stammered.

"Fuck Lakin," he said a tad too loudly, garnering the attention of some passing undergrads. "That guy couldn't hack it in the business world, so he came back here to teach," he said in a more measured voice.

"It's not Lakin. I'm used to people makin' fun of me for bein' Southern and assumin' I'm a ding dong," she said, playfully tapping Mike's arm as she let out a combination exhale/giggle before smiling slightly. Mike smiled down at her and squeezed her hand.

"So, what is it?" he probed. Caroline just sat there, drawing a few deep breaths before pulling her lips into her mouth as she tried regaining her composure. "C'mon. You can tell me anything."

"It's everythin'. I'm not cut out for this. I know what I want to say and I know what I think, but when I'm under pressure, I just... can't get it out."

"So you're not a debater," he said, shrugging.

"It goes way beyond that," she said, shaking her head. "It started when I was a little girl and came to a boil in high school. I was just tryin' to do the best with what God gave me," she said, pointing to her brain, her gorgeous eyes, and her ample breasts. "Not all of the other girls appreciated all that I had to work with," she said with a faint smile, "and made my life miserable."

"Well," started Mike, looking down at her breasts and raising his eyebrows. Caroline rolled her eyes. "Jealousy will do that," he said, rubbing his thumb across her knuckles.

"So I just learned to hold my tongue and avoid any sort of conflict," she sniffled.

9

"Can I ask why?" he asked kindly, looking into her eyes with concern.

"I grew up in a small town where your history and people's perceptions of you stick like white on rice."

Mike let out a small laugh at her use of the Southern expression and continued to soothingly caress her hand. Caroline let out a small giggle as he reacted to her phrase.

"It was just easier to push it all down and push it all aside," she continued. "I'm good when the goin's good, but when it turns south, I'm just a mess. I never really learned to stand up for myself and just dodge confrontations whenever possible. When a conflict is inevitable, I just... panic."

"Is there anything I can do to help?"

"No, but I appreciate knowin' you want to," she said, looking into his eyes.

"Well, if you're going to run your own business, which I know you are entirely capable of doing, you're going to need to learn to stand up for yourself and for what's right."

"My motto's gonna be 'Charm 'em and disarm 'em. Thrill 'em and bill 'em.'"

"That's all well and good and I have no doubt you'll do just that, but there are going to be times when you need to deal with shit," he advised.

"I know. I'm gonna try. Just consider me a work in progress," she said. She pursed her lips and nodded her head up and down before wiping her nose with her hand.

"Well, not everyone can be a model of perfection like me," he said, touching his hand to his chest. Caroline just shook her head back and forth, grinning.

"Feel better?" he asked, giving her a small pout and hangdog eyes.

"Actually, I do." Her mouth forming a perfect "o" as she exhaled sharply. Mike stood up and offered his hand to Caroline, who placed her fingers in his palm. He pulled her to a standing position and wrapped his arm around her, pulling her to his side while he kissed the top of her head.

"Good. Then my work here is done," he said smugly while he continued to rub her back and shoulder. "C'mon. Let's hit the mall and buy some perfume for that pig. My treat." Caroline just shook her head, sniffed loudly, and smiled.

●　　●　　●

The Boston winter snow had melted and the sun was finally shining in Cambridge. Caroline and Mike were studying for a particularly brutal statistics midterm when she finally broke the promise she had made when they first met, the promise not to sleep with him. After three hours of straight studying in Mike's spacious condo, he closed his book, rubbed his eyes, and refilled his coffee cup.

"So, this guy is flying in a hot air balloon over a beautiful countryside. But he's lost. So he lowers himself over a field and shouts to a man below, 'Hey, can you tell me where I am and which way I'm headed?' The man responds, 'Sure.'"

Caroline closed her book and looked at him quizzically, a small "v" forming between her eyes.

"'You're at 29 degrees, 6 minutes, 34 seconds north and 82 degrees, 7 minutes, 39 seconds west. You're 185 meters above sea level. You're hovering now, but on your approach, you were at a speed of 1.75 meters per second at 2.15 radians,'" he explained, reaching his arm up toward the sky.

Caroline looked at him skeptically before rubbing her temples. "What are you talkin' about?" she said with both exhaustion and exasperation.

Ignoring her question, Mike continued, "So the guy in the balloon says, 'Thanks. Are you by chance a statistician?'"

Caroline smiled, realizing that Mike was setting up a joke. She looked at him with brightened eyes, waiting for him to deliver the punch line.

"The second guy said, 'Yeah. I am. How did you know?'" Mike paused for a beat. "The first guy said, 'You've been completely accurate, given me more detail than I need, and told me in a way that is no use to me at all.'" Mike flashed a winning smile at her.

Caroline burst out laughing – a laugh that resonated deep in her belly, causing her entire body to shake. Before she knew what she was doing, she lunged across the table at him, her lips

11

and tongue completely consuming his mouth. Her hands twisted in his hair as he let out a slow moan. He too, ran his fingers through her hair, grazing her cheek and sending shivers down her spine.

Her legs straddled him as he pulled her into his lap. She could feel his erection pressing into her, working to break free of his faded blue jeans. He pulled his lips away from her mouth and trailed kisses and licks from her ear lobe down to her neck.

"Oh, God. I need this," she moaned.

"Me too," he panted.

He stood up and lifted her lithe body with his, carrying her into the bedroom, his lips never leaving her neck. He lowered her to the bed, desire pooling within him. Suddenly he stopped.

"Maybe we should…" he said, standing back, giving her the opportunity to change her mind.

"Take your pants off?" she replied, giving the belt loops on his Levi's a gentle tug. Within seconds, they were a twisted mess of naked arms and legs. As he eased himself inside her, Caroline grabbed his ass and pulled him more firmly toward her.

"You don't need to be gentle. I'm not gonna break," she whispered through labored breath.

"I know," he said, picking up the pace as his body started to possess hers. He started off slowly, but as their bodies adjusted to one another, moving in sync, he began a punishing rhythm which she matched thrust for thrust. Her hands roamed freely through his hair and down his neck and back while he continued to press his body deeper into her.

As his teeth grazed her nipple, he could feel her grip around him getting tighter, squeezing his already swollen member.

"Fuck," he muttered. "You feel so tight and wet. So. Fucking. Amazing."

"Oh, sweet lord, that feels good," she eked out between moans.

He arched his back up and his change in position only drove him deeper into a panting Caroline who wasn't sure how much more she could take. And Mike knew it. Between her trembling legs and fingers grasping at the sheet below, he knew how close to the edge she was – they both were.

"Look at me," Mike said, grasping her cheek, encouraging Caroline to open her blue eyes to meet his intense green-eyed gaze.

With one last thrust, he covered his mouth with hers, her garbled cry of pleasure mixing with his own and their intertwined tongues. They both collapsed together in a sea of sweat and heavy breath. Mike rolled off of Caroline, one arm still underneath her.

"Wow!" said Caroline, her heart racing as waves of pleasure spread throughout her body and her small frame trembled. She sat up a bit to look at him as he stroked the soft skin on her back.

"Yeah, wow," said Mike quietly, his heart beating erratically while he took deep breaths to calm his wracked body down.

"So..." said Caroline, unsure of how this would change things.

"That won't be happening again," said Mike.

"Nope. Huge mistake."

"Huge," agreed Mike as they lay intertwined together, both smiling and coming down from their moment of bliss.

It was a tension breaker that just had to be done. Despite agreeing immediately to never discuss it again, it would just come up – oh, all the time – when Mike, hoping to rile Caroline up, would remind her that she had slept with him once.

•　　•　　•

Caroline knew she had aced her last exam – retailing. The exhaustion of several weeks of late night cramming was rivaled only by the elation at having taken her last school exam ever.

As she walked into her small, one-bedroom Cambridge apartment, she saw a note folded and slid under the door. She bent down to pick it up and then looked around, wondering if she was being watched. After glancing around and seeing no one suspicious, she gave a small shrug and opened the letter up. It read:

I'm hiding in your apartment with a Nerf gun. The other is on the kitchen counter. Loser has to either cook dinner or pay. Good luck!

She looked over and saw an orange and yellow gun and a dozen darts. "Game on!" she shouted, loading the darts and pumping the air-powered hand grip. She slowly walked through the kitchen and living room on tiptoe, crouching under furniture and peering around corners like a cat burglar looking for an easy score. As she walked into her bedroom, it was over before it even began. Mike ejected himself from her bedroom closet, a Nerf gun in each hand. He looked like a movie soldier, locked and loaded. He fired a relentless stream of foam darts, assaulting Caroline and causing her to drop her gun and cover her face with her arms.

"Yes!" Mike exclaimed in triumph, raising his arms, still holding his guns, high in the air. "So," he said calmly, "what's for dinner?"

An hour later, Caroline poured the marinara sauce over the pasta as Mike tossed her freshly-made Caesar salad.

"So, I've made a big decision," he said.

"Celibacy? I don't think it's for you," she said, teasing and playfully touching his arm.

"Ha ha," he mocked, giving her an exaggerated sneer. "No, I'm being serious... for once."

"Sorry," she said, feeling chastised. "Go ahead."

"I've decided to move to L.A. I did a virtual tour of a great space today in an area called Brentwood. Lots of restaurants and yuppies with money to burn."

"Wow," she said, surprised. "That *is* a big decision."

"Do you think I'm crazy?" he asked, using a pair of silver tongs to gently place salad in bowls.

"Of course not. I'm just surprised is all. I just hadn't really thought about you movin' somewhere." She placed the plated pasta onto the placemats and handed Mike a bottle of wine to open. "I'm gonna miss you," she said thoughtfully, rubbing his shoulder, as Mike poured her a Chardonnay.

"Come with me," he said, taking a swig of wine from a stemless glass.

"Move to L.A. with you?" she asked with uncertainty.

"Yeah. I don't mean *with* me. I mean come to L.A. too."

"Well…"

"You could start your business from anywhere. You still have a ton of friends from college there and you obviously know the city," he said. "And think of all the money you'll save not having to pay for wine once the bar opens," he added, winking at her.

"Hmm. Well, that's definitely somethin' to consider." And consider Mike's offer she did, realizing that life was more fun when he was around. Caroline knew that girls were drawn to Mike because he was devilishly handsome, quick witted, and charming as hell. Guys hung out with him because he knew how to pick up girls. But she adored being with him because she never had to worry about what she said or how she acted, and he was the perfect, carefree foil to her overly accommodating personality.

•   •   •

It was more than two years ago when Caroline packed her bags – duffels, totes, shoulder bags, and purses – and ventured back to L.A. alongside her best friend Mike. While he was at the bar every night – except for Mondays when they were closed – tending bar, handling the finances, and giving out free drinks to hot girls whom he later wooed into bed, Caroline started her handbag line, *Clutch*. And business was growing. Her label was being sold in a major department store and local boutiques across the country, and a major fashion magazine had hailed her as a "40 under 40."

It was in discussing that magazine article one night that Aunt Mimi once again steered Caroline's life direction.

"You know, sweetie… <*cough, cough*> …that 'under 40' isn't going to last forever. It's time you start accessorizing your own life now."

As Caroline hung up, she knew that Mimi was right… with school, and her business start-up behind her, it was time to start designing her personal life. Much like a handbag, she believed a man was an accessory that needed to be perfectly matched. This is the true story of how she had to try out a number of different handbags to find the one she wanted to clutch – or hold onto.

Hobo

T he mob of metrosexual males and scantily-clad women in short skirts and high heels looked more like a crowd attending the latest after-hours dance club than an art exhibition. Yet they all lined up obediently to get their names checked off by the men in black suits and dark glasses who stood alongside the row of galleries in Santa Monica's artsy Bergamot Station.

Caroline noticed it would be a night of canopies and canapés, as tents from spirits and organic food sponsors dotted the outdoor plaza and waiters carrying trays of hors d'oeuvres weaved in and out of the crowd.

Caroline's golden hair was piled high and secured in a loose chignon on top of her head, small wisps falling around her cheeks in tiny ringlets. The look highlighted her elongated neck, made even lengthier by a low-cut red halter-style dress that hugged her bosom but flared out from the waist. Complementing her look was a buff-colored wristlet housing all of the night's essentials – cell phone, lip stick, ID, and cash.

Standing next to her, Mike was dressed in a pair of black pants, black pinstripe jacket, and white shirt open at the collar. He was the epitome of cool, looking calm and natural amongst the trendy crowd. But however confident and comfortable he looked, Caroline could sense his state of misery.

"Come on. It's not gonna be that bad. Kayle's gonna be here," Caroline said, brushing her hands on his lapels and trying desperately to convince Mike to stop his internal pouting and enjoy himself. She knew he'd had his eye on Kayle for quite some time now.

And what was not to like? First off, she was gorgeous. All honey-colored curls cascading down her back. And she was funny as hell. Seriously funny. She'd even taken a stand-up class last year at UCLA extension and nailed it. If anyone could get Mike to be monogamous, for a few months anyway, it would definitely be her.

"Uh…" he stuttered, a note of trepidation in his voice. She already knew where this was heading and couldn't help but look at him disapprovingly.

"You already slept with Kayle?" she asked.

"Last week," he admitted with a sly smile.

"And you didn't call her?" she said with a resigned sigh.

Mike smiled his most charming smile, all perfect white teeth, and pointed his finger at her. "Circle gets the square."

Of course he didn't call her. What was Caroline going to do with him? *And how was Kayle going to react when she saw him here? Wasn't it enough that he banged every waitress at the bar?* Did he have to "wham bam thank you ma'am" one of Caroline's best gal pals?

"What am I gonna do with you?" she said to him with a playful but exasperated tone.

"I can't help it if I'm irresistible. Remember, you slept with me–" he started.

Caroline interrupted him quickly, "Once. I know. I slept with you once."

Mike threw his head back and laughed. "What about Lydia? She's pretty hot. Will she be here?"

What? Lydia. He didn't think it was enough that he'd played love 'em and leave 'em with Kayle; now he wanted to drag Lydia into this. Seriously?

"You're incorrigible. You know that, don't you?" Caroline responded, shaking her head. *Be like the old lady who fell out of the wagon and just stay out of it,* she thought to herself. Mike just laughed more and gave her one of his "I'm-so-cute-you-can't-be-mad-at-me" winks.

After checking in with the men in black, they walked into the first of several art galleries showcasing works that evening. Caroline was quickly greeted by a group of ladies dressed in fashionable short dresses and high heels.

"Oh my God. You look so gorgeous," said Kayle. Caroline blushed.

"Oh, much obliged, but seriously, look at you. Your hair looks incredible," she responded. Lydia grabbed Caroline's wristlet.

"Is this new? What other colors does it come in? I love it," said Lydia, continuing to admire the bag and shaking her head admiringly at Caroline. "You are so talented."

Caroline blushed again. It felt good to have found her "girls." In high school, she hadn't really been part of a clique. Girls hadn't been very kind and had used every word and look like a weapon, however subtle. For example, in high school, if you didn't go to a party or other social function, the girls would say, "You missed such a great time. It was so fun." Now she had found some kindred spirits. If she missed an outing or experience, they would say, "We missed you. It wasn't as much fun as if you had been there." It was an important difference, and one that filled Caroline's heart with joy.

As Lydia continued to admire Caroline's wristlet and inquire about how she could get one from her – with the friends and family discount of course – Kayle and Mike locked eyes.

"Hi, Mike," said Kayle. She lowered her head and looked up at him with lustful eyes. Her lips parted and she slowly ran her tongue across the bottom of her front teeth. Mike flashed a smile at her.

"Hi, Kayle. Hi, Lydia." He nodded with his head, gesturing to the others. "Ladies," he greeted. The ladies looked into his warm green eyes and winning smile and giggled.

Walking toward him, her stiletto pumps tapping the gallery floor, Kayle said, "You didn't say you would call." She pulled her lips into a cross between a sly grin and a pout.

"No, I didn't," Mike replied dryly.

"I know. So I wasn't surprised," she confessed. Relief flooded over Mike, as he couldn't bear the thought of a scene, especially in front of Caroline. "Just disappointed," added Kayle, giving him a seductive and inviting smile. She turned and walked away slowly, turning back to look at him again as she went. Mike watched her with a small grin on his face.

As Mike went to grab a cocktail, Caroline walked around a corner, surveying the artwork and the chattering crowd as she went. Before her was a large white canvas, measuring about five feet wide and four feet tall. The canvas was empty save a large red circle painted in the middle.

"What are you thinking?" asked a handsome man in black skinny jeans, sneakers, a tuxedo T-shirt, and knit cap. He looked like an Urban Outfitters catalog model. Caroline was immediately attracted to him.

"I'm thinkin' this looks like the flag of Japan," she blurted out nervously, distracted by his good looks.

He gave a genuine and hearty laugh. "I could see where you would get that."

"Honestly, I just don't get it at all," Caroline admitted.

He studied her with a smile on his face. Keenly aware of his eyes on her, Caroline suddenly felt concerned that she may have offended him. "You're not the artist, are you?"

"No," he said gently. "I'm not the artist... of this piece."

"Oh, thank goodness," she said with a sigh of relief. "I would hate to have insulted you without knowin' it." Caroline had spent her entire life being guarded about what she said, always afraid to rock the boat or hurt someone's feelings. She wasn't about to start now, not with this handsome man before her.

"But I am an artist. I'm Jason. Jason Nash," he said, extending a hand to her.

"I'm Caroline Johnson," she said, lifting her hand to meet his and feeling a jolt of electricity as their skin connected. "I apologize for bein' so ignorant about all of this stuff."

"Nice to meet you, Caroline Johnson," he said, smiling and continuing to hold her hand in his. "I don't think you're ignorant at all. I actually think you're rather charming." Caroline blushed, and he slowly released her hand. "You're right. This does, at first glance, look like the flag of Japan. So that's a perfectly acceptable response."

"Well, aren't you kind," she responded, her head tilted down, looking up at him, all lashes. "Maybe you could tell me what it really means."

Jason walked closer to the painting and raised his arm, gesturing to the large red circle painted within. "The artist is making a social commentary about violence toward women. The red symbolizes the bloodshed and the white is the absence of chaos resulting in a systematic degradation of women in society."

Meanwhile, carrying two drinks, one in each hand, and chewing on a crab puff, Mike walked over and looked at the painting. "Oh look. A flag of Japan," he said dryly.

Caroline laughed and reached her hand out to touch his arm gently. "That's what I said!" she exclaimed, finding humor in their similar response.

Jason didn't seem to find the humor in the situation and responded to Mike with a hint of disdain, "It's not a flag of Japan. It's a biting social criticism of the treatment of women."

Mike gave him a look as if to say "Who the hell are you, you hipster loser." Before he could speak, Caroline obliged with introductions.

"Jason, this is my friend, Mike. Mike, this is Jason. He's an artist and was explainin' the larger significance of this piece to me," she said with growing admiration.

"An artist, huh? Which one of these *masterpieces* is yours?" he asked, taking another bite of his crab puff, making a sweeping gesture across the room and being certain to emphasize masterpieces with a hint of sarcasm.

Ignoring Mike's obvious attempts at belittlement, Jason replied, "I don't have any work on display tonight. But my studio is down in Venice." He turned to Caroline, "I'd love to show it to you sometime."

Caroline's breathing hitched. "That would be great," she said, giving him a warm smile and looking him directly in the eye. Mike rolled his eyes, not believing that Caroline would be interested in this artsy douche bag.

"Why don't I take your number and I can give you a call," he offered.

"Sure," said Caroline, her inner girl jumping up and down at the thought of this smokin' hot, creative, and talented artist being interested in her. Jason handed Caroline his phone, being sure to brush her hand as he did. The jolt of electricity between them was undeniable, and her breath quickened. Caroline took the phone, looking into Jason's eyes and smiling as she did. She programmed in her phone number while Mike piped up.

"Yes, that would be great. We would love to see your studio space," he said. Caroline turned to him with a quizzical look. "In the meantime, let's continue to explore these *amazing* works of art." He grabbed Caroline's arm and gently tried guiding her to other pieces. Caroline handed the phone back to Jason. He looked at it and smiled.

"I'll call you, Caroline Johnson," he said.

"I hope you do," she replied as Mike guided her around the exhibit corner.

•   •   •

A smoky, skunky haze sat like a fog over the threadbare rust-colored couch, patched together with silver duct tape, as Jason and his two buddies took turns taking hits from a bong. The floor was littered with empty Hostess donut wrappers and Big Gulp cups full of stale Mountain Dew. Jeff, a lanky, slim-built dude with narrow eyes and a hawk-like nose, grabbed a bag of Doritos. Feeling how light the bag was, he dumped out the last remaining crumbs onto the floor, disappointed. Small pieces of bright orange crisps rained down on a crumpled sleeping bag like confetti.

"Dude! I have to sleep there. Come on," Jason yelled, grabbing the bag out of Jeff's hand and throwing it on the floor.

"Taco Bell?" asked Jeff.

"Totally," replied Carson, a plump, red-haired hipster in a retro Pink Floyd concert T-shirt, who raised his hand for a high five but found it not met. "Jason? You coming?"

"No dinero," sighed Jason. "Spot me some?" he asked hopefully.

"Can't today, man. We'll see you," said Jeff as he and Carson walked toward the door. Jason took another hit of the bong. As he let the buzz wash over him, he flipped through his phone and dialed.

"Caroline? It's Jason Nash," he said upon hearing Caroline's voice.

"Jason. What a nice surprise. How are you?"

"I'm good. I was just working on my latest piece and was thinking about you."

"That's so nice to hear. What is it?"

"What's what?" he asked, confused.

"The piece?" she clarified.

"Oh. It's a painting."

"How lovely."

"Yeah. I was thinking that maybe you'd want to hang out."

"Sure," she said. She couldn't believe it. The thought of seeing Jason again, of feeling that current of energy run through her, was exciting. "When did you have in mind?"

"I know it's short notice, but are you free now?"

"Now?" she said, somewhat surprised. Now? She stood up and walked to the bathroom mirror. She grabbed a piece of toilet paper and dabbed at some stray eyeliner under her eye. "Well, I'm workin' right now."

"Oh, sure. That makes sense," he acknowledged. "You can't steal away for lunch?" he said with charm.

"Well, I suppose I have to eat, right?" She didn't want to come across as too desperate, but she certainly wanted to see Jason.

"My car is in the shop right now. Maybe you could come this way and I could show you the studio."

"Sounds fun. Why don't you text me the address and I'll come over in about an hour."

"Okay. I'll see you then," he said before hanging up the phone and taking another hit of his bong.

●　　●　　●

The noise of the metal studio door being dragged across its track startled Jason, who was napping on the studio's rust-colored couch. A young woman – she couldn't have been more than 20 – with a shock of lavender hair walked in and dropped a large plastic storage tub on the ground. She used her thin, tattooed arm to pull the noisy door closed and then slowly dragged the tub across the paint-stained floor. The screeching noise awoke Jason fully and he picked his head up off the duct-taped pillow.

"Hey, Cora," he said. Cora looked at him with disgust.

"You're not supposed to be staying here, you know," she sneered.

"Whatever," he replied with disdain. Cora rolled her eyes and walked to her corner of the studio. She was unloading her painting supplies when there came a knock on the door. She looked at Jason who sat immobile, sighed loudly enough for him to hear, and then walked to the door.

"Can I help you?" she asked with irritation.

"Hello. Yes, I'm here to see Jason," said Caroline, smiling. Cora called over to Jason, unable to hide the dislike on her face

"Jason. Someone's here for you," she shouted before walking away. Jason walked over to the door a bit surprised, until he remembered he had called and invited Caroline over.

"Hey there," he said, brightening up. He leaned in and kissed Caroline's cheek.

"Hi," said Caroline, walking in wide-eyed as she surveyed the incredible studio filled with creative pieces. "This place is amazin'."

"I'm so glad you're here. Come in," he gestured for her to come in further. "Let me just use the bathroom quickly."

"Okay."

Jason ran off to the bathroom while Caroline walked toward Cora. Before her were half a dozen tall, thin boards with shades of blue and green paint thickly applied. Although Caroline didn't recognize the impasto technique, she could appreciate how it impacted the play of light in these works.

"Wow. Are these all yours? They're beautiful," she said with awe.

"Thanks," said Cora, standing up and watching Caroline's reaction.

"I just love the colors. They make me feel happy and sort of melancholy at the same time."

"They're not finished yet, but that was what I was going for," Cora said, a rare smile crossing her lips.

"I'm really impressed."

"Well thank you. So..." Cora began hesitantly. "You're a friend of Jason's."

"Yes. We met at a gallery and he wanted to show me his studio."

"You seem like a nice girl. Just watch yourself," Cora said. "And your purse," she noted under her breath.

"What?" said Caroline, who had been distracted by a half-completed bronze sculpture on a nearby pedestal. Before Cora could repeat her warning, Jason walked in.

"Let's not bother Cora. She's kind of a bitch, especially when people are here during her hours," said Jason, glaring at Cora.

"Sorry," said Caroline, pulling in her shoulders. "I didn't know someone else would be here. So, which of these pieces is yours?" she asked, surveying the rest of the space.

"I have two paintings that I'm working on right now," he said, guiding her across the studio. Caroline looked to see two works in progress. The square canvases looked a chaotic jumble of lines and slashes. There was no rhyme or reason that she could discern. And while she certainly didn't know much about art, she did know it should evoke an emotional response. All Caroline felt was nausea.

"Wow. These are so interestin'," she said, unsure how to respond to her less-than-positive reaction to them.

"Thanks. I'm really going for the restlessness of the quarter life crisis," explained Jason.

"They do have a, um, restlessness quality to them," she responded. Meanwhile, Cora glared at them.

"We should probably get going," Jason said, returning Cora's scowl. "I'm starving. What about you?"

"Sure. I don't know this area very well. What do you suggest?"

"There's a great vegan cafe around the corner. We could just walk," he suggested.

"Sounds great. Lead the way. So how long have you been an artist?"

"I think I've always been an artist. But I've been doing this seriously for the past four years."

"Just bein' in that studio made me feel so creative. I feel like I just want to go back and sketch."

"Really. I didn't realize you were an artist."

"Oh, well, I'm not really an artist. Not like you anyway. I studied fashion design and own a handbag line."

"Oh, yeah. That's not the same, but it's cool," he said, looking down at her with a smile.

"How many people share the studio?" she asked, rounding the corner and approaching the café.

"There are twelve of us right now. We take turns when we work."

"That's great. It must be nice to have a place to go for dedicated work and then to be able to close the door and put work behind you for the day."

"Yeah. Well, I'm in between places right now, so I've been crashing there. I'm just waiting for my exhibition."

"An exhibition?" she asked with enthusiasm. "Sounds so excitin'. When is it? I'd love to come and support you," she said, turning to look at him as he opened the café door for her.

"I'm still working on the pieces. Then I need to get signed by a gallery. It'll happen. It just takes time."

•　　•　　•

Caroline had eaten half of her kale salad with fig compote, while Jason had already inhaled a veggie burger, French fries, side salad, and vegan chocolate shake.

Jason turned to the waitress, "Can I get another side of fries?" He then turned to Caroline, "Sorry. Living up to the reputation of 'starving artist,' huh?"

"Oh, don't apologize. I'm always hungry."

"Well, sometimes I just get so caught up in the work I forget to eat."

"How many hours a day are you workin' on your art? Do you do anythin' else for work on the side?"

"I spend almost all of my time at the studio. I can't imagine doing anything other than creating something that will stir the emotions of the audience. I was in college for a while studying psychology and then business, but art is really my passion. I worked on a lobster boat in Maine for a year and spent some time in retail, saving up some money. Now I'm solely focused on my art."

"I think it's very brave to focus on your passion when there are no guarantees."

"Well, then, you're brave too. You started your own business. That takes a lot of courage. There were no guarantees you would be a success. I'm assuming you are successful."

"I'm doin' all right, I suppose," she said shyly. "Thank you for sayin' that," she blushed.

They continued to enjoy lunch as much as each other's company. When Jason popped the last fry into his mouth, the waitress placed the bill, attached to a small piece of black slate, on the table.

"Shit!" Jason said, patting his back pockets. "I must have left my wallet back at the studio."

"Oh, that's okay," said Caroline, reaching into her metallic grey bucket bag. "I got this."

"I feel like such an idiot," said Jason, shaking his head. "Invite a beautiful woman to lunch and then forget my wallet."

"Seriously, don't worry about it. You'll get it next time," she suggested.

"There will definitely be a next time," he smiled.

●   ●   ●

There had been two more dates – the second being a romantic walk in the park and drinks at a boutique coffee shop on trendy Montana Avenue. For their third date, they found themselves at a free outdoor concert at UCLA. They talked about their childhoods, their aspirations, and their fears. Caroline was definitely feeling a connection to Jason and admired the way he talked about his work passionately.

They had just left the concert at UCLA's Fowler Amphitheater when Caroline said invitingly, "I don't live too far from here."

"Really, now?" replied Jason. She blushed. He took her hand and brushed his soft lips across her knuckles. A jolt coursed through her body.

They hurried back to her apartment and before the front door even closed fully, Jason pinned her against the wall, his muscular body pushed flush against hers. She could feel him hardened against her as his mouth claimed hers.

"Do you know how fucking sexy you are?" he growled while his tongue and teeth tormented her tender earlobe.

"Tell me," she said, as his hands unbuttoned her grey chiffon blouse and skimmed over a lacy cream-colored bra. She fumbled to open his oversized belt buckle and then dipped her hand past his waistband, rubbing his growing length.

"I've wanted you ever since you called that painting a Goddam flag of Japan," he rasped. "The color of that dot reminded me of your red lips and my cock twitched just thinking how those lips would feel wrapped around me while I come in your mouth."

"Oh, sweet Lord, that's hot," Caroline gasped. She tilted her head to the side, giving Jason more access to her neck and collarbone, which he gladly accepted with his tongue. Jason pulled his mouth away from her, the hunger in his eyes unmistakable. "Which way to your bed?"

Caroline lowered her chin and looked up at him through her long lashes. Her hand still stroking him, she grasped a bit tighter, turned her back to him and pulled him down the hall toward her room.

Jason grabbed a condom from his back pocket before his jeans and briefs hit the ground. Caroline laid down on the bed, now wearing nothing but her lacy bra with matching panties. She slowly inched herself up toward the headboard, not breaking eye contact with Jason who watched her intently and slowly licked his lips.

He stood over her and pulled her panties down her long tan legs, letting his fingertips caress her already sensitized skin along the way. He laid down, his leg between hers and wrapped his hands behind her back, unhooking her bra and letting the straps fall down her shoulders. He dipped his hands under her bra and massaged her hardening nipples as her legs writhed beneath him.

"Are you ready for me?" he asked, as his hand slowly moved down her taut belly and massaged that tender spot between her thighs. Feeling her wet with arousal, he said, "Oh fuck ya. You're so ready." Without warning, he plunged himself into her and while his hand still stroked her, he moved himself in and out of her like a piston. She wrapped her arms around his neck and moved with the rhythm.

With each thrust, stroke, and pinch, Caroline could feel Jason taking her closer to her release. "I'm so close," she panted.

"Oh, I can fucking feel it," said Jason as Caroline exploded around him, her throbbing body pulsing him into his own release. "Ahhhh. Fuck, Caroline." He lay on top of her, still inside her, as his forehead leaned to touch hers. "I knew it was going to be good with you," he breathed into her ear, licking her earlobe.

"More than good," she panted, remembering how amazing a non-self-induced orgasm could feel. Jason slowly edged out of her and rolled onto his side, his hand stroking her breast as his breathing calmed.

"Are you thirsty?" she asked, turning on her side and looking into his eyes.

"Sure." Caroline walked to the kitchen and returned with a glass of orange juice, setting it on a coaster on the nightstand table. Crawling back into bed, she nuzzled up against his chest and ran her fingers through the light smattering of chest hair.

"You can stay here the night," she offered. "You don't have to, of course, but I'd like you to, if you want to," she said, an inescapable grin plastered on her face.

"Yeah, sure. I'd like that too," Jason replied as he leaned up and kissed the top of her head. Caroline took a deep breath and drifted off to sleep.

The alarm clock buzzed at 6:30 and Caroline quickly shut it off, slipping out from under Jason's limbs. She hopped into the shower and checked on him before turning on the hair dryer. Jason remained blissfully unaware that anything was happening around him. Caroline stared at him as he slept, watching his chest calmly rise and fall. She smiled to herself and continued to get ready for work.

At 7:30, she gently touched Jason's cheek and roused him awake.

"Hey," he whispered. "What time is it?" he asked, his eyes blinking.

"It's 7:30," she said. "I need to go to work."

"Oh," he said, sitting up. "I'll..."

"No. You stay," she said, pressing her hand forward onto his chest. "Sleep."

"I may use your shower, if that's okay?"

"Make yourself at home," she said. "Just close the door behind you when you leave. It locks automatically."

"Okay," he said, looking up at her sleepily. "Thanks."

"Sure. I'll talk to you later." She leaned down and kissed his cheek. He grabbed her cheek, tilted her head to the side, and kissed her other cheek.

"I'll call you."

Caroline walked out of the apartment, unable to contain her glee. She bit her lip and took a deep breath, exhaling loudly as she walked toward her car. The day was a blur of invoicing, meetings, and one ill-fated trip to the photographer that would frustratingly result in a two-week delay to her website updates. On her way home, she swung by the market to pick up her weekly groceries.

She walked back into her apartment juggling two reusable Trader Joe's bags on her knee. Jason was sitting on her couch, eating a yogurt.

"Hey," he said, getting to his feet and helping her with the bags, looking through them as he did.

"Hey yourself," she replied, her mouth gaping open in surprise. "You're still here," she said in a tone that made it clear she was happy to see him in her living room.

"Yeah. I hope you don't mind," he said, shrugging. "I just needed some time to chill."

"Not at all. In fact, I'm happy to see you," she said as she bounded into his arms, wrapped her hands around his neck and pulled him in for a kiss. Her tongue glided across his lips, beseeching him to open up to her. His lips parted and his tongue met hers with an intensity that reverberated deep within her groin. He made quick work removing her polka-dotted sundress and carried her, with her legs wrapped tightly around his waist, to the couch where he gave her three intense orgasms before succumbing to his own release.

●　　●　　●

Taking his regular spot on the studio couch, Jason grabbed the joint from Jeff's hand and took a long drag, holding his breath and allowing the drug to have its strongest effect.

"Dude. My phone got disconnected. Let me borrow yours," he said, grabbing Jeff's cell phone. He took his own phone and looked up a number before punching it into Jeff's.

Caroline, sitting at her desk and typing promotional copy into her computer, looked at the ringing phone but didn't recognize the caller ID.

"Hello. This is Caroline."

"Hey. It's Jason. What are you up to?"

"Jason. Are you okay? I tried callin' you yesterday but I couldn't get through."

"Yeah, just having some problems with my phone."

"Oh good. I was a little worried. How have you been?"

"I'm good. But I miss you." *He missed me*, she thought. She smiled to herself, thankful she wasn't getting brushed off now that they had slept together. She hoped he would want to see her again, as he was as passionate a lover as he seemed to be about his art. "I'm really into one of my paintings right now but I'd like to see you. You've been inspiring me. Maybe I can come by tonight?"

"Sure. That sounds great. I should be free around six," she said, biting her smiling lip.

"Great. Why don't you pick up some takeout and we can just hang."

"Okay. I'll see you then." They both hung up. Caroline smiled to herself, excited to see Jason again. Jason smiled at Jeff.

"Dude, you are so set," said Jeff with envy.

"Yeah. She's got this sweet pad. Looks like I can say adios to this couch for a while."

•   •   •

It had been about three weeks since she started seeing Jason, or rather three weeks since he had become a permanent, albeit not always welcomed, fixture in her apartment. Caroline walked into Starbucks, finding it more crowded than usual for a Tuesday afternoon. Mike looked well-rested, having had the previous night off from the bar. Although judging by the topic of conversation, he likely hadn't gotten much sleep. While he regaled Caroline with tales about his latest piece of tail, Caroline rummaged through her leather-trimmed tote bag for her wallet.

"And she's a JAG lawyer – you know – for the army. It's very *A Few Good Men*, don't you think?" Mike said. He realized Caroline was distracted. "What?"

Caroline searched through her wallet, becoming increasingly agitated. "Huh. I thought I had a gift card in here. That's weird." Mike reached for his wallet.

"I got it."

"No, that's okay. I've got it," she said, pulling a twenty-dollar bill out of her wallet.

"She works at Beale Air Force Base in El Segundo. You should see her in her uniform. Super hot," Mike continued. Caroline remained lost in her thoughts. Mike waved his hand in front of her face. "Hello? Are you there? I know I can't be boring you. I'm too awesome."

She gave her head a small shake and then looked him in the eye. "Oh, I'm sorry. I just... I think Jason is stealin' from me," she confessed.

"Yeah, I can see that," said Mike, pursing his lips and nodding his head slightly.

"I had a Starbucks card in here and now it's gone. I also went to the ATM last week and am missin' a few twenties."

"You've got to dump that guy. He's a total bum. It's one thing to be a struggling artist but it sounds like he's just lazy."

"I know," she said, resigned. "He never seems to be workin' on his art. He's always hangin' out at my place, eatin' my food and watchin' TV. Even when he is inspired..." she used air quotes and emphasized 'inspired,' "I don't think he's very talented."

"So break up with him," he said flatly.

"I know," she sighed. "I will. Tonight." A troubled expression crossed her face.

"Yeah, good luck with that," he said sarcastically. Caroline glared at him, then gently punched him in the arm.

"Okay, so tell me more about..." she began.

"Katarina," Mike said, completing her sentence. "I'd let her court-marshal me," he said, raising his eyebrows. Caroline shook her head and laughed.

• • •

Jason, wearing a T-shirt and boxers, sat on Caroline's lush grey couch watching a movie – *Bill and Ted's Excellent Adventure*. His naked feet were propped up on her Jonathan Adler beech coffee table.

I've got to do this, she thought. *I've got to just say what needs to be said.* She mentally psyched herself up when her thoughts were interrupted by the doorbell. Jason leapt to his feet, paused the movie, and grabbed Caroline's wallet from her fringed buckskin shoulder bag. He bounded over to the front door and opened it for the pizza delivery man.

"Dude! I'm starving. What took so long?" he questioned.

"Sorry. Just a busy night," said the delivery man without a hint of contrition. He pulled a large pizza box from his insulated bag. "That'll be sixteen dollars."

Jason took a twenty, fresh from the ATM, from Caroline's wallet and handed it over. As the delivery man reached into his pocket to get change, Jason pushed his hand toward him and ushered him out. "Keep the change."

Jason closed the door and sat back down on the couch, grabbing a slice and shoveling it into his mouth. As he savored the melted cheese and spicy sausage, he clicked pause on the remote allowing Bill and Ted to continue with their air guitar riffs.

Caroline, completely frustrated, walked into the kitchen to get plates and napkins.

"Grab me a beer, will ya?" called Jason from the other room.

She took a deep breath as she opened the refrigerator door and took out a cold Corona Light. As she clicked the cap off, she resigned herself to the fact that it was time. She needed to tell Jason this wasn't working out. Fear and panic enveloped her. *Stay strong*, she thought. *You can do this. Just tell him, like you rehearsed in your mind.*

She handed Jason the beer, which he took from her and immediately lifted to his mouth. Taking a large swig, he then lowered the bottle down, condensation dripping on his hand, and placed it on the coffee table. Caroline drew another deep breath and moved the offending bottle to a coaster. Suddenly, a timer went off and Jason jumped up.

"Hey, pause the movie, will ya?" he called – more a request than a question. He walked over to Caroline's laundry closet and took his dry clothes from the dryer, replacing them with a wet load. Reaching for a dryer sheet, he pulled out the last one, revealing an empty cardboard box.

"Do you have any more dryer sheets?" he asked, sniffing the box. "I just love the way these smell. Pick some up tomorrow, will ya?" Jason walked back into the room, leaving his clean clothes on the floor beside the dryer. Meanwhile, Caroline had turned off the TV and was sitting on the couch facing the doorway.

"Listen, Jason," she started. "I think we need to talk," she eked out. Jason sat down and took another bite of his pizza.

"Is it about the paint on the carpet?" he asked, chewing. "I told you I'll pay you back for the cleaning."

"No, well yes… I mean… it's… you know… this… just isn't workin'."

"Sure it is."

"No, it's not," she said quietly and unconvincingly. She sighed, trying to say what was on her mind.

"I really thought we were connecting here. You've become my muse."

"That's sweet of you to say but… I… I think you should just go," she whispered, her voice trailing up as she completed the sentence, making it sound more like a question than a statement. *Why am I saying this like a question*, she thought to herself, *when what I mean is "get your freeloading, no-talent ass off of my couch and out of my life"?*

"Oh man. That sucks. Okay. Let me just finish this load and I'll be out of your hair." Jason leaned over the table and grabbed another slice of pizza. Taking a bite, he walked to the bathroom and turned on the shower. He started to disrobe and closed the door.

Caroline couldn't believe what was happening. Yes, she had broken it off, but he was still there…showering. She grabbed her phone and dialed. Mike answered on the first ring, sitting at his office desk in the bar's back room, pouring through receipts on his computer.

"Hey doll. What's up?"

"So I just told Jason we shouldn't see each other anymore."

"Yes!" said Mike enthusiastically, his hand balled into a fist. "I hope you told that no-talent mooch – and likely thief, I might add – off."

"Not exactly. I tried to articulate that he's well... you know... but just ended up sayin' he should go," she admitted meekly. "He said he just needed to finish his load of laundry and now he's takin' a shower."

"The guy's got balls, that's for sure."

"I don't know what to do," she whined.

"Walk in the bathroom, shut the water off, tell him to get his shit together – and I mean that both literally and figuratively – and get the hell out."

"You know I can't do that," she scoffed.

"Don't pussy out. Go tell him what you really think. If you give him half an earful of what you've told me about him, he'll run for the hills."

"I'm not good at this. I spent most of the day rehearsin' an eloquent way to tell him goodbye and goin' over various scenarios in my head. But when push just came to shove, I got tongue-tied and sounded like an idiot."

"Listen to me. By your own admission, when things are good, Caroline, you're unstoppable. I know you're smart, confident, successful, and charming. But with even a whiff of controversy brewing, you retreat like a frightened turtle into a shell. You care too much what other people think of you and that's just got to change."

"I know. I just don't know how to change that."

"Just say what you mean, consequences be damned."

"Like you? I don't think so."

"Come to think of it, I'm not the best role model, am I?" he joked. Caroline smiled to herself and shook her head no. "Well I think you just need to be less concerned with what other people think, unless that other person is me. In that case, you should agonize and fret over everything you do and say that could incur my judgment or wrath." Caroline laughed.

"I'll keep that advice in mind. Okay, the shower's off. I better go and help him gather his stuff."

"Be strong and kick his ass to the curb," he encouraged.

"Okay," she sighed. "Bye."

Demi-Bag

*c*aroline nervously handed the sample leather bags to Cynthia Hammer, owner of Hammer & Nails, a trendy women's boutique in downtown Manhattan Beach. Cynthia was a bored divorcée turned small business owner who wanted to keep busy while her three kids were in school and put to use the millions she got in the divorce from her movie producer husband.

In her mid-forties, she looked her age. Despite the regular Botox injections, years of living by the beach and enjoying the South Bay sunshine had taken its toll on her skin. Even her arms – toned from years of Pilates, spin classes, or the latest exercise du jour, looked leathered and worn. But she was a woman of discerning taste who didn't mince words. Caroline wanted to impress her. As she awaited Cynthia's feedback on the new designs, Caroline looked outside to see palm trees swaying in the breeze along the street dotted with shops.

"I'm like so loving these bags. This color is unreal," she said.

"Thanks, Cynthia. I'm so glad you like them," replied Caroline, with an obvious sense of pride and relief. Cynthia turned to a thirty-something blonde, wearing Lululemon exercise pants and flip-flops, pushing a stroller around the boutique.

"Isn't this color unreal? These are new to the shop," Cynthia said, now feeling proud herself.

"These are only samples…" began Caroline.

"But she can buy one today. Right?" said Cynthia, interrupting Caroline and making it obvious she didn't want to lose a sale.

"Absolutely," replied Caroline reluctantly.

As the woman with the stroller continued to examine the aqua distressed leather bag, Cynthia turned to Caroline and said, "Can I ask you a personal question?"

"Sure," said Caroline, taking her iPad out of her bag, preparing to process Cynthia's order.

"Are you seeing anyone right now?" Sensing Caroline's unease, she added, "I'm not asking for me. I'm totally into men… usually."

"Uh…" started Caroline.

"My cousin Craig just moved to L.A. from the Bay area. He's a really nice guy," she said, turning her head to the side and giving Caroline a hopeful look. Caroline returned Cynthia's gaze as her breathing accelerated and her palms became sweaty. She looked down at her knotted fingers.

"A fix-up? I don't know. I just broke up with someone a few weeks ago," she said meekly. Cynthia took her cell phone from her pocket and held it up to Caroline.

"He's really hot," she advised, pushing the phone toward Caroline.

"Whoa! Yes he is," said Caroline, her heart beating a bit quicker.

"He's a marketing manager for a software company that just relocated to Santa Monica. He doesn't know anyone else down here and I figured he would get along well with someone like you. You know, a smart business woman who knows how to get ahead."

Not sure how to respond, Caroline reluctantly said, "Okay. Give 'em my number."

"Awesome. Now about my order. I really love this. What other colors does it come in?"

•   •   •

Mike sat, casually dressed in khaki shorts, a snug fitting black T-shirt, and flip-flops, with two frozen mocha drinks before him. He flipped through emails on his phone as he waited for Caroline. She bounded through the coffee shop door, her blonde ponytail and pink canvas tote swaying in sync. She sat down and handed Mike a square-shaped tin.

"What's this?" he asked, taking the tin from her hands.

"Fudge. Mimi's homemade recipe," she replied.

"And she sent this for me?" he asked in surprise, putting his hand on her arm.

"No, silly. I made it for you usin' her recipe," said Caroline, shaking her head.

Mike opened the tin, took a small piece of the chocolate indulgence and popped it into his mouth. "Wow! This is really good," he said, chewing. "So, we're having some chick come sing at the bar tomorrow night. You should come by."

"Live entertainment? That's a first."

"It was Morgan's idea," he said, grabbing another piece of fudge and sinking his teeth into it.

"Ah, Morgan. She seems very into you," said Caroline. That wasn't unusual. Many, if not all, of the waitresses at the bar were into Mike.

"Yeah, maybe a little too into me. But she's a really good waitress. Probably the best I've ever had," he said, closing the fudge tin so as not to eat too much.

"When you say the 'best you ever had' are you talkin' about her waitressin' skills or other skills?" Caroline asked, unsure if she really wanted to know the answer.

"Waitressing. Although her other skills are pretty impressive. She does this thing—"

Before he could finish, Caroline interrupted, "I got it. I got it. But let me ask you somethin'. If she's such a good waitress, why would you muck it all up with sex?"

"Did I mention she does this thing..." he said, his voice trailing off as he raised his eyebrows at her. Caroline laughed and shook her head.

"So, live music tomorrow, huh? Well, I will be there to enjoy. I have a date and he's meetin' me at the bar."

"A date? I thought you were taking a break since the fiasco with the artist," he said, making air quotes. "And by artist, I mean douche bag."

"His name is Craig and he's the cousin of the owner of a boutique in the area. He's quite handsome and just moved to town. She wanted someone to show 'em around," she said.

"And you're comfortable being pimped out like that?" he scoffed.

"Pimped out? What are you talkin' about?" she asked quizzically.

Sometimes Mike was confounded as to how a woman so smart and savvy in so many ways could be so naïve in others. "She is one of your customers and she wants to fix you up with her cousin. Could you have said no?"

"I suppose so. I didn't even think about it like that," said Caroline, who now instinctively thought back to the conversation and Cynthia's words and tone: *"I figured he would get along well with someone like you. You know, a smart business woman who knows how to get ahead."*

"You just need to be careful mixing business and pleasure," Mike cautioned.

"Like you?" scoffed Caroline. "In addition to Morgan, how many waitresses at the bar have you slept with?"

"Exactly!" said Mike, raising a pointed finger in the air. "Do you want to end up like me?" he said, pointing to himself.

"No. I just want to meet a nice guy and be happy."

"I don't think a mercy date with one of your clients' cousins is the answer."

"I don't think Cynthia's like that. And maybe this will work out. Either way, I'm meetin' him at the bar tomorrow," she shrugged.

●　　●　　●

The bar was crowded with trendy twenty- and thirty-somethings with weekend time and money to burn. It was standing room only around the large rectangular bar that sat in the center of the large, industrial-style space, complete with exposed pipes from the high wood-beam ceiling. Two large skylights let in some light from the moon and neighboring office buildings and reflected the range of cocktail and spirits glasses that hung from the rafters over the bar.

Mike had selected this style and shape bar because it reminded him of the TV show *Cheers*, which he used to watch with Linnea after completing his homework. High tables with wood-backed bar stools and low tables with simple wooden chairs lined the red brick walls around the impressive space. Each was adorned with a small glass votive candle holder, creating an intimate ambiance.

Along a wall, centered between the men's and ladies' room doors, was a small 58-key piano painted green and distressed yellow. Its diminutive size and distinct hue were always a conversation starter among new visitors to the bar. Mike was happy to explain that it was a replica – and a good one at that – of the piano used in the movie *Casablanca*. It was one of his favorite movies and one he had introduced to Caroline during their final year of business school. Last he heard, the original piano had sold for millions at auction. He was just happy to have a small reminder in his establishment of one of the best bar movies ever.

Other memorable bar scenes and locations, such as Mos Eisley Cantina from *Star Wars* and the Bada Bing from the *Sopranos*, were memorialized in a series of original posters Mike had commissioned and that hung proudly on the restroom walls.

As Mike looked around, feeling pride in all that he had accomplished, he thought Morgan had certainly outdone herself. The place was packed thanks to her initiative. He'd have to remember to pay her the compliment. That might help smooth over the growing tension between them. Mike continued to pour drinks when his eye caught Caroline walking in.

She was dressed in a flowery, bohemian-style blouse with skinny jeans and a pair of high-heeled, sling-back tan sandals. The look was complemented by a matching tan fringed shoulder bag. She waved hello and, noticing how busy the bar was, gave him a thumb's up.

She glanced around the crowd looking for her date and found the handsome, curly brown-haired man saving her a stool at the bar. He had large, almond-shaped brown eyes, the color of milk chocolate. He turned and saw her, and she waved hello. He smiled at her, the same attractive, crooked smile she had seen in Cynthia's photo. Hope bloomed inside her.

"Hi, Craig. I'm Caroline. So nice to meet you," she said, reaching her hand out to shake his. Craig seemed to approve of Caroline's appearance, as he smiled a genuine smile that caused his eyes to crinkle.

"I'm glad this time I let Cynthia set me up with someone. You never know what you're really going to get," he said. Caroline thought back to previous set ups and nodded in agreement.

"I understand. Well, I hope you found this place okay."

"Yeah."

"My best friend Mike is the owner. Let me introduce you," she offered. "Mike! Mike! C'mon over here. Let me introduce you to Craig. Craig, this is Mike," she said, gesturing between the two. Mike reached out to shake Craig's hand, sizing him up as he did.

"Nice to meet you, man. Chardonnay for Caroline. What are you drinking? Let me refresh it for you," Mike said, pouring a glass of white wine for Caroline and placing it on a white paper napkin before her.

"Oh thanks. I'm having a scotch on the rocks," he said, pushing his empty glass toward Mike. "So, Caroline, Cynthia tells me you're an amazing designer. She really loves your bags and is so glad that she could support you," he continued. Mike gave Caroline a look, indicating that she was being pimped out. Caroline looked at him and subtly shook her head no.

"That's so sweet of her to say. She told me that you're a marketin' manager with a software company," she said.

"Yeah," said Craig. Caroline tilted her head to the side and grinned, waiting for Craig to continue. Meanwhile, Mike turned toward the other end of the bar, his attention having been caught by a waving hand. Caroline took control of the conversation upon realizing Craig had not elaborated.

"So, what kind of software do you make?" she asked.

"Video games," he answered flatly and then sat silently looking around the room. *Well, this conversation could be a bit easier*, thought Caroline.

"That's one topic I know nothin' about. But it sounds fun," she said, hoping he would talk about his work.

"It is." The two of them sat there for an awkward moment until Caroline spoke up again.

"Uh, she mentioned you moved here from the Bay Area. How long were you up there?" she asked, trying to think of some open-ended questions to help stimulate the conversation.

"Four years," Craig replied, before taking a sip of his drink and looking back up at Caroline with a grin.

"And did you like it up there?" she asked, before realizing she should have said, "*What* did you like about living up there?"

"It was okay," said Craig, clearly not giving her anything to work with.

"Well, I sure hope you like it down here. Santa Monica's a great place to work. You're near lots of shops and restaurants, never mind the beach," she added.

"Yeah," responded Craig. Before the awkward silence could stretch further, Craig said, "Which way is the restroom?"

"It's just back there," she responded, pointing to the back and left.

Craig hopped off the barstool and walked toward the back of the bar. This was the first time Caroline got a full glimpse of him. Quickly she noticed, as did Mike, that Craig was short. Very short. Caroline sighed deeply and took a swig of her Chardonnay, regretting her choice of evening footwear, as Mike walked to her.

"Correct that," he said with a throaty chuckle. "Maybe it's Cynthia who's getting short-changed in this deal." Knowing what Mike was doing, Caroline quickly sought to shut him down.

"Stop that right now," she admonished, pointing a menacing finger at him.

"C'mon. That was funny," he responded. Caroline looked at him disapprovingly. "You're right," Mike said, correcting himself. "That wasn't cool. How about drinks on me. Since he just moved here, your date may be a little short on cash."

"Michael Barnsworth! Grow up!" she said, threateningly and frankly a bit too loudly.

"Grow up?" Mike repeated, laughing all the while. Caroline tried to stifle a laugh. In a quieter, less menacing tone she said, "You know what I mean."

"Are you suggesting I shouldn't poke fun at his expense? Perhaps he's always getting the short end of the stick?" Mike said, before gesturing with his head that Craig was on his way back from the restroom.

Caroline laughed, but stopped herself before hissing under her breath, "Behave yourself."

"I'm a little hungry," said Craig. Mike smiled upon hearing "little," while Caroline tried to control her impulse to laugh by pulling her lips into her mouth and covering it up with the side of her hand.

"I'm gettin' a tad hungry too. What kind of food do you like?" she asked.

"Anything's fine," Craig said blandly, as he placed some cash on the counter.

"There's a great little Mexican restaurant around the corner. How does that sound?" she asked with a forced smile.

"Sure." Craig placed his hand on Caroline's back to guide her to the door. Mike leaned over to shake Craig's hand.

"Nice to meet you. Have fun," he said, flashing Caroline a knowing smile. She glared back at him.

"Thanks," said Craig, oblivious to the unspoken words between Caroline and Mike.

• • •

The next day, Caroline carefully carried the food tray holding two Chinese chicken salads and two iced teas to Mike, who sat saving a table at the crowded Century City Mall food court. She lowered the tray and Mike removed the items onto the table, licking his lips as he did. He stood and took the empty tray from Caroline, then motioned for her to sit down. After he returned the tray to the holding slot above the trash can, he grabbed napkins and two forks.

"Thanks for lunch," he said.

"My pleasure," she replied, smiling.

"So, tell me more about your date last night? Did you stay out late or cut it short?" he asked, with a completely straight face. Caroline knew all too well what he was doing and chose not to engage in such childish talk.

"You have just got to stop that. He's a very nice guy and we had a very nice time," she stated with haughty conviction.

Reaching his hand down to his knee, palm up, Mike smiled and said, "Low five!" He then nodded his head knowingly, acknowledging his hilarious joke.

"You're incorrigible," said Caroline, shaking her head.

"No, really. I'm happy for you. I hope it's not a short-lived relationship," Mike said with mock honesty. Caroline glared at him.

"I thought you didn't want to see me gettin' pimped out?" She placed her hand on her hip.

"I was being short-sighted," Mike replied. Caroline rolled her eyes, recognizing that was an easy strike for Mike.

"I walked right into that one, didn't I?"

"Yup," said Mike, chuckling.

"Be serious for a moment." She needed Mike to lay off the jokes and be her sounding board. "He's a really nice guy, but I'm just not interested in him in that way. And it's awkward because, now thanks to you, no less, I'm paranoid Cynthia will pull her orders."

"What's wrong with him?" Mike asked genuinely.

"Nothin'. I'm just not... attracted to him in that way," she responded. "You know, you just can't make a silk purse out of a sow's ear." Even if his conversational skills had been stronger, Craig didn't light a fire in her belly, or challenge her in any way.

"A purse expression. Sweet," Mike said, eliciting a smile from Caroline. "So, no attraction, huh? Is it because he's wee?"

"No!" said Caroline, interrupting him.

"Don't get short with me," Mike retorted, flashing her a dazzling smile. Caroline started to giggle before straightening herself up and looking at him seriously.

"It has nothin' to do with the fact he is short-statured," she said, straight faced.

"Good. That would be the height of hypocrisy." Caroline exhaled loudly.

"Are you done yet?" she asked disapprovingly.

"Almost. I have a great knock-knock joke," he said, hoping she would take the bait.

"Go ahead," she said, resigned. "Get it out of your system."

"Knock, knock." Mike looked pleased with himself.

"Who's there?" she said, humoring him, her head tilted to the side, connecting with Mike's eyes after rolling hers upward.

"Too short." His eyes twinkled and didn't break contact with hers.

"Too short who?" she said with smiling eyes, knowing it would be funny.

"Too short to reach the damn doorbell. That's why I knocked," he said with a shit-eating grin on his face. Caroline closed her eyes and put her fingertips on her forehead as she shook her head and laughed.

"Okay. Now please be serious."

"Okay." Caroline recognized his tone. He was ready to listen. "Seriously, what's wrong with the guy? Small dick?"

"What!" she exclaimed. She couldn't believe the conversation had taken this turn.

"You know. Short guy. Short dick."

"It was a perfectly platonic date," she said, shocked. "You are..." and her voice trailed off as she tried to find the perfect word. Mike, seizing the opportunity to lighten the mood yet again, responded.

"Hilarious? Clever? Devilishly handsome?" He smiled and put his index finger into his dimple, twisting it back and forth. "Dink," he said. Caroline shook her head.

"Exasperatin'," she said with a resigned sigh. Mike shook his head, considering her response. Then he nodded in agreement.

"Seriously," he said, once again attempting a thoughtful tone. "What *is* wrong with the guy?"

"Nothin's *wrong* with him. He's perfectly nice."

"You always talk about wanting to meet a nice guy."

"I do. I really want to be with a nice guy. But he is just so... bland," she said, struggling to find the right word to describe him.

"You say you want a nice guy, but what you really need is someone that makes you laugh, puts you at ease, pushes the envelope a bit and just..." his voice trailed off for a moment. "Gets you," he finished at the same time Caroline said, "Gets me." Of course, Mike was right and Caroline knew that.

"So what do I tell Cynthia?" she asked, trying to solve her problem.

"Don't put him down," Mike said with faux sincerity. He started to laugh. "Sorry. Last one, I promise. I don't really know why you need to tell her anything."

"Well, she's gonna ask if I had fun with Craig. I don't want her to think I'm not interested in him because... he's short," she said, the obvious pangs of guilt evident in her voice.

"So, you're saying you're a bigger person than that?" Caroline's expression was impassive as she tried to squash both the laughter and exhaustion about to erupt inside her. "C'mon. That was a good one," Mike laughed.

"I *am* a bigger person than that." She inhaled deeply to keep her frustration in check.

"So you tell her that you really liked Craig but just didn't feel that spark. That's all you need to say. You don't owe her a detailed account of your feelings. She'll understand that. And you can handle one sentence that shouldn't spark a drawn-out confrontation."

"Okay," she said reluctantly. "I'll give it a try. Thanks."

"Sure," Mike said with an equal dose of earnestness. "And if she gets angry with you, let's hope she has a short-term memory." Mike tilted his head back and roared with laughter. "You love me. You know you love me." Caroline shook her head.

"Incorrigible." Mike raised his eyebrows and gave her a knowing smile.

Coin Purse

C aroline stepped out of the nondescript rental car into the driveway of her parents' ranch-style home. It had been several years since she had been back for Christmas and even longer since she had last endured a South Georgian summer heat. But being back in Asbury for Mimi's 85th birthday bash was a given. In fact, it seemed as though the entire town was invited to celebrate this force of a woman.

And while she was excited to see her family and celebrate Mimi's big milestone, she was nervous about being back in town which would only dredge up bad memories. At least it was only for two days and then she could get back to her life in L.A.

Caroline grabbed a ponytail holder from her taupe leather messenger bag, which perfectly matched the Grecian-style gladiator sandals she wore with white linen shorts and a red and white polka dot blouse. She pulled her hair up off her neck, which was now starting to glisten with sweat from the humidity. Before she finished pulling her suitcase from the backseat, her parents came running down the walkway.

Hellos and hugs were exchanged as they made their way quickly into the air-conditioned kitchen. It seemed that every counter and surface was covered in homemade pies of every variety – from apple and huckleberry to key lime and rhubarb – made special for Mimi's party. As Caroline's mom swatted her hand away from taking a nibble of errant crust, Caroline turned to the sound of metal clanking on the floor.

Mimi bounded forward, as quickly as she could on 85-year-old legs while dragging an oxygen tank. Caroline moved toward her and carefully enveloped her in a hug.

Mimi guided Caroline over to the blue gingham-patterned couch and tapped a cushion next to her, indicating for Caroline to sit down. Mimi spent the next hour peppering Caroline with questions about life in Los Angeles – her new apartment, the office space she had leased above a trendy restaurant on Abbott Kinney, and her upcoming trip to Italy to meet with leather suppliers.

"Tell me more *<cough, cough>* about Mike," Mimi said, patting Caroline's knee and dragging in a deep breath.

"Mike? Why?"

"You've only been talking about him the whole time," Mimi said with a knowing grin, again taking in a large gulp of air.

"I didn't realize it. I guess because he's just a good friend and so ingrained in my life," Caroline replied with a shrug.

"So tell me," Mimi encouraged. Mimi of course had met Mike at the business school graduation ceremony. She knew his back story – rich kid looking to break away from his family and find his own path. She certainly could respect that and wanted to know more. As Caroline talked about the man he was – complicated, irreverent, playful yet focused, Mimi said, "Reminds me a lot of your Uncle Danny. Bring him with you next time you come visit."

"Here? You always say that Yankees are like hemorrhoids – a pain in the butt when they come down and always a relief when they go back up."

"You remember that <*cough, cough*>," she laughed.

"I remember everythin' you say," said Caroline, rubbing Mimi's knee lovingly.

"Can't say it ain't the truth," Mimi acknowledged.

"Well, he is a pain in the ass," joked Caroline.

"The good ones always are, Sweetie."

• • •

The party, being held in the recreation hall of the local chapter of the Knights of Columbus men's Catholic fraternal order, was in full swing and Mimi was in her element working the room like a skilled politician. Caroline's parents had done a wonderful job of transforming the dull, worn out, wood-paneled hall into a perky wonderland befitting Mimi's bright personality, complete with yellow and white balloons and streamers.

Family, friends, neighbors, old classmates and town staples danced to the tunes from the DJ (who doubled as the town lifeguard at the community center rec pool,) while they also pigged out on BBQ chicken, beans, coleslaw and cornbread, which had been catered from Jake's, a local favorite.

A dessert table ran perpendicular to the catering, with the homemade pies surrounding a three-tiered cake that read, "Happy 85th Mimi – Cake is Real." Caroline laughed to herself, recalling one of Mimi's favorite expressions. Whenever it was a birthday she would say, "Time is an illusion, but cake is real. So have a slice – or two – and enjoy."

As she turned around to watch a small group of little girls dancing with her dad, Caroline heard a familiar, sickeningly fake voice.

"Well, look what the cat dragged in." Standing before her wearing a too-short plum dress with a plunging neckline was Vicky Novak, the meanest mean girl that Asbury High School ever produced. She always reminded Caroline of kudzu, a highly-invasive Southern plant nicknamed "the vine that ate the South," because it takes over and destroys everything in its wake. Vicky was the personification of that green creeper.

Judging by the up and down once over she gave Caroline followed by the sneer and snarky, 'your style hasn't changed a bit,' comment, Caroline knew that Vicky was exactly the same as she had always been.

"Vicky Novak," she said, trying to control the range of emotions, from fear and loathing to exhaustion and frustration, bubbling up inside of her.

"It's Vicky Butler now. Troy and I married right after high school. He took over his dad's three car dealerships and is doing well. Very well," she continued with a smug smile. "We have two kids, but you wouldn't know by looking at me." She glided her hands down her thighs. Caroline had to fight the urge to vomit right there on the spot.

"How lovely for you two," Caroline responded drawing on all of the manners her Southern mother and Mimi had instilled in her. "Well, if you'll excuse me, I have to go check on some things in the kitchen." She hurried away and found a hiding place between the industrial refrigerator and stainless-steel counters. She scrubbed her hands over her face, being careful not to mess up her eye make-up. Suddenly she felt two hands glide up from her thighs to her hips. Before those foreign hands could reach her breasts, she turned around and gasped.

"Troy!" she exclaimed in shock.

"Heeeeey sweet Care-line," he slurred, a small amount of spit escaping his mouth and hanging on the corners where his lips curled up into a drunken smile. The smell of whiskey on his breath brought Caroline to another desire to vomit. Ironic, she thought that *both* the Butlers made her want to puke.

"Hey Troy," she said, trying to pull away from his surprisingly strong hold given how wasted he was.

"Yer as hot as I renemmbberr," he said, swaying slightly. "I always had a crush on you. Shoulda married you," he continued. Caroline managed to move out of his embrace and started to back up toward the door.

"Oh, well, you know…" she started, unsure of what to say to his drunken confession and wondering how to remove herself from the awkward situation. He stumbled toward her and she slowly walked backward. Her back hit the sink, full of soapy water and pans soaking from the caterers.

"Vickys a bitschhh and she wot suck my dick. Wouldyou suck my dick sweet Care-line," he started. He lunged for her and suddenly was pushed back by a pair of masculine hands. Before she could take in what was happening, Troy was on the floor, rubbing his jaw and what looked like a version of Alex Tuggle, a slight and gawky boy Caroline had gone to school with, stood over him, his fist poised to strike again if needed.

"Are you okay?" Alex asked.

"Uh, yeah," she said, but she definitely wasn't. Her small frame trembled, and she was on the verge of tears. Alex shepherded her out of the kitchen, through the hall and outside into the warm summer air. He sat her down on the stone steps, his hands gently holding her shoulders. Caroline took a deep breath and felt her body calming down. She looked up and got her first real glimpse of Alex.

Unlike the boy she remembered from high school, Alex was now a man. A manly man. He had grown a good four inches, his body finally catching up to his lanky arms. He had filled out nicely and she could see broad shoulders, toned biceps and likely a six-pack set of abs underneath his black fitted T-shirt. He still had kind eyes, like those of the boy she had known, but his face had matured, and his cheeks were covered in a light dusting of stubble which only gave him a slightly dangerous look.

Caroline tried to stand, but her legs were still shaky. "Just sit," said Alex, who took a place next to her. He placed a gentle hand around her shoulder and rubbed her back. "Take a deep breath."

"I'm okay," she nodded her head. "Thank you."

"I'm just glad I was there. What a dick wad."

"I'm glad you were there too," she said, the enormity of what had happened just now fully hitting her. She shuddered and Alex drew her in closer.

"It's okay." He continued to soothe her. Caroline took one last draw and let out a big exhale.

"No. I'm okay," she said. "But again, thank you. You have great timin'." Alex started to chuckle and shake his head. "What?" said Caroline, unsure of why he was reacting that way.

"Oh, nothing."

"No, it's somethin'. C'mon. Tell me," she coaxed, giving him her most charming smile, which wasn't too difficult as she continued to admire how attractive little Alex Tuggle had become.

"It was just that back in high school, I had a big crush on you," he said, glancing down at his worn black boots.

"Oh, that's sweet," said Caroline, a blush creeping over her. Alex knotted his fingers in his hands and kept staring down.

"I had finally worked up the courage to ask you to the homecoming dance. It was a Tuesday and I had just finished American history class. You were wearing a denim mini skirt and a pair of polka dot knee socks." He looked up to Caroline who was flattered by his attention to detail. "I almost lost the courage right there because you were just so cute," he said, letting out a nervous chuckle. She remembered that day.

"I walked up to your locker and I was about to ask you, but you turned around all flushed and fanning your face with your hand," he continued. "You said, 'oh my, Alex, Eddie Hoffman just asked me to the homecoming dance. Can you believe it?' I just stood there cursing myself for not asking you sooner, not that you would have said yes," he said, glancing down.

"Oh, Alex," she said breathlessly. She felt on the verge of tears.

"It's okay. Just bad timing, I suppose," he added, trying to comfort her when she knew it should be the other way around.

"I'm so sorry."

"Hey. Really. It's okay. It was a lifetime ago."

"It does feel that way, doesn't it?"

"Can I ask you a question though?" Caroline knew where he was heading with this. "If I had asked you to the dance, would you have gone with me?"

Caroline knew she had to lie just as she had lied all of those years ago. She had known Alex was going to ask her to the dance but didn't want to go with him. She lied about Eddie Hoffman, to preempt his proposal. While he was a sweet boy, he had been shy, awkward and nerdy. She knew she would have endured relentless abuse for going on a date with him and would have – politely of course – declined.

She didn't feel proud of those feelings, but she knew they were the truth, albeit a truth sweet Alex didn't deserve to know. "I don't know if this will make you feel better or worse, but of course, I would have said yes." Alex took a deep breath and shook his head.

"Perhaps you can make it up to me. Have dinner with me tomorrow?"

"I'd love to," she said, unsure if she was trying to make up for her past poor behavior or assuage the guilt she felt for knowing that given the choice, she would sadly do it all over again. "But for now, we should probably get back inside." Alex got to his feet and extended his hand to Caroline, helping her up. She looked into his kind eyes and smiled. "Thank you."

As they walked back inside, Caroline saw Vicky and one of her bitchy buddies standing at the bar. Vicky's eyes lingered on Alex and Caroline before she turned and whispered something in her friend's ear. Caroline felt the bile rise in her throat again.

● ● ●

"I hope you don't mind eating here," Alex said as they pulled up to Poochy's, the local hamburger joint in town where kids used to hang out after school. Nothing about the restaurant had changed since Caroline was last there more than ten years ago, including the oversized rooftop sign – a big, sad puppy dog, its eyes doing double duty as the "o's" in the name Poochy's. "It's just me working through some old unresolved issues," he added playfully.

"Not at all," she responded kindly. While the thought of eating greasy chili cheese fries at Poochy's was repulsive to her, she didn't want to burst Alex's bubble. He had been so kind to her the night before, confessing his earlier feelings for her and saving her from Troy's drunken advances. This was the least she could do for him.

They sat outside on the worn, circular metal seats connected to a round table bolted to the concrete. The chipping blue paint could have used a good sand blasting and replacement, as they looked and felt exactly as Caroline had remembered. Cars slowly drove down Route 5, on which the restaurant sat, as high school students and even older locals cruised the street, taking in the scene.

Over burgers, fries and a surprisingly good chocolate milkshake, Alex and Caroline caught each other up on their lives since high school. Caroline was saddened to learn that Alex's dad died of a heart attack shortly after graduation. Alex put his plans for college at Georgia Tech on hold to help his mom keep the family's local dry-cleaning business from going under.

Flash forward and he was still in Asbury, struggling to keep the family business afloat, with little hope of making a change. He didn't seem to mind though and instead shared stories of small town life and a few off-color stories about people in town who had some rather interesting dry-cleaning stains.

Caroline shared stories about school and life in LA, trying her best to temper her enthusiasm, as she knew if the roles were reversed, she would be jealous that Alex had escaped life in this stifling small town. But Alex seemed enthralled and happy for her, which only endeared himself more to her.

Caroline was glad she had agreed to go out with Alex. He was sweet and funny and grown into a lovely man, but he wasn't the man for her.

When the evening came to a close, he walked Caroline to her parents' door. He was visibly nervous about how the date would end. Caroline was equally nervous, hoping that Alex wouldn't try to kiss her goodnight. Despite being physically attracted to him, she couldn't shake the feeling that whatever happened in this town became fodder for the gossip mill the next day. And she didn't want to add any more fuel to the fire, as surely someone had seen her and Alex together this evening and was spreading rumors like jelly on a roll.

Caroline leaned forward and gave Alex a chaste kiss on the cheek. "Thank you for dinner and for rescuin' me last night," she said, pulling back quickly to avoid him pursuing anything further.

"It was great to see you Caroline," he said, rubbing the back of his neck. He turned on his heels and started to walk back to his weathered truck. "Take care of yourself in the big city," he said.

"I will. You take care too," she said, giving him a small wave.

•　　•　　•

Caroline slid into the front seat of Mike's sporty two-door Audi (a graduation gift from his parents that they insisted he accept despite their disappointment with his career choice) and buckled in as he placed her suitcase in the trunk. He pulled away from the airport curb as she stared out the window.

"What's wrong?" he asked. "Aside from the obvious."

"And what would the *obvious* be?" she asked.

"Let's see. You just spent two days at home in the shitty small town you grew up in where nothing and nobody ever changes and everyone but your folks and Mimi did a number on your self-esteem."

"Well there is that," she said, acknowledging that was part of her issue. "I just keep thinkin' about this boy I used to know in high school who I had dinner with while I was home."

"Can't stop thinking of him in a good way or a bad way. Or maybe a sexual way," he said wiggling his eyebrows up and down. Caroline slugged his arm and shook her head.

She then proceeded to spend the forty-minute, traffic-filled drive to her place telling Mike about her weekend – the time with Mimi, the party, Vicky and Troy and her *date* with Alex. Once she finally finished, Caroline rubbed her temples.

"We clearly have a lot to discuss," Mike said grimly. "So what's bothering you the most?"

"I feel badly for not wantin' to date him," she admitted, absent-mindedly playing with the air conditioner vent.

"Because he..." Mike started, putting on a fake Southern accent, "doesn't have two nickels to rub together." Caroline laughed at his poor impersonation of her.

"Gosh no. You know I don't care about that stuff. You were my bestie long before I knew you were..." she exaggerated her accent even further, "livin' high on the hog." Mike tilted his head back and laughed a full-on belly laugh.

"I know. I'm just giving you a hard time."

"I clearly couldn't date him now. He lives in Asbury and I would prefer a slow meander through the depths of hell before I'd ever move back there. I just feel like a bad person for not wantin' to date him *back then*."

"You're not a bad person because you weren't able to deal with bullies," he scoffed.

"Now I just feel like I want to help him," she said,

"You mean, give him money?" Mike questioned, taking his eyes off the road to glance at her, not convinced that was a good idea.

"I don't know what I mean. He's definitely too poor to paint and too proud to whitewash."

"It's been a while since I read *Huckleberry Finn*," he jokingly scolded her. Caroline laughed and shook her head, happy to have Mike playfully comforting her. "Let me ask you this. Did he ever say he was unhappy with the way his life has turned out?"

"No," she responded.

"Did he *seem* unhappy?" he probed. Caroline pondered the question, thinking back to Alex's body language, his demeanor and his behavior.

"No, he didn't."

"Did it bother him when you were no doubt talking about your fabulously glamorous life battling the downtown traffic on the 10 to visit Mood Fabrics and spend hours hunting through bins and bolts of cloth?"

"No," she conceded with a laugh.

"What about traversing every day past those two homeless dudes you named after the characters in *Trading Places*..."

"You mean Randolph and Mortimer?" she clarified.

"Yeah. Those guys. What about having to get past them every day just to get to your office? Did he seem enamored with that professional dream?"

"No," she laughed. "He most definitely did not."

"Well, don't take this the wrong way, but maybe these feelings you're having aren't about him at all. Maybe you're projecting your own feelings about life in Asbury onto him."

"Hmm." She considered Mike's analysis. "You could be right." She smiled a genuine smile, feeling a sense of relief. "Thank you."

"That's what I'm here for," he said, patting her knee. "Now, tell me more about this Troy character," he said, his fingers gripping the steering wheel a bit tighter.

"I really don't want to talk about that SOB," she shuddered. Mike let out a little snort. "What?"

"Oh, it's just...never mind." He shook his head.

"No, tell me," she implored.

"Well, you called the guy a SOB. That's not really an insult to him. That's more of an insult to his mom," Mike laughed.

"What?"

"Think about it. You're really just insulting his mother. Come to think of it, most insults are really just insults to someone's mom."

"Yo mama!"

"Exactly. Or Bastard," he said, pointing his finger in the air in a triumphant gesture. "Or motherfucker," he nodded in pride at having thought of another one.

"You're right," she considered. "We need to come up with a better way to insult men."

"We do," Mike agreed. "I must say, I'm surprised you aren't making some comment here that our current slurs are misogynistic and offensive to women."

"They are. I just don't have it in me today to fight that fight."

"He really did a number on you, didn't he?"

"That's enough for today, Dr. Phil," she said, not looking to rehash that particular nightmare.

"I could be Dr. Ruth if you prefer. I'm sure there's some sexually-deviant behavior we could discuss," he said in a playful tone. Caroline just laughed, rolled her eyes and patted his knee in return.

Messenger

The following week, Caroline sat at The Last Drop, sipping on a Chardonnay. She couldn't help but notice Mike arguing with one of the waitresses, a petite, slim-built blonde who clearly had used her tip money to enhance her... assets. Mike stood over her, his green eyes looking down at her with sincerity. He mouthed something to her, which Caroline desperately tried to overhear, but couldn't above the chatter of the bar crowd. Suddenly, the tiny blonde teared up and ran to the back room. Mike took a deep sigh, ran his fingers through his hair, and walked back to the bar.

"Still breakin' hearts, I see," said Caroline disapprovingly.

"I told her from the start not to get attached," Mike replied, shaking his head and again running his fingers through his hair.

"Boy, am I glad I never got involved with you," she said, playfully tapping him on the arm and rolling her eyes.

"Well, you did sleep with me once," he said, flashing her a smile.

"Once," she repeated, rolling her eyes again.

"Yeah, but you're a smart girl. Don't get into Harvard without being one."

"True," she winked at him. "So, why is she so upset?"

"We've hooked up a few times and... well, you know the rest."

"Sadly, I do."

"So, I've been meaning to ask you. What ever happened with the buyer and her short cousin?" he asked, using a towel to absent-mindedly wipe down the bar.

"Oh, you mean Cynthia. Spoke with her yesterday. She asked if I had a good time with Craig. I did what you said." She pointed at Mike. "I told her that he was a really nice guy, but I just didn't feel that spark."

"Good for you," he nodded. "I know that probably wasn't easy. I can just imagine you up all night worrying about talking to her."

"You do know me well," she said, shaking her head slightly and taking a sip of her Chardonnay.

"And how did she take it?" he asked, wiping out glasses.

"I think her exact words were, 'Yeah, he's pretty short and boring,'" she said, emphasizing the "ing" in boring, her lips forming into a thin line as she slowly nodded her head. Mike roared with laughter.

"Then why the hell did she set you up with him?"

"Good question," Caroline noted, her eyes widening and her head nodding.

"Did you ask her?"

"Goodness, no!" she said, letting out a gasp and clutching her hand over her heart.

"Too afraid of the confrontation?" he asked, already knowing the response.

"Like I said, you do know me well. That's not a confrontation I had rehearsed in my mind beforehand. No good comes from startin' an argument in an empty house."

"Yeah. I have that expression stitched on a pillow on my couch," said Mike dryly. Caroline laughed and playfully tapped his arm. "Well, at least you told her the truth that you didn't like the guy."

"Baby steps, right?"

"Right," Mike confirmed.

•   •   •

Fresh from her early evening workout, Caroline's skin still glistened with sweat as she pulled her shopping cart into the check-out line at Trader Joe's. She squatted down, holding onto the shopping cart handle, stretching out while she waited. A sudden tap on her shoulder caused her to lose her balance and falter. She turned around to see a tall blond man with a golden tan and perfect smile standing before her.

"Tyler!" she exclaimed with enthusiasm. "How the heck are you?" she said, hugging him tightly.

"Wow. This is such a surprise. You look… great." He took a step back to admire her. Caroline took mental note that she was wearing a tight-fitting pair of yoga pants that left little to the imagination and blushed.

Tyler had been a junior and volleyball setter at UCLA while Caroline was at FIDM. Tall, handsome, and eternally tanned, he was the epitome of California living. She remembered thinking guys that looked like him only existed in the movies. Maybe they did and that's why Tyler was in Los Angeles.

He was dating Julia Fredericks, a classmate of hers, who was neither a nice person nor a good designer. *Julia was so stuck up, she'd drown in a rainstorm*, thought Caroline. But she did have nice boobs, which was why a good-looking and popular guy like Tyler was probably so into her. Not that Tyler was entirely shallow. But even Caroline, a staunch heterosexual, admitted to having fantasized once or twice about Julia's boobs.

"How's Julia?" Caroline asked.

"We broke up more than a year ago," Tyler responded, specifically looking directly into Caroline's eyes. Caroline unconsciously raised an eyebrow. "We realized we just wanted different things. I heard she's a buyer at Bendels in New York. What about you? Where are you working these days?"

"Believe it or not, I started my own handbag line. I recently got picked up by Bloomingdale's, so things are hummin' along nicely," she said with pride.

"Next," called out the cashier, and the two of them moved up in line as they continued their reunion.

"That's fantastic. Wow! I'm really happy for you," He smiled broadly. "Boy, it's really great to see you. I've got to say, I had such a crush on you back then." Caroline blushed and looked down at her hands, before swatting him gently on the arm.

"What? You did not."

"I did. I have this image branded on my brain of you wearing these belly dancer pants and a pink tank top." Caroline's eyes widened at his admission.

"I totally remember those safari pants. That's hilarious," she chuckled. "Well, I hope you won't judge me for my poor fashion choices back then." They continued to move up in the line as the cashier began to ring up Caroline's items.

"Judge not, that you be not judged," he said. "I'm sure I wasn't the king of fashion in my cargo pants and backwards ball cap."

"Oh, I remember you bein' pretty stylin' back then," she said giving him a playful smirk and being sure to connect with his eyes.

"Well, I don't know about that, but I do remember Julia trying to dress me," he admitted. Caroline pulled her credit card out of her wallet and slid it through the grocery pin pad, not paying attention to the total. She signed, as Tyler continued to talk.

"I didn't seem to mind it back then, but it's not what I'm looking for now." His eyes looked at her with interest.

"And what are you lookin' for now?" she asked, tilting her head to the side and smiling slightly.

"Dinner with you, if you're free," he said as the cashier began to ring up his order of dried pasta and canned goods. "It would be great to catch up properly."

"I'd love to grab dinner sometime. Why don't I give you my number." She took his cell phone from his hand and programmed her phone number in. She handed it back to him, being sure to let her skin touch his. Tyler took his phone and looked at it with a broad smile on his face.

"I'll call you."

"Bye." Caroline waved slightly and walked away, all the while knowing that Tyler was following her black yoga pants with his eyes. As she got to her car and balanced a grocery bag while trying to open her car trunk, Caroline's cell phone rang.

"This is Caroline," she said, the bag teetering perilously on her hip.

"Hi Caroline. I said I would call," said Tyler from across the parking lot. "So, are you free for dinner Saturday night?"

"I am."

"How about I pick you up at seven?" Tyler suggested.

"Sounds great. I'll text you my address."

"Perfect. I'll see you then."

●　　●　　●

The waitress cleared away the dishes as Caroline and Tyler sat completed sated from an incredible French cuisine meal at an unassuming bistro. Caroline was glad she had worn a loose-fitting floral maxi dress, as she felt a small tummy bulge from the chocolate soufflé the two had shared.

"Wow. Sounds like you've really done well for yourself. I shouldn't sound surprised. I could tell back then you were going to be a star," Tyler said. He took his credit card out of its slot in his wallet and slid it into the faux leather check holder.

"You're just too sweet," she said, raising her hand to her heart. "And you're such a good listener. I feel like I've been lettin' my mouth overload my tail," said Caroline, taking a sip of water. "I mean, I feel like I've been monopolizin' the conversation."

"'If one gives an answer before he hears, it is his folly and shame,'" replied Tyler.

Admiring his beautiful words, Caroline said, "That's just lovely. Sounds very Shakespearian."

"Proverbs," Tyler clarified.

"I like it. So, besides managin' the sales department, what else do you do? Are you still playin' volleyball?" she asked, thoughts of a sweaty, bronzed Tyler dancing through her head, making a straight line to her groin.

"I'm on a team through Westside Volleyball. We practice on Wednesdays and have games every Saturday. You should think about joining. It's really fun."

"Oh, I don't think I'm much of an athlete," she scoffed playfully. "But maybe I could come watch sometime," she said, as the waitress returned with Tyler's receipt and credit card. Tyler's long tanned fingers stroked Caroline's hand.

"That would be great," he said, smiling into her eyes. "We could use a cheerleader."

"I think I could manage that," she responded, each stroke of his fingers matching the throbs erupting down below. "Thank you for dinner."

"My pleasure. Where to now?" he asked.

"Have you been to The Last Drop? It's not far from here. We could grab a drink?" she suggested.

"Sounds great." Tyler rose from his chair and pulled out Caroline's chair for her.

A short car ride later in Tyler's nondescript Toyota and they were at the bar. It was crowded for a Saturday night, but

Tyler and Caroline managed to find a small table near the back. He pulled out the chair for her and she sat.

"What can I get you?"

"I'll have a glass of Chardonnay. Thank you." Tyler walked to the bar while Caroline took out a small compact mirror, checking her eyeliner and lipstick.

"I see you're here with our fair Caroline," Mike said to Tyler.

"Indeed. The Lord really works in mysterious ways. I was at Trader Joe's picking up last minute items for a food drive at my church and bumped into her," Tyler volunteered.

"Lucky you," said Mike. "What can I get you?"

"Can I get a glass of Chardonnay and a club soda with a twist of lime."

"Nothing stronger for you?" asked Mike, knowing what brand of Chardonnay Caroline preferred.

"'And do not get drunk with wine, for that is debauchery, but be filled with the Spirit,'" said Tyler with flair. Mike looked a bit confused, unfamiliar with that saying. He started to pour the drinks. Tyler, noticing his confusion added, "Ephesians 5:18."

"Ah, Ephesians 5:18," said Mike, nodding his head to acknowledge he now understood it was Biblical reference. "Probably not the best line to quote to a bartender, eh?" he suggested with a playful raised brow. Tyler, recognizing his folly, laughed softly and knowingly.

"'Judge not, that you be not judged,'" he said.

"Cool man. That one I can embrace," Mike responded with a smile that reached his eyes. "Have fun with Caroline. I'm sure it will be great." Tyler nodded, laid down some cash, took the two drinks, and returned to his date.

• • •

Caroline and Tyler were splayed out on her plush couch, with him leaning on his side, propped up on one arm, the other in Caroline's hair. His tongue explored her mouth as his hand slowly massaged her head and cheek.

"You taste so good," he breathed.

"Ahhh," was all Caroline could muster in response. She clicked off her platform sandals and ran her foot in between Tyler's legs. He reached down and placed his hand at the hem of her dress, lifting it up, his fingers making slow circular motions as they climbed from her ankle to her thigh. He reached her panties, and slid his hand up through the bottom, caressing her bare behind.

"Oh, sweet lord," Caroline panted, her body responding to Tyler's increasingly erotic touch. Tyler, suddenly bolted upright, leaving Caroline unclear of what was going on.

"'You shall not take the name of the Lord your God in vain,'" he admonished.

"What?" said Caroline, her labored breath flush with confusion.

"'You shall not take the name of the Lord your God in vain.' Exodus 27. 'For the Lord will not hold him guiltless who takes his name in vain,'" Tyler repeated.

"Seriously?" questioned Caroline in disbelief. "You're quotin' me scripture?"

"I'm only following my truth," he replied. Tyler leaned in to kiss Caroline again and began his march up her thigh. She gently pushed him away with a look of confusion across her face.

"Is this somethin' new, because I don't remember you bein' so religious when you were doin' Jell-O shots off of Julia's navel durin' spring break," she questioned, her hand pressed against his chest. Tyler sat up, removing his hand from her body.

"Two years ago, I was nearly killed in a car accident. I'm pretty sure that God opened the door for me to be reborn," he explained, moving aside further so she could sit up more comfortably.

"So you found… God?" she asked hesitantly.

"I did. I am but a messenger of Jesus Christ's love."

"And God is okay with us doin'… what we were doin'?" she asked, the words coming out slowly, as she was unsure how Tyler could reconcile his behavior with his beliefs.

"Jacob was a cheater, David had an affair, and Paul was a murderer. God doesn't call the qualified. He qualifies the called," Tyler explained, looking directly into her eyes.

"And what if *I'm* not reborn?" she questioned, her eyes narrowing.

"My priority is to serve in the Lord's name" he stated simply, shrugging his shoulders and pulling his lips into a thin grin.

"Umm, I think it's... great... that you have found... Jesus... but I..." Caroline stuttered. Certainly this was not something she had anticipated and her discomfort grew, matching her racing heartbeat while she tried to articulate her feelings.

"I understand if this path isn't for you. All I know is that this is my testimony," said Tyler, sounding a bit defeated.

"I..." started Caroline, unsure of how to move beyond this awkward impasse. Thankfully, Tyler knew what to say.

"You want me to go," he said – both a question and a statement. Caroline tentatively nodded in agreement.

"Okay," she said. Tyler rose from the couch and took his jacket from behind Caroline's West Elm chair. She leaned in and gave him a chaste kiss on the cheek.

"Goodbye, Tyler, I hope you find what you're lookin' for." After he walked out of her apartment, Caroline flopped onto the couch, exhaled sharply and shook her head.

$$• \quad • \quad •$$

Caroline sat at the end of the bar, sipping on a glass of Chardonnay. She watched with amusement as Mike flirted with a group of women seated at a nearby table. Mike walked back to the bar and lined up five shot glasses, which he filled with Patron.

"So, I was watching that vampire trilogy on TV the other day and a thought occurred to me," he started.

"This ought to be good," she said tilting her head to her side and exhaling through her nose. He looked at her expectantly. "Go ahead," she said, sweeping her upturned hand across her body.

"Will a vampire get AIDS from sucking on the blood of someone who's infected?" She practically choked on her wine.

"What?" she spluttered.

"You know. If they suck out the blood and it gets into their system. Will they get the disease?"

"What on God's green earth possessed you to think of that?" she said, a small "v" forming in between her brows as she pressed her fingers to her forehead and shook her head slightly.

"I don't know. Just thinking," he said nonchalantly, shrugging his shoulders.

"Sometimes I worry about you," she said, shaking her head.

"Just sometimes?" He looked at her with a playful pout and puppy dog eyes. Caroline laughed and continued to move her head back and forth in amusement.

"So, no plans tonight? What happened to that guy who you were here with last night?" he asked.

"His name is Tyler," answered Caroline, not offering up more details.

"Ah, yes. Tyler. What is he, like a professional surfer or something?"

"He's in sales," she replied simply, again not interested in pursuing this line of questioning.

"Sales, huh? 'For the love of money is a root of all kinds of evils.' At least the Bible says that," said Mike. Caroline was taken aback by Mike's mention of the Bible. In all the years she'd known him, he had never once quoted the Bible. In fact, if anything, Mike was against organized religion.

"The Bible?"

"Yeah, you've heard that expression." He took the shot glasses to the table of attractive ladies. The women cheered and hollered, taking all but one of the glasses from the tray. Mike took the final shot and leaned it in to clink with the others.

"To Diane," the women cheered in unison before they all downed their shots and cheered again. Mike threw back his shot and collected the glasses. He smiled at the ladies before walking back to Caroline at the bar.

"Anyway, what happened with Tyler?"

Still disarmed by his canonical reference, Caroline forgot that she didn't feel like rehashing her uncomfortable evening with Mike and started to talk.

"Tyler and I knew each other in college. He was datin' a girl that went to FIDM with me. You'd like her. She had nice boobs."

"I'm intrigued," he replied with mock seduction. "Go on." Caroline laughed, knowing her statement would have elicited such a response.

"Tyler and I bumped into each other last week. We had dinner followed by drinks here, as you know. Everythin' was goin' great. We went back to my place and..." she began.

"Yes," said Mike expectantly.

"We were gettin'... amorous..."

"Amorous?" said Mike, his eyes bugging open, finding humor in her choice of euphemisms.

"Do I have to spell it out for you?" Caroline asked, clearly becoming exasperated.

"I wish you would," said Mike, raising his eyebrows and giving her more mock-seductive looks.

"You're incorrigible, you know that?" she hissed in frustration.

"I do," Mike declared. "I just wish you would drop the fake Southern thing." Caroline looked at him, feigning insult and moved her hands up and down in front of her body.

"Oh honey, this is all real."

"Yeah, you're right. I know that's all real. I slept with you once."

"Incorrigible, I tell you," she retorted.

"Okay, finish your story. You were getting *amorous*," he said, using air quotes, "when, what?"

"He started quotin' Bible scripture to me. He's become very religious since college." Mike raised his hands in the air, like a preacher praising the Lord.

"'Go into all the world and preach the gospel to all creation,'" he said emphatically.

"Now you're quotin' scripture to me? And since when do you know anythin' about the Bible?" she said with frustration. Mike leaned his head back and laughed with fervor.

"He was quoting passages to me when he came up to get your drinks last night. I figured he was a Bible thumper," he shrugged. Caroline reached her arm across the bar and swatted Mike on the chest.

"And you looked up Bible quotes to throw out at me today?" Her blood boiling, she placed her hand on her hip and cocked her head to the side.

"I did," he responded smugly. "Gotta love Google. Pretty good, huh?"

"Why didn't you warn me," she said, as she once again swatted him from across the bar.

"And miss out on this conversation? Never," he laughed.

"You could have helped me avoid an awkward situation. I clearly wasn't prepared to tell this man I wasn't interested in bein' involved with someone who's also in a serious relationship with God."

"Oh, to have been a fly on the wall for that one," said Mike, chuckling to himself.

"Hrmpf!" responded Caroline, her hand instinctively resting again on her hip.

"Well, I'm all for a good bromance, but that might be going too far," he declared. Caroline laughed and grasped ahold of her Chardonnay.

"I agree. I may be Southern, but I'm no Baptist. Lord, give me coffee to change the things I can," she lifted her glass, "and a tall glass of Chardonnay to accept the things I can't. That's about the only gospel I can get behind."

"Amen," added Mike as they both laughed.

Doctor Bag

*c*aroline stood at the bar, her yellow bucket bag hanging off her tanned shoulder. She was dressed in a casual pair of Capri jeans and a yellow and white striped tank top, with a light navy sweater slung over her arm. She watched Mike as he chatted, seemingly breezily, with a male bartender whom he had recently hired. It was a Thursday night and the bar was filled with people in casual business wear enjoying the happy hour specials.

Mike walked back to Caroline, who enthused, "I can't believe you're takin' a night off."

"Opening night of a Tom Cruise movie will always be a reason to take the night off," he responded.

"Boy, Linnea really did a number on you, didn't she?" she replied, shaking her head. Mike smirked, thinking back to fond memories of the blonde au pair to whom he lost his virginity, age fifteen, after their first joint viewing of *Risky Business*.

"She did. Give me five minutes and I'll be ready."

Mike walked to the backroom, undoubtedly double checking that all was in place for a successful night at the bar. Despite his constant dalliances with staff and patrons, Mike was quite conscientious about his work. The bar was an unabashed success, no doubt based on his years of research and keen business sense.

As Caroline waited patiently, she glanced around, her eyes falling on a large group of ten or twelve men and women in powder blue medical scrubs. One of the men stood and walked toward the bar. Caroline noticed he had a youthful face, punctuated by a few stray lines around his eyes. With his smooth, shaved head she guessed he was in his late thirties at least. He carried an empty pitcher of beer and placed it on the polished wood counter. Raising two fingers in the air, he motioned for the bartender.

"Another pitcher, please. We're celebrating."

"Well congratulations...on whatever it is you're celebratin'," said Caroline, offering a genuine smile.

"We just brought a man back from the dead. It's a good day," he said confidently.

"Oh my. Resurrectin' the dead certainly seems to be cause for a celebration, especially if you're the one who died,"

Caroline replied. He gave a small laugh and reached his hand out to her.

"True. I'm Dr. Stanhope, but you can call me Sam."

Caroline met his hand with hers. "Hi, Sam. I'm Caroline. What kind of a doctor are you?"

"I run the ER at Santa Monica hospital." He shrugged his shoulders and gestured with his hand like it was not a big deal.

"Wow. That's impressive. I imagine you see a lot of serious cases there," she replied, tilting her head, her mouth gaping open slightly.

"Between gunshot victims and drug overdoses, we stay pretty busy," he said, again shrugging it off.

"Not too busy, I see. You certainly do have some time to enjoy life."

"There was a bus that overturned on the freeway this morning and we handled triage and the red cases." A small "v" formed at Caroline's forehead.

"Red cases?"

"Those are the most emergent cases, where skilled emergency physicians with experience in major trauma are needed."

"Wow. That's *very* impressive."

"All in a day's work. So, what about you, Caroline. What do you do?" he asked, as the bartender set a pitcher of beer on the bar counter.

"Nothin' as important as savin' lives. But I do help victims of fashion emergencies. I'm a handbag designer," she said, her Southern charm oozing through. Sam laughed a low laugh.

"Well, fashion emergencies I'm sure can be very serious. Likely not fatal, but serious."

"So true," said Caroline, nodding her head in agreement and giving a smirk to feign seriousness. Mike walked out of the backroom and motioned to Caroline that he would be a minute longer. She smiled back at him with Sam taking notice.

"Looks like your boyfriend is almost ready for you."

"Oh, he's not my boyfriend. He's just my best friend." She smiled brightly at Sam.

"Oh, in that case, maybe you'd like to go out sometime?"

"Sure," she replied. "If you give me your phone, I'll put my number in." Sam handed Caroline his iPhone after unlocking his home screen. She typed her number in and glanced up at him, and their eyes locked before she returned it to him.

"I work some pretty crazy hours, so don't be offended if I don't call right away," he said. "But I will call."

"I'll look forward to it." Sam slipped his phone into the back pocket of his scrubs, took his pitcher of beer and walked back to his colleagues. Caroline smiled, feeling excited about the possibility of dating someone handsome, important, and, thankfully, taller than her. Within seconds, Mike walked up and touched her arm.

"Ready?"

"Yep, let's go." As they walked out, Sam looked over at Caroline and gave a wave. Caroline waved back and gave herself an internal hug.

• • •

The group of twelve-year-old walking hormones stood around Mike as he tried to come up with words of encouragement and support. Their baseball jerseys, reading "Scared Hitless" on the front and with The Last Drop's logo on the back, were covered in dirt, sweat, and, in one kid's case, snot.

It was the last game of the season and they had missed making it to the playoffs by a score of 12-0. Surprisingly, that was their closest match of the season.

The boys couldn't stop staring at Morgan and Loren wearing tight The Last Drop baseball-style T-shirts with blue sleeves that were gathered and knotted on one side, showing off their trim abs. Morgan took out a box of popsicles from a cooler as Mike ran his fingers through his hair.

"Okay," he began. "You fought hard. You tried your best and, hopefully, you had some fun," he said. "Hey! Hey! Eyes on me," he shouted as the boys (and some of their dads) ogled Morgan who was sucking seductively on a red, white, and blue turbo rocket popsicle in a vain attempt to get Mike's attention.

"This was a tough year. A building year," he continued. "But next season we're going to come back stronger." Noticing that not one of the boys was now paying attention to him, he said, "Okay. Go," and released the team to the waitresses who were waiting with the frozen treats.

Caroline, watching from the other side of a chain-link fence, walked over to Mike.

"Have fun?" she asked.

"Yeah. I did. You?"

"Absolutely! What could be more fun than watchin' you channel your inner *Bad News Bears*."

"At least in the movie, the team scored some runs," he said with disappointment.

"Maybe they need a better coach," she teased.

"Yeah, maybe they'll fire me," he scoffed.

"Or dock your pay," she added, swatting his chest lightly. One of the boys walked over and looked Caroline up and down hungrily.

"Hi," he said in a forced low tone while raising his eyebrow at her.

"Hi yourself," said Caroline, chuckling slightly, surprised by his audacity.

"Hey. Eyes off her," said Mike, annoyed at how these horny pre-teen boys couldn't keep their greedy eyes off his girls. "What is wrong with you?"

"Thanks, Coach Mike, for everything," he said, giving Mike a high hand shake that turned into a bro hug.

"Sure thing, Kyle. Next season, we're gonna work on those flies. Okay?"

"Yeah," Kyle replied and walked away to his parents.

"Thanks, Mike," called out Kyle's dad, as he ruffled the hair on his son's head. "Appreciate all the hours you put in." Mike smiled and waved back.

"I'm really proud of you," said Caroline, her head tilted to the side and her eyes crinkling from her broad grin.

"An 0 and 14 season. Yay," he said, lifting his hands in the air and waving them in jest.

"No, it's wonderful that you donate your time like this."

"It's good PR for the bar," he said, brushing aside her compliment.

"Layin' the groundwork with future customers, are you?" she mocked.

"Something like that. And, well, the chicks dig it." He glanced over at Morgan, who desperately continued trying to get his attention with her bordering-pornographic popsicle display.

Caroline, knowing how much *she* liked seeing him be the wonderful man he was, rubbed his arm and said, "Yeah. We do."

●　　　●　　　●

A few weeks later, Caroline and Sam strolled into The Last Drop after their third dinner date, taking a seat at the bar. Caroline rested her burgundy metal-studded wristlet on the counter. She waved at Mike with a smile. He motioned to an attractive brunette that he would be a minute and walked down toward Caroline and Sam.

"Hey doll. Chardonnay?" asked Mike.

"Of course." Turning to Sam, she continued, "He knows me so well. Sam, this is my very best friend Mike. Mike, this is Sam." The two men reached forward to shake hands, each sizing up the other.

"Caroline has told me a lot about you, Sam," Mike said while pouring a Chardonnay for Caroline. "It's nice to finally meet you. What can I get for you?"

"Oh, just a club soda with a twist of lime for me. I'm on call for level 1 trauma," he offered, lifting his head up and pulling his shoulders back, meeting Mike's gaze straight on.

"Club soda coming up," Mike said, not blinking and returning Sam's stare before bending down to pull a fresh glass from underneath the counter. "So, what are you two up to tonight?"

"We're just gonna grab a drink here and then have dinner across the street at Fabio's. Sam needs to stay in the general area in case he gets called in," she said with a little pout.

"I thought doctors on call had to stay at the hospital?" Mike asked.

"It's not like it seems on TV," scoffed Sam. "Most of the ER doctors have to stay there, but since *I* run the unit and am only on call for level 1s tonight, I can be off site as long as I'm nearby and able to get to the ER pretty quickly."

"I see," replied Mike, a fake grin sprawled across his face while he considered the arrogance of the man standing before him. "Well, lucky for you. Hopefully your date won't get interrupted."

"I'm used to it. When you save lives for a living, you really get your priorities in order and set aside your own selfish needs for the greater good," he declared. Caroline looked up at him, an impressed grin on her face, as she hung on every life-saving word he said. Mike was far less impressed. He put on the smile he reserved for dinners with his father's business associates and nodded his head in acknowledgement. "It's not something you would really understand with a regular job like Caroline has," continued Sam, "although she's been very patient." Caroline looked down at the ground, as if a bit uncomfortable.

"Don't let Caroline here undersell herself. She's quite remarkable," said Mike, giving Caroline a genuine and supportive smile.

"Oh, don't get me wrong. She's great. She's gone on and on about how great you are too. She said you two went to business school together," said Sam.

"We did. We met on the first day of class at Harvard," he offered in an effort to compete with the good doctor.

Recognizing that Mike only name-dropped Harvard because he was feeling subconsciously insecure, and wanting to diffuse a potentially tense situation, Caroline piped in, "Mike walked into the lecture hall and plopped right down next to me with a tall latte. He's been servin' me coffee and Chardonnay ever since."

"Harvard? You didn't tell me that, Caroline," said Sam, showing her some level of adulation.

"She's very modest," said Mike.

"But you're not?" replied Sam with a hint of annoyance in his voice. The moment of awkward silence ended when Sam continued, "Just kidding, man. But let me ask you. If you went to Harvard Business School, what are you doing running a bar?" he asked, looking to take Mike down a peg or two.

Caroline slapped Sam's arm. "Sam!"

"No. It's okay. I get that question a lot... especially from my dad. We only have one chance in this life. So we should do what makes us happy and be with the people that make us happy," Mike explained.

"You're right. Life's short. When it's your time, it's your time. Unless I'm around," Sam responded, puffing out his chest slightly and plastering a smug grin on his face.

"Now look who's being modest," said Mike, tilting his head to the side and flashing a grin. "Ha! I'm just kidding too," he added after a beat, crinkling his nose and nodding his head. He took a bar towel, rubbed some condensation from the wood and turned to walk back down to an awaiting brunette. "You guys enjoy."

•   •   •

The outdoor beach café was barely crowded, owing to the fog emanating from the coast. Caroline pulled her pale pink sweater, which perfectly matched her floral print fabric tote bag, closer across her body. Mike took off his denim jacket and placed it over her shoulder.

"Thanks," she said.

"Do you want to see if we can move inside?"

"I'm okay now, as long are you are," she replied, appreciative of Mike's concern.

"I'm warm enough."

"So chivalrous. A girl could get used to that."

"Well, you deserve someone treating you well. Speaking of which, I can't believe you've been seeing that guy for over a month. When are you going to dump that arrogant asshole? Coming into the bar with his scrubs on, always talking about his job like he's some hero," said Mike with increasing agitation.

"He's not arrogant and he's not an asshole," she replied firmly.

"The guy has a god complex. And after that Tyler dude, I thought you would have had enough with that," he retorted.

"Well, he does save people's lives," said Caroline, trying to keep her growing anger at Mike in check.

"I know plenty of humble doctors. Believe me, that guy is a douche."

"You're drivin' me crazy!"

"I don't need to *drive* you crazy. You're close enough where you can walk there all on your own," he said, shaking his head. Caroline laughed.

"If that wasn't so damn funny, I would be really angry with you," she said between fits of giggles.

"But you're not. Because I'm adorable," he said, batting his eyelashes at her.

"Incorrigible, maybe," she said back, smiling at him. Caroline's phone rang and upon recognizing the number, she drew a deep breath and her expression turned serious.

"This is Caroline," she said in her most charming Southern voice. She listened intently and nodded her head. Mike watched her expression harden and her resolve strengthen as muffled sounds through the phone were heard. "I see. Well, my attorney assures me the contract is valid. And I have no problem askin' her to pursue its enforcement." Mike looked at her in awe. "I'm glad we see eye to eye. I will expect that shipment on Monday, as scheduled. Thank you." Caroline hung up the phone, her hand trembling.

"What the hell was that all about?" said Mike, still amazed at Caroline's words.

"A vendor doesn't want to meet his deadline. I'm literally shakin'. I can't believe I just did that."

Mike clapped his hands. "Bravo! I've never heard you speak like that to someone before. Well, except me."

"I haven't, except for you," she replied, her voice shaky. "But I've been seein' a therapist and she's helpin' me to find my voice. Everyone assumes that I'm just some sort of Southern bimbo and they can take advantage of my kind nature. But I'm takin' baby steps to stand up for myself."

"Therapist, huh? See, you're not that far from crazy after all." Caroline rolled her eyes at him. "Seriously. That's good. So now you're just a ruthless business woman wrapped in a charming *fake* Southern accent."

"I've worked hard to get where I am. And just because I sound so sweet and charmin' with my *real* Southern accent," she said, laughing and clearly more relaxed, "doesn't mean I don't deserve to get what I've worked hard for. That's what Dr. Watanabe keeps tellin' me."

"Maybe *you* should go work for my father," said Mike, disdain dripping from his voice as he glanced down to the left and looked at the pavement.

"Have you spoken to him lately?" asked Caroline, her mouth open in surprise.

"No. I talked with my mom a few weeks ago though, and she tried to convince me to come home," he answered, looking back up and shaking his head back and forth while exhaling sharply through his nose.

"I can't imagine not havin' my family's support. I talk to my parents every week, sometimes three or four times a week."

"You just don't know my parents... Too bad you can't be my proxy. I think you would fit in just fine with all of those hard-nosed financial types. You did ace statistics and accounting."

"That's true. I do well with the numbers. But a brokerage firm? No thanks. Too borin'. Do you see me fittin' in there?" she scoffed.

"You've got a head for business and a bod for sin."

"What?" she questioned, that "v" forming on her forehead again.

"It's from *Working Girl*. Not a Tom Cruise film but one of Linnea's favorites. Melanie Griffith played a smart secretary who tried to make it big in business."

"Sounds like my kind of movie," she considered.

"Come over Monday night unless you're going out with *God*," he said in a mocking tone, "and we'll watch it."

"Sam's on call, so that's perfect," she replied, ignoring his fussiness.

•　•　•

Mike's apartment was the typical bachelor pad. Located in Brentwood and therefore an easy walk to the bar, it housed a leather couch and matching recliner chair, oversized TV, and stereo sound system. From a decorating standpoint, it was rather sparse, save for the framed posters from Tom Cruise movies that lined the back wall.

Carly Simon's "Let the River Run" blared through the speakers as the credits rolled up the screen, while Caroline sat on the edge of the couch and Mike leaned back into the soft cushion.

"Well? What did you think?" he asked anxiously.

"I... *loved* it," she replied, clapping her hands together rapidly. "She's sassy and smart and so brave. I can't believe I had never seen that movie before."

"I knew you'd like it." Caroline stood up and walked toward the bathroom.

"I'll be right back." Mike grabbed the empty popcorn bowl and half-drunk glasses of wine and walked toward the kitchen. Caroline's phone rang and Mike reached to answer it.

"Caroline's phone."

"Uh, is Caroline there," said a confused voice on the other end.

"Yeah, just hold on a minute," he replied. Caroline walked back into the room as Mike handed her the phone.

"For you."

"This is Caroline," she said in her usual friendly tone.

"It's Sam. Where are you?" he demanded.

"Hi, Sam. I'm over at Mike's watchin' a movie. Have you seen *Workin' Girl*?"

"Mike?" asked Sam in disbelief.

"Yeah," said Caroline, unclear why this would come as such a shock.

"You know, I just don't think this is going to work," he said to Caroline.

"What are you talkin' about?" she said, a lump forming in her throat.

"I just got off of a thirty-six-hour shift and called you to find out you're on a date with someone else," he said sternly.

"It's not a date. We're just friends," said Caroline imploringly.

"You keep telling yourself that."

"Sam, you're bein' ridiculous. There's nothin' goin' on here," she said in her most convincing tone.

"I'm not willing to take that chance. Listen, I work sixty to seventy hours a week saving people's lives. I've got enough drama in the ER. I don't need it in my personal life. Goodbye, Caroline."

"Sam…" she said, before realizing he'd already hung up. She stood before Mike, dumbfounded. "He just dumped me," she said, her mouth gaping open, the phone resting in her listless hand.

"What?" said Mike, not believing what he was hearing.

"He said he has enough drama at work and doesn't believe that you and I are just friends," she said, pacing around the room.

"Good riddance. He thought he was better than everyone and never seemed to respect you or your work."

"He didn't even want to listen," she said, stopping in place.

"Like you could have changed his mind? Honestly, did you think you could go head to head with that condescending megalomaniac?"

"I'm makin' progress. You've seen it," she responded harshly.

"Well, you've never had a problem arguing with me," he retorted angrily.

"No. That's always been easy," she said with a smile, trying to diffuse the growing tension between them. Caroline paused for a moment. *Maybe*, she thought, *Sam was right. Maybe it was weird that she and Mike spent so much time together.* "Maybe he's right," she said out loud. "Maybe this…" she gestured between the two of them, "is weird. Maybe I shouldn't…"

"What? Us?" said Mike, not liking where Caroline's mind was headed. "We're not weird. And stop over-analyzing the he said/she said right now. He wasn't good enough for you." Caroline once again started to pace around the room. Mike grabbed her shoulders and looked into her eyes. "Hey! Look at me. It's not weird. There's never anything wrong with being with someone who makes you happy."

Unsure of her feelings on the matter, Caroline responded tentatively, "You're right."

Of course I'm right, thought Mike. "We can be friends and nothing more. Believe me, I'm not interested in you in that way."

Feigning insult, Caroline retorted, "Oh really? Because as I recall, we did sleep together once." It felt good for her to throw that in Mike's face for once.

"Yeah. Only once. Wasn't worth repeating," he said, flashing her a smile.

"That's hitting below the belt," she sneered.

"That sounds dirty," Mike retorted, his eyebrows wiggling up and down.

"You're a perv," she huffed.

"Do you prefer the expression 'low blow' because that's sounding pretty pervy too. Seriously, though. First, you're adamant that we're just friends and now you're upset that we aren't more than friends," he said, clearly making fun of her.

"I don't know. I don't want it to be weird that we're just friends, or that we once…" Her voice trailed off.

"Did the deed?" asked Mike, raising his eyebrows at her.

"Thank you for restrainin' yourself with that one," she replied facetiously. Mike roared with laughter again.

"You just want to be the one deciding we're just friends, not me," he scolded her playfully.

"Exactly! Who doesn't want to be wanted?" she replied with an equally playful tone.

Mike shook his head at her. "And you say I'm incorrigible!" he scoffed. "Well, I'm sorry about Sam, but I know you're better off without him."

"Perhaps," she responded thoughtfully.

"There's someone else out there for you. Someone better," he said confidently.

"I hope you're right," she replied as he hugged her.

Baguette

axine sat at the newly-assembled desk Caroline had purchased from IKEA (and Mike had begrudgingly put together) clasping her hands in excitement. She couldn't believe that Caroline had really hired her to be her assistant. She had just graduated from college at Cal State Long Beach and was thrilled to find a job in fashion.

Maxine seemed very eager and fashionable – two things Caroline felt would be important. Even though she didn't have much business experience, Caroline was confident that Maxine would pick things up quickly.

Caroline's only real concern about Maxine was how Mike would react to her. She had made him promise not to hit on Maxine and even if Maxine came on to him, which was likely given he was...well Mike...he could not sleep with her. He promised to keep his charms to a minimum and assured Caroline he could control himself. After meeting the auburn-haired, green-eyed beauty, Mike understood why Caroline had made him agree on a hands-off policy in advance.

The timing of Maxine's arrival couldn't have been better, as Caroline was set to leave a few days later for a week-long trip to Italy to meet with her leather supplier, bring back samples and do some trend research for her upcoming line. She figured the meetings would last two to three days and built in a few days to tour around Florence.

• • •

After touching down in Italy and surviving a harrowing cab ride to the hotel, Caroline checked into her modest room, running her fingers along the simple blue and white bedspread. While business was strong enough to enable her to hire an assistant and make a personal visit to Italy to sample leather and negotiate a purchase order, she still had to be mindful of budgets.

She stared out the window, her cheek brushing against the gossamer curtains, and admired the view. Laid out before her was a stunning site – Florence's famed Duomo which housed the city's main and most famous cathedral. She looked in amazement at the pink, white and green marble exterior and wondered how different it would look at night. She would find out soon enough. But for now, she needed to wait downstairs for the car service that would drive her to meet Vincenzo Marcucci, her leather supplier. While they had never met in person before, she had enjoyed their phone and email correspondences. She was eager to put a face with the voice and virtual experiences.

Her time with Vincenzo didn't disappoint. A thin, elderly man who was a seventh-generation tanner and leather supplier, he kissed both of Caroline's cheeks and offered her a glass of wine before spending the next four hours touring her through his leather factory and explaining his family's long-held secrets and methods for providing Italy's finest leather to designers like her.

Spent from her afternoon with Vincenzo, Caroline returned to the hotel and had a quiet dinner in the restaurant downstairs. She went to bed early, exhausted from a combination of travel, jet lag and the detailed description of the Marcucci's new family process of tanning without the use of harsh chemicals, which was not only better for the environment but was proven to better prevent decomposition. Caroline almost wished she had taken some chemistry classes in college to better understand what Vincenzo was talking about. But she felt confident enough in him and his products to take his word at face value. She had a few more hours of meetings planned with Vincenzo and his daughter, Geovana, the following day to go through samples and place her order. After that, it would be time to explore the city and soak in all of the amazing culture and food Italy was best known for.

•   •   •

Caroline was thoroughly enjoying browsing through the outdoor San Lorenzo markets. Stall after stall was filled with leather goods, clothing and souvenirs. She had already purchased a case of red wine to send home to her parents in Asbury. While they were unlikely to appreciate the quality, they would certainly appreciate the thoughtful gesture.

Now she was engaged in a fierce bargaining battle with a vendor over two leather strap bracelets with engraved initials for Kayle and Lydia. These, along with the leather wallet for Mike and handmade candle for Maxine would help round out her gift list. The only person she had yet to find the perfect gift for was Mimi.

After securing the bracelets for what she determined through her online research was a fair price – half of what the vendor had initially quoted her – she saw a stall selling silk scarves. A pink and purple leopard print caught her eye and she knew she had found what she had been searching for.

As she carefully placed the folded scarf in her large cloth shopping tote, a blue scooter zoomed past her, knocking her on her behind. Dazed, but unhurt, she started to stand and realized the scooter driver had pulled over his motorized bike to assist her. He held out a strong hand and pulled her to her feet. She looked up to find the biggest, darkest brown eyes she had ever seen.

"Le mie scuse. Stai bene?" he said, still holding onto Caroline's hand. Caroline just stood, staring at the thick and beautiful lips that just uttered what had to be the most romantic words ever spoken in the history of language. Of that she was certain. "Parli Italiano?" Caroline stood frozen. "Parlez-vous français?" Time stood still. "American?"

Hearing something familiar, and not nearly as beautiful as what had been previously said, broke Caroline out of her reverie. "Yes. I'm American," she said, blinking her big blue eyes rapidly, a smile creeping across her lips.

"Are you okay, American?" the handsome stranger asked with a thick European accent.

"Yes, I'm fine," she breathed. She leaned down and picked up her tote bag with trembling fingers. Caroline didn't know if she was shaking from her near-death experience or because she was standing in front of the sexiest man she'd ever seen. Take away the accent and he still ranked up there in the top five.

"You don't seem okay, American," he said with smiling eyes. "Perhaps a caffé will help." Caroline nodded in affirmation and let the raven-haired sex god, or at least she had already built him up that way in her mind, lead her a few blocks over to a small café where he ordered two coffees and some biscotti.

"So tell me American, what are you doing here in Florence?" he asked.

"First off, my name is Caroline" she clarified. He took her hand in his and brought it up to his plump red lips, gently pressing them against the back of her hand. Caroline shivered.

"Un beau nom pour une belle femme," he murmured. "I am Sasha."

"That was beautiful. What did you just say?" she asked in awe.

"I said it was a beautiful name for a beautiful woman." Caroline blushed and took a sip of her coffee.

"In Italian?"

"French. I am from Maisons-Laffitte outside of Paris, here for a few weeks on holiday." Caroline was drawn to his lips, which seemed to caress the ceramic coffee cup as he sipped his drink. She wondered what those lips would feel like on her skin.

"Sounds wonderful," she said, coming out of her daydream. "I'm here for business but added a few days to tour around. It's my first time in Florence."

"You do not speak Italian?" he asked.

"No."

"Clearly not French. Spanish?"

"No. Just English."

"Ahh. Typical ethnocentric American, only speaking one language. Too bad. Language can be so beautiful."

"Well all of these languages certainly sound beautiful when you speak them," she said, glancing down at her lap.

"So, here in Florence, what have you done so far?" he asked, draining his cup.

"I've been to the cathedrals, piazzas and palazzos so far," she explained. "I don't know how anyone can get anythin' useful done around here. I'm so distracted by all of the beauty around me." Sasha stared directly into Caroline's eyes.

"I seem to be distracted by beauty as well," he said. Caroline exhaled sharply and then looked away, unable to maintain such intense eye contact.

"Have you been to the Uffizi Gallery yet?"

"Not yet, but it's on my list of things to do before I leave on Saturday."

"Come," he said, reaching his hand out to hers. "Let us go now." Caroline couldn't resist his offer and placed her hand into his, hoping that her sweaty palms were hardly noticeable.

After a four-hour tour of the Uffizi with Sasha, Caroline had a new appreciation for Michelangelo, Botticelli and da Vinci. She also was finding herself completely smitten with the Frenchman.

She knew she would be leaving Florence in two days and that a long-distance relationship was out of the question. She couldn't imagine dating someone who lived in the Valley, let alone across an ocean. But for now and the next two days, she was going to enjoy as much of his company and beautifully-formed lips as he was willing to give her.

●   ●   ●

Men and women bustled along the busy, winding streets of Florence, heading to and from work, home, meetings and shopping. But all Caroline and Sasha could do was sit on a bench in the park and kiss. Caroline was closely nestled on his lap and his lips completely consumed hers.

"Tu es si belle, Jenet," he said as he pulled her lower lip into his mouth.

"I could listen to you speak French all day," she murmured. "What did you say?"

"You are so beautiful," he translated as his hands ran through her blonde strands. Caroline sighed.

"Je pourrais t'embrasser toute la journée, Jenet," he moaned into her mouth, his tongue gently caressing hers.

"And that?" she breathed. "What does that mean?"

"I could kiss you all day," he said, pulling back a moment and staring into her eyes. "You silly American girl," he said shaking his head. "So typical only knowing English," he scoffed.

Before Caroline could absorb the insult, he leaned in and kissed her again. All thoughts beyond the pleasure his mouth was bringing to her body went out the window.

"Mmm, Jenet. Tes lèvres sont le plus doux nectars."

"English, please," she moaned. "Don't stop the French. Just add in a little translation," she said with a smile.

"Your lips are the sweetest nectar," he groaned as his lips continued to tangle with hers.

And so it continued like this for hours, with Caroline and Sasha taking breaks from kissing to walk around Florence and enjoy its sights, sounds and tastes.

When Sasha tried to coax Caroline to spend the night with him before her morning flight home, she replied, "These two days have been amazin'. I want to remember them for bein' just as perfect as they are right now."

•   •   •

Surprisingly, the flight home passed by quickly, as Caroline's thoughts were wrapped up in memories of Sasha. She had been sad to say goodbye to him and could still feel the bit of sting on her skin where his stubble had rubbed against her cheeks and chin for hours as they kissed throughout the city.

On one hand, she regretted not sleeping with him. Not many women get the chance to bed a handsome, sophisticated and sexy Frenchman. He was so skilled with his lips and tongue she would have enjoyed having them on other parts of her body. If he kissed that well, chances were he was a skilled lover in general.

On the flip side, the kissing was so perfect she didn't want to risk the memory of that perfection with bad or even mediocre sex. She was quite certain she'd be able to survive for months off of the fantasy alone of sex with Sasha.

•   •   •

Mike walked up to Caroline who sat at the outdoor café, speaking into her phone repeatedly and then scowling at the screen. He placed a tray with two salads and two iced teas down. She glanced up and gave him a smile.

"What are you doing that's got you all hot and bothered?" he asked.

"I'll take the 'hot' part as a compliment," she said with a wink. "I'm tryin' to figure out what a word means in French."

"What word?" he asked, placing a paper napkin in his lap.

"Je-nay," she said, trying hard to enunciate and clearly articulate the French word.

"Jenet?" he repeated.

"Yes."

"Why?" he asked in confusion, digging into his salad.

"Sasha kept saying it while we were..." her voice trailed off.

"While you were getting it on with Frenchie," he finished, his statement tinged with mild disgust.

"We were just kissin', not that it's any of your business," she said, her salad-speared fork held in midair. "But it was so beautiful and romantic and he kept murmuring it," she explained, waving the fork around slightly with a wistful look in her eye as she recalled her marathon make out sessions with Sasha. He was both passionate and tender, which didn't seem contrary to her in the slightest. "I didn't have the guts to ask what it meant, so I thought I would try to look it up. I'm either not spellin' it right, not sayin' it right, or my accent is gettin' in the way because my translation app isn't workin'."

"Mmm," Mike hummed, acknowledging her words but not commenting on them.

"You don't happen to speak French, do you?" she laughed, giving his hand a playful tap before she took a sip of her iced tea.

"Mais bien sûr, je parle francais. Gwen Barnsworth a envoyé son fils aux pensionnats les plus prestigieux où le français était obligatoire," he rattled off nonchalantly before placing a mouthful of salad in his mouth and giving her a look that demanded "bring it on." Caroline's eyes widened and she gave him a mock exasperated look.

"I take it that's a yes," she said, nodding and grinning.

"Oui," he said, his eyes sparkling with humor.

"Of course, you speak French." Caroline rolled her eyes as Mike continued to munch on his lunch. "What did you say?"

"I said that of course I speak French. Gwen Barnsworth only sent her son to the finest boarding schools where French was mandatory. Not that it's come in handy much at the bar, but you never know."

"You're like an onion, Mike," said Caroline, fascinated by learning something new about him.

"A French onion?" he suggested. Caroline laughed at his joke, as she always did.

"Yes, a French onion. So many layers. I had no idea." She shook her head not in disbelief, but in amusement. "What other hidden talents do you have?"

"Oh, I think you already know," he said, waggling his eyebrows up and down. Caroline, rolled her eyes, as she always did when Mike made lascivious comments about their one mistaken hook up.

"Not in the mood to go down that road," she said, wagging a disapproving finger at him.

"Route," he corrected her. "That's road in French," he said winking. "So tell me more about your meetings in Italy."

"Not so fast," she insisted. "What does 'je-nay' mean?" Mike shifted uncomfortably in his chair and his uneasiness was clearly visible to Caroline.

"Why does it matter? You already said you didn't exchange anything with the guy but some spit."

"You're so romantic," she scoffed.

"I mean, you didn't even get his last name. It's not like you're going to stay in touch. So why does it matter? I want to hear more about Italy."

"It must be really bad. Tell me. What does it mean? Bad kisser? Bad breath? Oh Lord. What does it mean?" she said, growing more and more agitated as she spoke.

"Jenet is French for the name Janet," he said, looking down at his salad.

"So he was kissin' me and callin' out another woman's name," she said, too calmly for Mike's liking.

"Bad breath is looking pretty good right about now, huh?" he said with a shrug, trying as always to diffuse the situation with humor. Caroline lowered her head into her hands.

"How humiliatin'." She couldn't even look up to meet Mike's eyes. She quickly raced to the ladies room and threw up. *Why does this shit keep happening to me*, she thought. She shook her head while staring at her reflection in the mirror. Disgusted with what she saw staring back at her, she rinsed her mouth out with water and walked back to the table to tell Mike she was heading home.

•   •   •

She honestly didn't know how long she'd been in her bed. She did know she'd heard him at her door at least three times, pounding his fist and calling her name.

"Caroline. Come on. It's me. Open up. I have your spare key. Don't make me use it," he threatened. Caroline walked over to the door, opened it and walked back to the bedroom. Mike's eyes were burning with anger and frustration.

"You haven't returned my call in two days," he said, his voice starting out harsh and authoritative before becoming more measured – more sympathetic – as he continued, "I've been worried about you."

When he saw her swollen eyes and the half-eaten/half-thawed pint of ice cream on the nightstand, he took a deep breath and exhaled sharply through his mouth.

"Why are you wearing your period pants?" he said, squinting his eyes, his mouth pulled into a grim line.

"Period pants?" Caroline questioned.

"Yeah," he said, pointing at her sweatpants, "those ugly worn-out black sweatpants that are now more of a shade of dark grey, that you wear on the first day of your period."

"I do not," she huffed, affronted by his rude accusation.

"You do," he replied, nodding his head.

"That's disgustin'."

"Yes, those sweatpants are," he agreed.

"Not the sweatpants," she huffed. "That you think I wear them when I have my period."

"It's not disgusting sweetheart. It's the truth. And I know for a matter of fact you do not have your period."

"How do you know I don't have my period?" she asked, with a mixture of both curiosity and disgust.

"Because I know your cycle and you're not due to be on the rag for another two weeks."

"You *know* my cycle?"

"I do. It's called self-preservation! You think it's just lucky that I bring you chocolate chip cookies and ice cream every month precisely when you need it?" Caroline gasped.

"So what gives?" he asked, his hand cocked on his hip.

"Sasha," she whispered. Mike shook his head, not believing that Caroline was wasting her energy and further depleting her fragile self-esteem on that guy.

"At least you didn't sleep with him," he offered with a small shrug of his shoulders.

"What a lovely silver linin'" she scoffed.

"He's French. Clearly he's stupid." Caroline laughed quietly to herself and displayed an enigmatic grin. "What?" said Mike, knowing there was something interesting behind that Mona Lisa smile.

"I'm just thinkin' of somethin' funny Mimi once said. She and my Uncle Danny had gone to Paris for their 35th weddin' anniversary. She came home and told me how brilliant the people were because even the little kids could speak perfect French." Caroline's grin broadened at the memory.

"That's hilarious. I hope to God she was joking," he responded.

"Of course," said Caroline. "Despite being born and bred in the deep south, Mimi was as progressive as they come."

"Well, I don't think speaking French makes you smart. Just look at me," he offered.

"Sasha made some snide remark while we were together that like a typical American, I only spoke one language. I dismissed it, because, well, I was enjoyin' his kiss, but now that I think about it, he was quite rude."

"Pretty typical of the French to bash Americans. Know what they would be calling Paris if it weren't for us *Americans*?" he asked smugly. Caroline shrugged. "Berlin!" At that, she let out a raucous laugh and knew she would get through this.

Diaper Bag

*T*he five girls were seated at the bar, and Caroline marveled at how hard Mike was flirting with Lydia, flashing his winning, panty-dropping smile. Caroline just shook her head and took a sip of her Chardonnay, listening to him recount his one-year stint at the prestigious Allendale Academy. While she had heard the stories numerous times before, she still found herself chuckling at all the right spots. And Lydia, despite knowing all she knew about Mike, was flirting back with equal enthusiasm, laughing seductively and gently touching his arm.

Caroline turned to see how Kayle was faring with this scene unfolding before her, but Kayle's eyes were elsewhere. She was checking out a raucous group of men dressed in smart business pants and button-down shirts, with the sleeves rolled up who were sitting at a nearby table.

A tall African American man with warm eyes and gleaming white teeth was taking an equal interest in Kayle, who was dressed in a Kelly-green halter top which accentuated her wavy honey-colored locks. The man turned to his friend, whispered something in his ear, and approached Kayle.

"Hey ladies," he said, not taking his eyes off of Kayle. "Today is my buddy Damien's birthday and we're trying to give him a good time. I'm sure he would love it if you came over to wish him a happy birthday," he said invitingly. Kayle took her eyes off him only for a moment to look at the group of well-groomed men, laughing and enjoying themselves.

"Sure. Why not?" she said, smiling. She motioned for Lydia, Caroline, and the two other girls to follow, which all but Lydia did obligingly.

"I'm Alex, by the way," he said to Kayle. She smiled and introduced herself in return. Caroline smiled as she watched the electricity between the two of them unfold. She slid into a chair next to a man with light brown hair that was beginning to gray at the temples. He had warm hazel eyes and a boyish smile.

"Wow! You're pretty," he said to her as he put down a shot of tequila and sucked on a lime. Caroline blushed and gave an embarrassed smile. "Am I not supposed to say that out loud?

It's been a while since I've been out. Am I not supposed to say stuff like that?"

"No, you can tell me I'm pretty," she said, feeling flattered.

"You're *really* pretty." He put down his lime, wiped his hand on his pants and reached out to shake Caroline's. "I'm Damien."

"I'm Caroline," she responded, meeting his hand and his gaze. "Nice to meet you. Happy birthday by the way," she said brightly as she noticed happily that Lydia had joined the group.

"Thanks. I've had a bit more to drink than usual so I apologize in advance if I say anything I shouldn't," he said with mock warning.

"Like I'm pretty?" she asked, batting her eyelashes at him.

"No. You really are pretty." A flush of red crept up his cheeks as he looked away slightly.

"Thanks." Caroline glanced down at her lap and then looked back up to meet his eyes. "So, what's your story, Damien?"

"I'm a management consultant for a big firm. In fact we all are. The guys didn't want to let my thirtieth birthday go by without making a big deal out of it."

"Thirty, huh? Well, you don't look a day over twenty-nine, if that makes you feel better," she joked.

"I'm not sure that it does, but I'll take it."

The next hour or two were a blur of laughing, drinking, and flirting among the group of attractive men and women crowded around two bar tables pushed together. Kayle got up to use the ladies' room and Alex leaned over to Damien, whispering something in his ear. Damien shook his head no, but Alex nudged his arm and nodded his head up and down. Damien turned to Caroline.

"Listen, before I drink too much and either embarrass myself or forget, I was hoping I could call you sometime," he said nervously. Caroline found his shyness charming.

"Sure," she responded and reached for his cell phone on the table. She programmed her number in and then looked up to see Damien – and his buddy – smiling. "Will you excuse me for a moment. I need to visit the ladies' room."

In the restroom, Caroline met up with Kayle, who was fixing her lush waves in the mirror. "Well, you seem as happy as a dead pig in the sunshine," Caroline said.

"He's hot," said Kayle, giving Caroline a big smile. "I'm going home with him."

"Oh really?" said Caroline, both impressed and slightly surprised.

"Yeah, he doesn't know it yet, but that man and I are going to do some serious damage together." She smiled and gave Caroline a quick squeeze on her shoulders. "I'll see you out there," she continued and walked out.

Caroline looked into the restroom mirror and used a wet paper towel to gently wipe some smudged eyeliner from beneath her eyes. She readjusted her ponytail and walked back out toward the bar to say hello to Mike.

"Looks like you're having fun," Mike said.

"I am. He's pretty drunk but very sweet. He keeps tellin' me how pretty I am. You know I'm a sucker for a good compliment."

"Yeah, you're pretty easy. And I should know," he remarked. Caroline responded with her all-too familiar eye roll.

"Is he in here often?"

"Never seen him before. One of his buddies comes in frequently. Single malt, neat. But I haven't seen…"

"Damien. His name's Damien," she said, filling in the space.

"Damien," confirmed Mike.

"Well, I better get back over," she said, blowing Mike a kiss.

"Have fun," he replied, giving her a small smile.

The night wore on and, before she knew it, Mike was ringing a brass bell and shouting for last call. Alex helped Damien out of his chair and steadied him. Damien swayed slightly, the tequila shots and beers having left their impression on his equilibrium. Kayle, concerned that Alex would be leaving to get Damien safely home, helped prop up the drunken businessman. She smiled at Alex who seemed to understand her motivations.

"Okay buddy. I think it's time to get you home," said Alex.

"Okay. Caroline?" Damien spluttered, slurring his words as he scanned around the table. "Caroline. I'll call you."

Shifting Damien's weight onto him and guiding him toward the door, Alex said, "He'll call you, Caroline." He turned his attention back to Damien. "Okay," he said, dragging him away, flanked by Kayle on the other side, "okay, here we go."

Caroline watched Alex and Kayle help a drunken Damien out the door. "Bye, Damien. Hope you had a fun birthday. Call me tomorrow, Kayle." Kayle turned back to her and winked. Caroline glanced around the bar and saw that Mike was busy closing out the night's receipts. She waved goodbye and put her hand to her ear, indicating she would give him a call, before walking out the door.

•   •   •

Caroline stood in her kitchen slicing an apple. Her hips bumped up and down to Nellyville's "It's Getting Hot in Here" as the sharp blade cut through the tender fruit. Her shoulders started to rise and fall as she danced around her apartment. Her impromptu dance party was interrupted by her ringing cell phone. She lowered the music and glanced at the phone on the counter. Not recognizing the caller ID, she answered in her sweetest voice.

"Hello. This is Caroline," she said, her body still moving to the music.

"Hi, Caroline. This is Damien," the disembodied voice on the other end of the phone said nervously. "We met at The Last Drop a few weeks ago."

Caroline shut the music off and steadied her body. "I remember," she said flatly, unsure if she was happy to hear from Damien or angered that he had taken three weeks to call her.

"First of all, thanks for not hanging up on me. I'm sorry I didn't call you sooner. Believe it or not, I've been hung over this whole time," he said, hoping she would find him charming.

He succeeded and Caroline laughed. "Well, you did have quite a bit to drink."

"I did," he continued. "And as much as I don't remember a whole lot about that night, I do remember how sweet and pretty you were and that I promised to call you." Caroline found his honesty and sincerity to be refreshing and knew at that moment all was forgiven.

Eager to see where the conversation led, she said, "You certainly know how to flatter a girl."

"Good to know I didn't blow it. It's been a while since I've been out there."

"Well you're doin' just fine," she advised. She recalled this wasn't the first time he had mentioned being a bit inexperienced in this area. She could relate, having suffered a broken heart before and mild humiliation not so long ago.

"So, I was wondering," he began with a shaky voice, "if you were free on Saturday night to have some dinner...with me?" His voice rose a bit too sharply at the end, betraying his attempts at confidence.

Saturday night? Saturday night? She racked her brain to think if she had plans for Saturday night. Nothing other than hanging out with Mike at the bar sprung to mind. "Saturday night would be great. What did you have in mind?"

"Why don't I plan to pick you up at seven and I'll make a reservation somewhere. Would that be okay?" he continued tentatively.

"That sounds lovely. Why don't I text you my address."

"Good. Good. Okay then," he said, satisfaction in his voice. "I'll see you Saturday."

•　　•　　•

Damien stood outside of Caroline's apartment building, dressed in a pair of dark-washed jeans and a button-down shirt. He breathed into his hand, checking his breath, and let out a large exhale. Psyching himself up, he balled two fists side by side and said, "You can do this. Don't be a pussy." He inhaled sharply again, shook his head vigorously, and then rung Caroline's doorbell.

Caroline's heart raced when she saw Damien. She hadn't fully remembered his hazel eyes and was struck by their immediate warmth.

"Wow. You look amazing. Even prettier than I remember," he said, clearly in awe of Caroline's beauty. She wore a blue chiffon blouse that made her eyes look the color of unspoiled ocean.

"Well, you're just as charmin' as I remember," she replied. Damien leaned in awkwardly to hug her and she kissed his cheek sweetly.

"Sorry, I just…" he started.

"You're doin' just fine," said Caroline, putting her hand on his arm and giving him a reassuring smile.

Damien had selected a traditional Italian restaurant in downtown Los Angeles for their date. White linen tablecloths sat below empty bottles of Chianti with candles stuck in them. As they dined on shrimp scampi and linguine with clams, the conversation flowed, as did the wine.

"C'mon. Just tell me," he implored.

"Harvard," Caroline replied reluctantly, glancing down in her lap.

"You went to business school at Harvard? Harvard Business School?" asked Damien in disbelief.

"You're surprised?" she asked, unsure how he would take this admission.

"No. Totally turned on." Caroline blushed and looked down at her lap before glancing up to catch Damien staring at her with both awe and hunger.

After finishing dinner and a sharing a delectable chocolate gelato, Caroline and Damien found themselves sitting in his car outside of her apartment building. In that moment, with his kind and tender eyes shining with a heady combination of sincerity and lust, she knew she was going to be putty in his charming, albeit slightly clumsy, hands.

As they made out in the front seat of his car like horny teenagers, Caroline felt his hand fumble for the buttons of her blouse, as his moist breath tickled her neck. His tongue gently fondled her earlobe, the feeling making a beeline for her groin. And while Caroline was thoroughly enjoying his company and the feeling of his lips on her skin, she knew she needed to stop now or risk waking up with him the next morning.

"Sorry. Just need to slow things down a bit," she said, pulling back and panting, as she ran her fingers through his greying hair.

"Oh, yeah, sure. Sure," he said, his labored breath mirroring hers. "Can I see you again?"

"I think all of this should be a pretty good indication that you have permission to call me again," she said with a hint of spirited sarcasm.

"Well, I didn't go to Harvard, so I'm not that bright," he retorted playfully.

"Hey, MBA from UCLA night school isn't too shabby." She continued to stroke his hair with her fingers. She gazed into his eyes once more, then stopped and turned to exit the car.

"All right. I'll call you. And it won't take weeks this time," he said, leaning over to give her another kiss.

"Better not," she retorted, pointing her finger at him menacingly. "Goodnight," she said as she leaned over and gave him a quick chaste kiss on the cheek, before catching his gaze again for a beat or two.

•   •   •

Caroline sat at the bar, nursing her glass of Chardonnay as Mike shifted through a pile of papers looking for an invoice. It was still early and the bar was fairly empty. The Saturday night crowd didn't really show up until around 8:30 or 9:00, so there was time to catch up on some paperwork while he waited for the relief bartender to show.

"So, I take it things are going well with that guy..." his voice trailed off.

"As I've told you twenty times already, his name is Damien," she said, exhaling loudly and crossing her arms over her chest. "And yes, things are goin' well," she continued, now smiling at the thought of him.

"So well that you're hanging out at the bar with me on a Saturday night?" he asked.

"We don't need to be around each other all of the time in order to be a couple," she responded a bit too defensively.

"If you say so," said Mike, glancing down at his pile of papers.

"What does that mean?" she snapped.

"It just means that if you're happy with how your relationship is progressing, then that's good," he replied, not wanting to raise her ire.

"I think he's just really busy with his job. He's not able to talk a lot on the phone, but he texts and emails me during the day. And on the weekends I think he just... well, he said a couple of times that he hasn't been out there datin' in a while, so maybe he's just takin' things slow."

"If you say so," replied Mike, pursing his lips.

"Stop sayin' that," she snapped again. Calming down, she continued, "You just need to get to know him and you'll see what I mean." Mike was about to speak when Caroline interrupted him. "And don't say, 'If you say so.'" Mike just smiled at her and went back to his paperwork.

• • •

Caroline was thrilled to be visiting the bar this evening, as she would finally be able to introduce Mike to Damien. Damien had been so busy with work lately it seemed like forever since they had enjoyed a proper weekend date. Clutching a gold-toned satchel that matched her gold-toned flat sandals, she bellied up to the bar and motioned for Mike.

"So, Damien. This is my very best friend, Mike, owner of this fine establishment," Caroline proudly announced. Damien leaned over and shook Mike's hand.

"Nice to meet you, man. Caroline's told me all about you."

"All about me, huh?" replied Mike, flashing a winning smile. "Glad you still wanted to meet me." He began to pour a glass of wine for Caroline. "Chardonnay for Caroline. What can I get you?"

"I'll just take whatever you have on tap," Damien said in his easy-going manner. He motioned for his wallet and Mike gestured with his hand to put his money away. Damien nodded in acceptance. He placed his phone on the bar counter and got up to use the restroom.

"I'll be right back," he said, giving Caroline a gentle kiss on the cheek. She smiled and watched him walk away, feeling a warmth spread through her, as she had grown quite fond of him.

"Isn't he lovely?" she asked, dreamily looking at the ceiling and taking a deep breath.

"Yeah, lovely," muttered Mike, pursing his lips. "You hungry?" he said, hoping to get Caroline talking about something other than her most recent beau.

"No. We just gorged ourselves on tacos and guac. Have you been to Carlito's? It's amazin'," she said, unaware of Mike's motivations to change the subject. Suddenly, a faint buzz vibrated on the bar counter. Damien's phone received a text. Caroline glanced at it. It read:

Christa: When will you be home. I miss you. XOXO

The words were followed by multi-colored heart icons. Caroline's face fell and a low gasp escaped her mouth.

"What?" asked Mike, looking at her with concern.

"It's..." she began. Before she could continue, Damien returned.

"I like the cool movie posters you have in the men's room," he said, lowering himself onto the barstool. Damien turned to an ashen-faced Caroline. "What's wrong?" he asked with sincere concern. Tears began swelling in her eyes.

"Who is Christa?" she said quietly.

"Uh, wha..." he spluttered.

"Who is Christa and why does she want to know when you'll be home?" she repeated, this time with a tad more conviction, her hand on her hip. Damien looked over at Mike, who stood motionless, watching the interchange unfolding before him.

"Can we talk about this outside?" he asked, glancing over at Mike.

"Anythin' you can say to me, you can say in front of Mike," she said with a haughty tone, straightening her shoulders and lifting her head up.

"Christa's my daughter," he said, exhaling sharply.

"Your daughter?" Caroline repeated, in utter shock, her shoulders sagging.

"Yeah. She's nine."

"I'm going to let the two of you talk," said Mike, sensing the start of an uncomfortable situation. He walked down to the other end of the bar but kept a close watch on Caroline's reactions.

"You have a nine-year-old daughter?" she whispered, looking down at her lap.

"And a three-year-old son," he finished, trying to catch her gaze.

"Two kids. You have two kids," she repeated in shock. A wave of nausea flooded over her. "And is there a wife to make this family complete?" she asked, her body trembling slightly.

"No. No wife," Damien replied softly. "She left last year and we haven't heard from her since."

"We've been datin' for three months. And exactly when were you gonna tell me that you were married and had two kids?"

"Well, I think it's important to note that I *was* married. I'm not married anymore," he said, correcting her.

"But you're still a dad. A full-time dad. Is that why you never pick up the phone when I call you? Or why I've never been to your place?" she asked, finally looking up at him.

"It's complicated," he sighed.

"Sounds like it," she sighed back.

"It's been a tough year for my kids and for me. They're pretty fragile – especially Christa. I just don't want to introduce them to someone who might not stick around. I'm sure you can understand that."

"I can," she began. "But why wouldn't you tell *me* about *them*?" she said, furrowing her brow.

"I don't know. I guess I didn't know how you would react and I didn't want to take the chance that you wouldn't want to go out with me if you knew I had two kids. Why don't you come over for dinner tomorrow night and meet them," he said, gently touching her hand. "They're great kids."

"Wait, what?" she said, recoiling from his touch and trying to process all of this new information.

"Listen, I really like you. A lot. I don't want this to be a reason that we stop seeing each other," he pleaded.

"But you've been lyin' to me for months now," she said meekly.

"I explained why. I know it was wrong, but I had a good reason." Caroline sat there, motionless except for her rapid heartbeat and erratic breathing.

This just doesn't make sense, she thought. *Why the hell wouldn't he tell me?* Confusion and conflict engulfed her. *First, he didn't want me to know he had kids and now all of a sudden he wants me to meet them,* she thought. *And his little girl is fragile? He's afraid another woman is going to come and break her heart. That's a lot of pressure. Damn!* She wanted him to respect her enough to be honest with her. And she wanted him to like her enough to introduce her to them because he wanted her in his life, not because he was afraid of *not* having her in his life. *Hell, he doesn't know whether to check his ass or scratch his watch*, she thought. But she couldn't get the words out – or any words out for that matter.

"What do you want from me, Caroline?" he asked, growing frustration in his voice. He reached his hand to cover hers. Tears streamed down Caroline's face. She again withdrew her hand from his touch and turned to look him straight in the eye.

"I want you to go home to your kids and I... I want to have another glass of wine," she spluttered before looking down in her lap, knotting her fingers and picking at a piece of nail polish.

"And there's nothing I can say to change your mind?" he asked, shaking his head slightly, trying to get her to look at him.

"No. There isn't." She took in a deep breath and turned her eyes back toward him. She leaned over and gave him a chaste kiss on the cheek. "Goodbye, Damien." Damien shook his head, grabbed his phone, and walked away. Mike watched with interest, waiting for the door to close behind Damien before approaching Caroline.

"A kid, huh?" he said, refilling her glass with Chardonnay.

"Kids, with an 's'," she corrected him, her forehead resting on her fingertips.

"Wife?" asked Mike, fearful of the answer.

"No. She apparently walked out last year," she responded quietly, not looking up at him.

"Not ready to be insta-mommy?"

"I love kids. You know that," she said, looking up into Mike's concerned eyes. "And I think I would have been okay datin' someone with kids. But he didn't give me a chance," she sniffled.

"Yeah. You're great with the team," he responded smiling, recalling how much the boys loved having Caroline around to cheer them on. And despite not enjoying being an onlooker to Caroline's ever-changing love life, he not only wanted to see her happy but also felt some sympathy for Damien who seemed like a decent guy. "Maybe you should give the guy a break. His wife did just leave him," Mike suggested.

"Don't piss on my leg and tell me it's rainin'," she snapped.

"Hey, don't get pissed at me." He held up his hands in surrender mode.

"I know. I'm sorry," she said, remorse for her harsh comment evident in her tone and eyes.

"Seriously, he seemed like a good guy. Cut him some slack."

"He said it's been hard on his kids and he didn't want to introduce them to a woman who might not be around for the long haul. We've only been datin' for a few months. But he should have told me he had kids. All of a sudden he wants me to meet them. First, he doesn't like me enough to know I will be around and then, all of a sudden, when he's backed into a corner, he can't bear the thought of losin' me. I don't know what to believe. I just don't think this is gonna work out if I can't trust him to be honest with me."

"So why didn't you tell him all of that?" he said, shaking his head at her.

"You know why," she said, resigned.

"I thought you were working on this?" he said, looking in her eyes.

"I am. I just wasn't prepared for this."

"No one ever is," he said, pursing his lips. "But you gotta figure this out if you're ever going to have a successful relationship."

"You're givin' *me* advice on havin' a successful relationship?" she said, raising an eyebrow.

"I know, ironic, right?" he smiled. "But seriously. Being able to talk honestly and openly with your partner is the cornerstone to any solid relationship."

"Who are you and what have you done with Mike?" She shook her head, hoping to lighten the mood and shift the conversation.

"Okay, okay." She looked down at her lap, and he gently tilted her chin up with his fingers. "What can I do?" he asked with concern.

"Just keep my glass filled. And don't get mad when I complain that I'm alone."

"Okay. I can do that."

●　　●　　●

The line wrapped around the block as Caroline and Mike got behind a man with a blue Mohawk and smattering of piercings dotting his pale face.

"How long is this gonna take?" she huffed.

"Hmm. Judging by how far back we are, I'd say a little more than an hour."

"An hour?" she exclaimed. "You're puttin' me on."

"Sadly, no. I'd say we have at least an hour, probably more."

"For a hot dog? You're gonna make me wait an hour in line..."

"More than an hour," he interrupted, correcting her.

"More than an hour," she emphasized, "for a hot dog."

"Yup." Caroline let out a loud, exhausted exhale. "I can't believe in all of the time you've lived in Los Angeles, you've never been to Pinks."

"This better be one helluva hot dog," she said, shaking her head in disbelief.

"Trust me." The line moved slowly as Caroline's frustration increased – both from the long wait and her recounting to Mike how Maxine was not catching on to proper business procedures as she had hoped. Mike did his best to entertain her with stories of his latest series of dates with a delightful yoga instructor he met at the gym.

"She's great – very flexible – but it's run its course."

"Your three-date rule?" she asked with a disgusted sneer.

"Yup," he replied smugly.

"You know, for most people the three date rule means waiting three dates to sleep with someone. Not three dates before they dump them."

"Lucky for me, I'm not most people," he said as they reached the front of the line. Caroline just rolled her eyes.

Mike put his arm on her shoulder and said, "Trust me to order for you?"

"Sure. Knock yourself out."

"We'll have two chili cheese dogs with mustard and onions, one order of chili cheese fries and two Dr. Brown's cream sodas." Caroline's mouth watered as she watched the meaty chili being poured on top of a hot dog fresh from a steaming hot pot.

With a wax paper wrapped hot dog in one hand, a cold bottle of soda in the other, Caroline followed Mike into the seating area. She unwrapped her hot dog, smearing some chili on her finger in the process. She wiped it off on a napkin and looked up to find Mike's disapproving stare.

"What?"

"You don't waste Pinks chili on the napkin," he said, wiping some errant chili off of the wax paper and licking his finger. Caroline closed her eyes tight and laughed. She lifted her hot dog to her mouth, took a bite and let out a slow moan.

"Ohmygod," she blurted.

"Worth the hour wait?" Mike asked, already knowing the answer.

"More than an hour," corrected Caroline smugly.

"Worth *more than the hour* wait?" he clarified.

"Mmm. Yes," she moaned. Mike cleared his throat and shifted in his seat, as Caroline's response to her chili dog was a bit arousing.

Caroline shoveled a handful of chili cheese fries into her mouth as she felt her phone ring in her snakeskin cross body bag. She wiped her fingers on a napkin – smiling at Mike as she did – and took a quick swig of her cream soda.

"Well, hey there. How's the most amazin' man in the world?" she asked smiling. Mike put his hands up in protest.

"What am I? Chopped liver?" Mike snipped. Caroline pushed her hand forward and shook her head. Mike looked confused until she mouthed, "my dad," at him.

"Tell him I said hi," said Mike stepping away to grab some more napkins.

"Hey princess. Listen, I have some bad news. Are you sitting down?" her dad asked.

"I am sittin' down," she said. "What is it?" she asked, a knot forming in her stomach.

"It's Mimi," he said. "I'm sorry, princess." Caroline dropped her phone on the table and raced to a nearby trash can to throw up. Mike rushed over to her and rubbed her back. She looked up at him, tears in her eyes as other restaurant patrons looked on with hushed whispers.

"You okay?" he asked with concern. When Caroline lifted her head out of the trash can, he added "I told you. We don't waste Pinks chili," trying to get her to smile.

"Mimi," she whispered. "Mimi."

"Fuck!" he said. He helped her back to her seat and picked up her phone upon hearing the muffled voice of her dad.

"Caroline. Princess. Are you there?"

"Hi, Mr. Johnson. It's Mike."

"Mike. Thank goodness you're there with her."

"She's in shock. I'm going to take her home. Let me have her give you a call in a little while."

"Yes, yes, of course."

●　　●　　●

After returning to her apartment and getting through a good cry, Caroline called her dad back to find out the details of Mimi's passing. She had drifted quietly in the night and the doctor was certain she hadn't suffered.

"Hmm. Not like Mimi to do anything quietly," said Mike with a tilt of his head. Caroline let out a little laugh.

"How true. Came in like a lion and went out like a lamb," she added. "I'm gonna miss her," she said, staring off into space.

"Me too. Do you know, despite having only met me a few times, she sent me a birthday card every year?"

"Huh. That actually doesn't surprise me. She loved you."

"The feeling was mutual," he said with genuine feeling.

"Do you know she wrote me a hand-written letter every week while I was in Los Angeles for college and in Boston for graduate school?"

"Mmm," Mike hummed, wanting to acknowledge her statement, but not interrupt her flow of thought.

"I could never tell what she was saying in them because her handwriting was so atrocious," she said, giving a knowing laugh. Mike put a consoling hand on her knee. "A few years ago, we got her an iPad, so she started emailing me a letter every week. She would still write it like a letter with the 'To My Darling Caroline' and signing it 'Love you to bits, Aunt Mimi'."

"She was something special," Mike agreed.

"I just can't believe I'll never get a letter from her again." Mike put his arm around her as Caroline cried into his chest. When she finally finished and pulled back, he spoke up.

"So when are you heading home?"

"I'm gonna leave tomorrow," she said, making a mental check list of all of the things she would have to do quickly to prepare. She stood up and walked to her hall closet, pulling out her suitcase and rolling it toward her bedroom.

"Do you want me to go with you?" he offered. Caroline stopped rolling the suitcase and ran into Mike's arms. Tears rolled down her cheeks.

"Thank you," she said. "Thank you, but no. I'll go on my own. But I appreciate you offerin'."

•　　•　　•

A balding man in his mid-fifties, Fred Jenkins led the Johnson family into the cramped conference room located in his small-town law offices. Legal boxes were stacked up against one wall, and mismatched chairs, no doubt brought in from nearby offices, were crammed around the scratched wooden table.

"Thank you all for coming in today," he began as they all took a seat. "My condolences to you all," he continued. "Mimi was a special lady. Lotta folks 'round here are really gonna miss her." Caroline's parents thanked him for his thoughtful words.

"Mimi had come in to see me a while back and put together a video message for y'all. As her attorney and executor, I've been instructed to play it for you." He placed a DVD into a player and pushed a few buttons on a remote. The television screen sprung to life and a date, from more than a year prior, displayed on the screen.

From there, Mimi appeared, wearing her signature oversized glasses and equally large costume jewelry. A plastic tube ran across her nose and into a large tank, providing her with much needed oxygen. A disembodied voice could be heard saying, "You're all set, Mrs. Johnson. Whenever you're ready." Mimi nodded and then spoke.

> If you're watching this, then I have left this world for the next one <cough, cough>. I have no doubt that St. Peter was waiting for me at the Pearly Gates with a mint julep in hand <laugh, laugh, cough, cough>.
>
> I'm sure it won't come as much of a surprise, but I've got everything planned out, so you don't have to worry about a thing.
>
> There is to be no funeral. Last thing I want is for people to be sitting around talking about me and feeling sad.

I've arranged to be cremated. I've always known I'm one hot number, so now it will be official <laugh, laugh, cough, cough>.

My ashes are to be buried in a biodegradable urn and planted in Asbury Park next to a bench with a plaque bearing my name. Don't worry. Fred Jenkins, my attorney who should be sitting there with you right now, has all of the details worked out with the city. Had to grease a few palms to make it happen, but it's a wonder what some cash and a huckleberry pie or two can get you.

Mimi continued to talk, addressing specific people around the room including Caroline's parents and her cousins Buzz and Mitchell. But Caroline wasn't listening. All she could think about was how she would never talk with Mimi again. When she heard Mimi saying her name, Caroline looked back at the screen.

And to you, Caroline sweetie <cough, cough>. I've told you your whole life to find something you love and hold onto it. I know this is the secret to happiness because that's what I did with you. I love you sweetie, more than you'll ever know.

When you think of me, I hope it will be with a tear on one cheek and a smile on the other because that's what life is about. So do something every day that scares you a little and don't forget to live, laugh and love.

The sight of Mimi blowing a kiss to her through the camera took Caroline over the edge and she lunged into her father's arms for comfort. Fred clicked the video monitor off and pulled papers out of a manila folder. "As you heard, Mimi has prearranged her cremation and burial. The only thing we really need to go through is her will."

Buzz and Mitchell sat up a little straighter, eager to hear if Mimi had bequeathed them anything. She kindly left them her stake in some local businesses, no doubt purchased by her late husband over the years.

The remainder of her assets – stocks, savings, jewelry and even her house – were to be given to Caroline with the expectation she would use the money to purchase a home in Los Angeles or further grow her business.

•   •   •

Over the next few days, Caroline spent time at her parents' home helping them receive visitors who had come by to pay their respects over Mimi's passing. She did her best to avoid Vicky and Troy Butler, who stopped in with a platter of cold cuts from the nearby diner. Alex Tuggle dropped in the day before she had planned to return back to LA.

"Hey Caroline," he said, giving her a gentle hug.

"Thanks for stopping by Alex. Mimi always liked you," she said, giving him a grin.

"I knew Mimi for twenty-eight years and I loved Mimi for twenty-eight years," he acknowledged, his head bowed slightly with a grim expression on his face. Caroline just nodded her head up and down, her face scrunched up as she held back her tears. She gripped his shoulder and led him into the living room to take a seat.

"I'm sorry for the reason you came back home, but I'm really glad to see you again."

"Thanks Alex," she said. "You're a good friend." Caroline sensed Alex tense up at the word 'friend', but pretended not to notice.

They visited for about a half hour before Alex excused himself to get to the dry cleaners for work. "Thank you for coming by Alex. I know it would have meant a lot to Mimi," she said.

"I hope it meant a lot to you." He stared down at his worn boots.

"It did," she said, giving him a light peck on the cheek. "Goodbye." Alex walked out the front door with a sad look on his face, figuring it would be a long time before he would see Caroline again.

•　　•　　•

Caroline grabbed a cab at LAX and instructed the driver to her apartment. She pulled her phone out of her black leather satchel and dialed Mike.

"Hey doll," he said. "When are you heading back?"

"I'm actually in a cab on the way to my place now," she replied.

"Aww, you should have told me. I would have picked you up."

"It's okay. But thank you. For everything. The flowers you sent were beautiful. I can't believe you remembered that lilies were Mimi's favorite."

"Well, they're your favorite too." Caroline started to quietly sob. "Shit! I didn't mean to make you cry," he started.

"It's okay," she interrupted. "I'm clearly just in a really emotional state right now." The cab driver glanced back at her through the rear-view mirror causing her to take a deep breath and try to keep her emotions in check.

"I'm on my way into the bar now. Let me take care of a few things there and then I'll come by with dinner," he offered.

"That would be great."

"Okay. See you soon."

"Mike?" she asked, unsure if he had already hung up.

"Yeah, I'm here."

"Thank you."

"No need to thank me."

•　　•　　•

Caroline shoveled a forkful of Pad Thai into her mouth and gave a little moan. "Oh that's good," she mumbled through overstuffed cheeks. She swallowed and took a sip of green tea. "Five days of nothin' but fried food and sympathy cake," she began, "was startin' to take its toll."

"Constipation?" Mike asked with humor in his voice.

"No!" she scoffed in disgust.

"Oh. The opposite?" he said with an overly dramatic shudder.

"No! I just meant..." she started.

"Never mind," he said, shaking his head. "I don't want to know." Caroline rolled her eyes. She spent the next hour recapping her trip to Asbury and her official goodbye to Mimi. Mike listened patiently, nodding at the appropriate times and placing a consoling hand on her shoulder when needed.

"Thank you," she said finally.

"Happy to bring you dinner anytime," he said with a smile.

"No. Well, I mean yes. Thank you for dinner. But thank you for listening. You're a good friend." If she wasn't mistaken, Caroline sensed Mike tense up at the word 'friend' just as Alex Tuggle had done. She quickly dismissed it as being her imagination. Yet she couldn't help but think about all of these male friends in her life and how she very much wanted to find someone to be more than that to her. She thought back to Mimi's advice to do something every day that scared her a little bit. Starting tomorrow, she resolved to do just that.

● ● ●

The next day, Caroline took a deep breath and picked up her cell phone. She hit the call button and shakily held it up to her ear.

"Caroline," said Damien. "This is a surprise."

"Hi," she breathed. "I hope I haven't caught you at a bad time." Caroline had been sure to call Damien in the afternoon when he wouldn't have to worry about answering while his kids were around.

"No. This is fine. I'm just grabbing some lunch. How...how are you?"

"I'm doin' okay," she said. "How are you?"

"Uh, I'm fine," he replied, surprise in his voice continuing as he grabbed a pre-made salad and continued down the cafeteria line.

"So you're probably wondering why I called," she said, pacing around her office.

"Yeah, I do admit, I'm a bit curious. I mean, last time we spoke, you were pretty adamant that you didn't want to talk with me," he continued, picking up a chocolate chip cookie and walking his tray over to the register.

"I didn't want to talk with you last month. Everything came as a big shock to me and I wasn't really in a place to address it."

"I thought about calling you after, you know. I didn't want things to end like that. I didn't want things to end at all," he continued, taking a seat. "I'm so sorry that I hurt you."

"I was actually calling to apologize to you," she responded. "I think I was a bit hasty in not letting you explain things and I'm sorry."

"No need to apologize. I should have told you a lot sooner."

"Well I was wondering if you wanted to, you know, try again," she said.

"Oh, wow, Caroline. I...I, um, I just started seeing someone."

"Oh," she said, her heart sinking. "Of course. I should have figured you moved on."

"It's early, but she's really great. She's a single mom with a little girl that goes to preschool with Connor," he explained.

"That's wonderful for you, Damien," she said, trying to keep the tears from flowing. "I'm so happy for you. I hope it works out."

"Thanks Caroline. I hope you find what you're looking for too." With that, he hung up the phone. Silent tears fell down Caroline's face as she slumped into her chair, her head hanging in her hands.

Fanny Pack

*T*he bar was exceptionally busy for a Thursday night. Caroline figured it was the live music drawing in the crowd. When Mike explained that the acoustic duo performing was called 'Free Beer' and had heavily promoted their appearance at The Last Drop through social media, Caroline realized the majority of patrons were there thinking the booze was free.

"Last time I let Morgan vet the talent," he said in exasperation.

"Perhaps she was distracted from her duties," suggested Caroline, taking a little dig at Mike for his work dalliances.

"Perhaps," he said, looking off to the side as if he were truly considering what Caroline was implying. "I just think it's important to be precise when it comes to things like this," he added in frustration.

A wide grin crossed Caroline's face as she recalled a particularly fond memory from graduate school. Professor Moss had told the students they could bring in a 3x5 card with notes for the final. Mike had brought in a 3-foot x 5-foot poster board that contained a shrunken down photocopy of every case study they had covered that semester.

Professor Moss had turned to him and said drolly, "You're quite precise, Mr. Barnsworth. You sure you don't want to go to law school?"

Mike had basked in the whispers and chattering from his classmates and had replied, "Nah. I'm good," before settling himself into his seat and propping the large poster board against the wall so he could easily refer to it during the exam.

As Caroline sat, grinning and chuckling to herself in the bar, Mike sensed where her head was at and asked, "Three by five card?"

"Mm hmm," she responded. Mike smiled.

"Good times." Mike nodded his head up and down at the memory of it. Caroline looked at him and shook her head.

"I'm gonna use the ladies room. Save my seat?" Mike nodded. As Caroline walked away, Mike noticed a man sitting two stools down, leering at her behind as she proceeded to the restroom.

The man stroked his index finger back and forth over his lip as her hips swayed, her bottom accentuated by a pair of dark-wash skinny jeans and brown leather knee-high boots. Once she disappeared from view, the man just grinned. As he turned back to the beer he was nursing, he noticed Mike watching him. He gave a small smirk. Mike responded with a head nod before turning around, an eerie feeling coursing through him.

When Caroline returned to her seat, the man smiled at her and Caroline gave a friendly smile back. Mike leaned into her.

"That guy was totally checking out your ass when you went to the restroom," he said with outrage and disgust. Caroline chose to chalk Mike's tone up to jealousy and frustration at how the night was unfolding.

"Well then it's a good thing I've been hitting the yoga studio," she responded sweetly. Caroline took a sip of her Chardonnay while Mike handed out more free beers. The man keenly interested in her derriere asked the patron sitting between them to swap seats, placing him right next to Caroline.

"Hi," he said.

"Hi," Caroline responded.

"So do you come here often?" he asked leaning in so she could hear him over the noisy crowd before slapping himself on the head and following it up with, "Jeez. That sounds like such a cheesy pick up line."

"You're right. It does," Caroline shouted, giving a playful sneer. "But yes, I do come here often."

"Really?"

"My best friend Mike over there," she said, pointing a finger at Mike who was watching them from the other side of the bar, "is the owner and keeps me coming back with free Chardonnay."

"So it's not just free beer?"

"What?" she said, pointing her finger in the air indicating she couldn't hear him.

"It's not just the free beer," he repeated a bit louder.

"I think that's the name of the band performing. Kind of a marketing gimmick," she explained.

"Makes sense. Are you in marketing?"

"No. I'm a handbag designer. What about you?"

"I used to be a college writing professor but now I'm semi-retired and working on the great American novel."

"How novel," Caroline said flirtatiously.

"I'm Beckett, by the way," he said reaching out to shake her hand and leaning in even closer, so they could hear each other.

"I'm Caroline," she replied, shaking his hand in return. "So what kind of novel are you writing?"

"Oh it's about an average guy dealing with the stresses of life and trying to overcome his internal demons."

"So a comedy."

"Exactly," he laughed, his fingers brushing against her arm leaning on the bar. "You nailed it."

"Well, good luck with that," she said, taking a sip of her wine.

"So, that accent of yours. Let me guess. You're British, right?" he joked. Caroline nearly choked on her drink and started to laugh.

"You are so perceptive," she said, her mouth agape and her arms outstretched in front of her. "I can't believe you deciphered that from just this brief conversation."

"I know," he replied smugly. "I'm good, even with all of this noise." The two of them laughed. "I know this is kind of crazy, but would you like to come back to my place. Just to talk. Where it's a bit quieter."

"Ahhh," she started. "I don't make it a habit of goin' home with strange men that I meet in bars. I'm sure you understand."

"Of course. That's probably smart. I just really am enjoying your company and would like to hear more of that adorable British accent before you lose your voice with all of this shouting. What about dinner? Do you eat dinner with men you meet in bars?" he started as Mike walked over to check on Caroline. "Perhaps some bangers and mash?" Caroline laughed at his reference to the stereotypical British meal while Mike grimaced at the thought of this odd guy talking with Caroline about "banging" and "mashing."

"Dinner would be lovely, but I'd prefer somethin' a bit more…" she paused, trying to think of the right word before settling on "edible." Beckett laughed.

"Saturday night?"

"That would be great."

"Okay. Why don't I give you a call tomorrow," he shouted, pointing to his phone. He unlocked it and handed it to Caroline. She programmed in her number and passed it back to him. He looked at the number and rubbed his finger across his lip. He leaned in and whispered in her ear, "I'll call you tomorrow."

"Cheerio, govnah," she said, smiling back at him. Beckett laughed before throwing some cash on the bar and walking out. Mike's eyes followed him as he left.

"What was that all about?" said Mike, glaring at the door.

"He seems like a nice guy and he asked me to dinner this weekend," said Caroline matter of fact.

"I don't like it," muttered Mike. He turned to Caroline who looked at him with a tilted head, waiting for him to say something. "Something about that guy is off."

"You're just being overprotective," she groaned. "And I think you're just on edge because of all the free beers you've been givin' away tonight," she added, sweeping her hand across the crowd filling The Last Drop.

"No, seriously. That guy is giving off a weird vibe. I don't want you going out with him."

"I'm a big girl, Mike. I can decide who I want to date," she scoffed.

"Don't go out with him, Caroline," he implored. She pushed her hand forward toward him.

"Stop bein' a big brother."

"Do me a favor then. Please. Meet him next door at the Japanese place for dinner. Don't let him pick you up."

"Mike…" she started.

"Please. Have I ever asked you something like this before?" he asked with pleading eyes.

"Well, no," she conceded.

"Then please. For me."

"Seriously? The odds of him being a psycho are so slim."

"You're right. But the odds of that are more than the odds of you winning this argument, so please just trust my gut." Caroline put her hands up in surrender.

"Okay, okay. I'll have him meet me next door."

●   ●   ●

Caroline stood in the lobby of the sushi restaurant waiting for Beckett to arrive. Her phone pinged, and she wondered if Beckett was planning to cancel or would be late.

Mike: Let me know when you get home tonight from your date. Or better yet, just come by the bar after dinner. I'll be here all night.

Caroline: Yes dad!

Mike: Don't make me take you over my knee!

Caroline: You'd like that too much!

Mike: You know me well.

Caroline: Better than you know yourself.

Mike: Lucky you!

Caroline: What an ego!

Mike: And your point is???

Caroline: Ugh! You are incorrigible!

Mike: And you love me.

Caroline was about to respond when she sensed someone watching her. She turned and saw Beckett, standing behind her, his eyes roaming up and down her backside.

"Hi," she said with a smile.

"Hi yourself," he said, leaning in to give her a chaste kiss on the cheek. "I hope you haven't been waiting long."

"Not at all." Beckett motioned to the hostess that they would need a table for two and ushered Caroline ahead of him, watching her walk as they made their way to a table in the middle of the restaurant.

"What are you in the mood for tonight?" Based on his tone and the way he was looking at her, Caroline wondered if he was talking about the food or something else. She giggled nervously.

"I could definitely go for some teriyaki chicken," she said. "And some white rice. The stickier the better."

"Sounds good," he responded. "Can I interest you in some Sake?"

"Sure," she agreed quickly. Beckett and Caroline both looked around trying to attract the attention of their waiter when Beckett's eyes caught a woman enter the restaurant. She had long blonde hair pulled back into a ponytail tied together with a velvet scrunchie. She wore a pair of black pants and a Kelly-green cardigan sweater that set off her hourglass figure. As she walked past the table and saw Beckett with Caroline, she raised an eyebrow and then continued briskly to her seat.

'Green Cardigan' joined three other women who were seated at a booth. Although the woman's back was turned to her, Caroline could see the table from her vantage point. Caroline noticed Beckett shift uncomfortably in his seat and a small bit of perspiration form on his upper lip. He tried to subtly wipe it away with his finger, but Caroline could definitely sense something was amiss.

She tried to keep her conversation with Beckett going, maintaining a light banter, but all the while kept an eye on the woman in green. She noticed the woman stand up and speak to a server who pointed her to the back of the restaurant.

Caroline surmised the woman was heading to the ladies room and politely excused herself. With shaking hands, she opened the door and stood by the sink, pretending to check that nothing was in her teeth. She heard the toilet flush and watched as the woman walked toward her to wash her hands.

Caroline's mouth went dry, but she shook out her hands and began to speak. "Excuse me," she started, her voice cracking. "Excuse me," she said more clearly. The woman turned to her and pulled her lips together in a grim line.

"I'm sorry to bother you and I apologize in advance if this is out of line, but I couldn't help but notice that you knew Beckett," she began. The woman took a deep breath and opened her mouth as if to say something, but then shut it just as quickly. "I know this is going to sound a bit crazy, but I was just wonderin' if there was somethin' goin' on between you two," Caroline said, her hands shaking. She glanced down at the ground as the woman placed her hands on her hips with a shocked look on her face.

The woman let out an insulted laugh. "There's nothing going on with me and Beckett," she assured Caroline.

"Okay, but I couldn't help but notice he was a bit unnerved when he saw you. And you're just so beautiful. I'm just not interested in bein' the other woman."

"I'm not his girlfriend," she said as she began to walk out. Caroline shifted to block her exit.

"Clearly there is some history there," Caroline said. "Is there somethin' I should know about because seein' you definitely upset him. I mean, I just not too long ago got out of a relationship where someone wasn't honest with me and I just don't want to go through that again. I just need to know where I stand." Caroline shook her head in frustration at her babbling. "I'm sorry. I'm bein' out of line." She moved aside to let the woman pass.

"I'm not his girlfriend. I'm his probation officer," said the woman. She brushed past Caroline, opened the door and walked out. Caroline stood dumbfounded. *Beckett was a criminal*, she thought. *But he seems so nice and normal.* Caroline took a deep breath and returned to the table.

Beckett looked up at her, glanced over to 'Green Cardigan' and immediately sensed he was about to have a serious discussion.

"So you've spoken to Hillary," he said, shaking his head in agitation. "What did she tell you?"

"I happened to notice you got uncomfortable when she walked in and when I bumped into her in the restroom, I asked how you two knew each other," Caroline explained. Caroline's heart rate accelerated. She didn't know what Beckett had done or what he was capable of. She wasn't sure if sitting with him and talking about this with him was a wise idea. *Mimi used to say, 'Curiosity killed the cat.' I just hope it doesn't kill me*, she thought.

"She just said that she was your..." Caroline leaned in and whispered, "probation officer."

"That's all she said?"

"Yes. Listen, I..."

"I made a mistake, Caroline. A stupid mistake and I've been paying for it for a while now," he began. "Please let me explain."

Caroline's instincts told her to leave and trust her gut. She realized at that moment she should have trusted Mike's gut and he wasn't going to let her live it down. But she was here, in a public place, and she really wanted to give Beckett the benefit of the doubt.

"Go ahead," she said. Caroline listened patiently as Beckett explained his 'mistakes' and the steps he had gone through – both legal and personal – to make amends and a course correction.

"I hope this doesn't change anything between us," he said, reaching across to take Caroline's hand in his. Caroline recoiled, knowing that she couldn't sit here any longer.

"I need to go and I need you to let me go. And I need you to not call me again," she said as she stood.

"I understand," he acknowledged. "Take care of yourself Caroline." He hung his head in shame.

•   •   •

Caroline rushed into the bar, her eyes searching for Mike. Loren, the waitress, sensing Caroline's urgency, pointed to the back room. Caroline rushed to the door and knocked gently before letting herself in.

"Hey doll," he said, only glancing up from his computer monitor for a quick second before sensing something was amiss. "What's wrong?"

"My date...with Beckett," she started, her voice shaky.

"What did that fucker do?" Mike said, tension radiating off of him, his hands balling into fists at his side.

"Calm down, Conan! He didn't do anything," she said, holding her hand up, realizing that she was unnecessarily riling Mike up. She took a deep breath.

"Conan?"

"Yeah. As in the Barbarian."

"I'll take it as a compliment. So tell me what's got you all rattled," he implored her.

"Beckett and I were next door about to order dinner when this woman walked in and he got visibly uncomfortable," she began. She wrapped her arms around herself and rubbed them up and down. "They sort of acknowledged each other but it was really weird."

"There's definitely something off about the guy. I'm glad you ditched him," he said, moving over to put an arm around her shoulder.

"There's more," she said, taking a deep breath. "We ordered an appetizer and some Sake and I noticed this woman go to the ladies room so I followed her in there."

"Shit," Mike breathed. "And..."

"And I asked her if there was somethin' goin' on between her and Beckett. She laughed at my assumption that there was anythin' romantic between them and told me she was his...probation officer."

"Fuck!" Mike shook his head and muttered under his breath. "Knew I shouldn't have let you go out with that guy." He looked up to see her taking a few deep breaths. "Well I'm glad you came straight here. Nothing's going to happen to you now."

"Oh, I didn't come straight here. I went back to the table to try and figure out what the heck he did."

"You're a smart girl, Caroline, but that was just plain stupid."

"It's okay. Bottom line," she started before breaking into a laugh.

"What's so funny?"

"Not to make light of a serious situation, but it really was the bottom line. He was arrested for groping the butts of some women he worked with. Apparently, he had some sort of butt fetish, but he claims it's under control with therapy," she explained.

"Sexual harassment and assault is no laughing matter. Ever."

"I know," she exhaled. "I think I'm just in a bit of shock."

"He didn't touch you, did he?" Mike asked, fire burning in his eyes.

"No. And he didn't try to stop me from leavin'. He said he understood my reservations about him and would leave me alone. But still, it's sort of freaked me out." Mike turned Caroline so she was facing him head on, one hand on each of her shoulders. He leaned his head down so they were eye to eye.

"I want you to tell me if he ever comes near you or contacts you again. I mean it Caroline."

"Okay. I will," nodding her head up and down.

"You sure you're okay?"

"Yeah. I'm fine. Just hungry. I didn't eat anything and now I'm famished."

"Come on," Mike said. "I can slip away for an hour and take you to dinner. There's a great new seafood place nearby. I heard the specialty is their hali-BUTT." He roared his head back in laughter. "Come on. I know better than to laugh at women being exploited. But you didn't think I was going to let the butt fetish part go unnoticed, did you?"

"Let me just use the ladies room," she said, giving a small chuckle. Mike walked out into the bar and whispered into Loren's ear, letting her know he was going to step out for a while and she would be in charge. As he pulled away from her ear, he noticed Beckett sitting at the bar.

Beckett looked up from his beer and saw Mike giving him a nasty look. Mike pointed to the "We have the right to refuse service to anyone" sign above the bar and gestured with his head for Beckett to leave. Beckett put his hands up in surrender, threw a ten-dollar bill on the bar counter and walked out.

A moment later, Caroline returned from the ladies room, her nose red and her eyes puffy, no doubt from a good cry. Mike put a consoling arm around her shoulder and walked her out of The Last Drop.

•   •   •

After a delicious seafood dinner at which Caroline opted for the tilapia, she returned to the bar with Mike. Over the course of a few hours, she polished off a bottle of Chardonnay while sitting at the bar and pondering her bad luck with men. Mike returned from bringing a last round of shots to a group of attractive young women celebrating a 21st birthday.

"Whatcha thinking, doll?" he asked Caroline, removing her empty wine glass and putting a tall glass of water in front of her.

"If I eat a pound of M&M's why won't I only gain a pound?" she pondered aloud.

"Don't eat a pound of M&M's," Mike advised. "It will only make your butt big."

"I only trust people who like big butts because they can't lie," she choked out between fits of laughter. Mike shook his head and laughed at her. When a guy walked over to Caroline, who was swaying on her stool, Mike warned the guy off with a dark look. "Maybe I need more junk in my trunk?" she suggested, slapping her thigh with her hand.

"More butt than the end of a rifle?" Mike replied.

"More ass than...than a donkey breeder?" she giggled.

"More crack than a drug dealer?"

"Yer funny," she said. "He's funny!" Caroline shouted, standing up and pointing her finger at Mike.

"Sit down."

"Am I makin' an assa myself?" Caroline started to laugh uncontrollably. "Am I getting too...cheeky?" She laughed so hard she fell off her stool. Mike ran around the bar to help her up as other patrons laughed at her.

Mike returned to his place behind the bar and rang a loud bell. "Last call!" he shouted. The bar turned silent as it did every night around this time. Mike cranked up the speakers on the bar's sound system and a guitar and piano instrumental flowed forward. Suddenly, everyone in the bar erupted in song, just as they did every night at last call, singing and shouting out the first few bars to Semisonic's "Closing Time" and about not having to go home but not finding shelter at the bar.

"Wiseeveryone laughin' at me?" Caroline slurred.

"Because you're standing on a bar stool, drunk as a skunk, as you would say, and singing at the top of your lungs."

"Oh," she said before cracking up.

"Oh," he confirmed. "C'mon drunk girl. Let's get you home."

"Becasth its closin' ti and I can't stay here."

"Right."

"I dote wanna go home. Let's go dancin'" she said, as he lifted her off the stool.

"Okay. Let's go dancing," he said as she swayed slightly and then passed out in his arms.

• • •

Caroline rolled over, her head throbbing. She opened one eye and noticed dark grey sheets. This wasn't her bed. A slow panic started to rise within her. *Where the hell was she? What the hell happened last night? It really didn't matter. This headache was going to kill her.*

She sat up slowly, opened her eyes and looked around. Relief washed over her as she realized she was in Mike's bedroom.

"Mike?" she called out. Mike walked into the bedroom wearing a Nike Dri-fit tank top and basketball shorts. He looked sweaty as if he has just worked out. He placed a glass of orange juice and bottle of Tylenol on the nightstand.

"Morning. How are you feeling?"

"Like a tap dancin' jackrabbit and jackhammer are battlin' it out in my head." The night came back to her. "Beckett. And the booze. Not a dream, huh?"

"Nope," said Mike taking a seat on the bed, facing her. "All true. You okay, really?"

"The Beckett stuff? Yes. The headache? No." She reached over for the bottle of pain reliever. "Thank you."

"Figured you could use an *Ass*pirin," Mike said, raising his eyebrow at her. Caroline let out a loud laugh and then rubbed her temples.

"Don't make me laugh." She took two pills and washed them down with the juice.

"Do you want to talk about it? This is a conversation I can really get behind," he said with a serious expression on his face before a smile split across his mouth.

"No," she sighed.

"Sorry. I don't mean to *butt* in. It may help to talk about it."

"I think I've officially hit *rock bottom*," she said, nodding her head up and down.

"Nice one," Mike acknowledged. "Let's just chalk it up to another dating dis*ass*ter."

"I am pretty *bummed* out right now," she said with a grin. Mike laughed a knowing laugh.

"Well it's all *behind you* now. Come on. I just finished a workout and could use breakfast."

"Thanks," she said with sincerity, placing a hand on his thigh and looking into his eyes.

"Sure thing, doll."

Briefcase

*C*aroline excitedly awaited her flight to Chicago, as she had been upgraded, by a fluke, to first class. Had she known in advance, she would have arrived at the airport earlier to enjoy the first-class lounge amenities. However, she wasn't complaining. When the automated check-in kiosk spit out a ticket indicating her seat as Row 2, Seat A, she did a little happy dance. Caroline boarded the 747 and was met by a warm woman with cropped grey hair, dressed head to toe in navy blue, whose nametag read "June."

"Welcome aboard, Ms. Johnson," she said, glancing at Caroline's ticket and guiding her to the left of the aircraft door. "Can I take your bag for you?" she offered.

"Much obliged," said Caroline, enthused by the congenial treatment she was receiving. "I'm not used to flyin' in first class. I could get used to this," she said. The flight attendant gave her a friendly smile as she hoisted Caroline's tan calfskin leather weekend bag into the overhead bin. "How lovely for upgrades," Caroline continued as she slid into the plush leather window seat.

As she buckled, a tall dark-haired man stood in the aisle, staring down at her with a sly smile on his face. He had a strong, angular nose, dark brooding eyes, and an intensity she was immediately drawn to. She guessed he was a lawyer or financier, as he wore the hardcore businessman's uniform – a dark pinstriped Zegna suit, crisp white dress shirt, and polished black leather loafers. The only color she noticed was his bright blue tie and the flush of red that crossed his face as he looked down at her with what she could only describe as lust. It had been a long while since she had been with Damien, and while she enjoyed what a gentle, albeit slightly bungling, lover he had been, he never sent shivers down her spine like this walking aphrodisiac in a suit.

"Hello. I guess we'll be seatmates for the next few hours," he said, smiling down at her with hooded eyes. He took off his tailored suit jacket and handed it to the waiting flight attendant, all the while sexily ogling Caroline.

"I suppose so," she said, smiling shyly and glancing down in her lap to avoid his intense gaze. "So, are you headin' to

Chicago for business or pleasure?" she asked, her fingers fidgeting in her lap.

"Business, but I'm not opposed to some pleasure if the opportunity presents itself." Caroline's breathing hitched as she felt warmth extend from her face down below her waist.

"I'm travelin' on business, but wouldn't mind a little pleasure either," she said, her voice a tad shaky.

"Dunham Carter," he said, thrusting his hand out to hers. "I'm a senior vice president with UNT Financial Services. I've got a few days of meetings in Chicago. What about you?"

"I'm Caroline Johnson. I'm a handbag designer and am meetin' with Marshall Fields to try and convince them to carry my new line," she said, straightening herself up.

"That sounds very exciting," said Dunham, continuing to gaze into her eyes.

"Probably not as excitin' as talkin' about surety bonds or tax-free investments," she said, batting her eyelashes subtly.

"Don't tell me you understand all of that terminology?" Caroline nodded her head and then cocked it slightly to the side, shrugging slightly. "Beauty and brains?"

"I was once told I have a head for business and a bod for sin." She couldn't believe she just made that movie reference out loud. Mike would be so proud.

"Really," said Dunham, gazing at her lustfully. *Holy shit*, thought Caroline. *What am I doing?*

"You know," she said, trying to explain herself, "from the movie *Workin' Girl?*"

"What kind of work is she doing?" Dunham asked provocatively, raising his eyebrow at her.

"Oh, it's not like that," said Caroline, playfully tapping his arm. "You're terrible."

• • •

The feeling and the sound of him slamming into her brought Caroline close to the brink as he dug his fingernails into her hips. She braced herself against the non-descript hotel chair as he continued to pound.

"C'mon. Give it to me, Caroline," he grunted.

"Ah, ah," she moaned.

"Say my name," he commanded.

"Oh, Dunham," she panted.

"That's right. Say my name," he said through gritted teeth.

"Dunham," she gasped as she neared the tipping point.

"Again," he growled.

"Dunham!"

"Yes! That's what I want to hear." He could feel her getting close as her legs began to tremble and she tightened around him.

"C'mon," he said, slamming into her harder from behind. "C'mon. I want to hear you." And that last thrust sent Caroline spiraling out of control. As she let out an inaudible groan and he could feel her pulsing around him, Dunham let go. "Oh yeah, baby. That's right," he cried out.

He pulled out of her and Caroline moved over to the bed, her unbuttoned blouse dangling from her arms and her panties still hanging loose around one ankle. She tried to catch her breath but this unexpected and vigorous encounter had taken its toll on her composure.

"Well, I can officially confirm both the head for business and bod for sin," he said, sitting down on the bed and catching his breath.

"I can't believe we just did that. I never do stuff like this," Caroline responded, laughing.

"Well I'm glad you decided to break tradition today."

"Me too. So…what next?" Caroline wasn't used to having such raw, animalistic sex, and with a man she just met, no less. "Like I said, I never do stuff like this."

"Next we take care of business in Chicago and I'll call you when I'm back in LA." Caroline wondered if he really meant it or whether this was just a fling. She decided to surrender to the moment and just go along for the ride.

"Okay," she said, taking a few deep, steadying breaths.

"But for now, I'm going to take you this way," he said, pushing her down onto the bed and climbing over her. He trailed his skillful hand up her leg, landing at that sweet spot below her belly. He thrust one finger, then two, inside her quickly and then moved them slowly, deliciously slowly – in and out, in and out as she bucked her hips up to increase the pressure.

Next, he lowered his face and placed his tongue on her – circling and flicking at her most sensitive spot. She tilted her head back in ecstasy and grasped onto the hotel bedspread in a vain effort to control herself. Dunham continued his oral assault, bringing her to the edge of another intense orgasm.

"Yeah, I own you," he said.

"Ah," she panted, knowing her release was near.

"Tell me!" he commanded.

"You own me," she panted before exploding around him.

"Yeah, that's right," he said, wiping her arousal from his mouth as she lay on the bed immobile.

● ● ●

Later that evening, now back in her own hotel room, Caroline sat on the bed replaying her unexpected afternoon with Dunham in her mind. Famished from her encounter, she ate a grilled cheese sandwich and chocolate milkshake from a room service tray. She turned the TV on, trying to distract her thoughts from his impressive performance. He was just so intense. And masterful. Her breathing hitched just thinking about it. *No*, she thought, *I've got work to do.* She opened her laptop and started revising her presentation – correcting all of the typos Maxine had missed – for tomorrow morning's meeting with the large Chicago retailer.

She was pacing around the room, rehearsing her pitch and a charming anecdote or two that she could casually throw into the conversation when her phone pinged with a text message.

Dunham: What can I say? This afternoon was a welcome surprise.

It was him! Her breathing became more erratic as her fingers fumbled on her phone's keypad.

Caroline: It was definitely a pleasant surprise for me 2.

Dunham: Pleasant? Is that all?

Caroline: More than pleasant. I suppose that's just the Southern girl in me coming out. ;)

Dunham: I like you coming out.

She felt flush. She'd never engaged in this kind of sexual banter via text before. He was just so sexual... intense... aggressive. She thought back to their recent tryst. His skillful hands were an abrupt change from her last sexual encounter with the fumbling but gentle Damien. She pushed Damien out of her mind, trying instead to think of a witty comeback – "*Comeback*," she said to herself, laughing. This wasn't really her area of sexpertise. Perhaps she should call Mike. Surely he'd know the perfect thing to say in response. *No, don't be ridiculous*, she thought.

Caroline: I noticed.

Dunham: Yes, it certainly was hard 2 contain my enthusiasm.

Caroline: "HARD" 2 contain your enthusiasm? That's an understatement.

She gave herself a mental pat on the back. *I am getting the hang of this after all,* she thought.

Dunham: Oh Caroline. The things I could do 2 you...

She fanned her face with her hands. *Like what*, she thought. *Should I ask? Could I handle knowing?*

Caroline: Oh my!

Dunham: When it comes to your body, I can't control myself.

Caroline: I seem to be feeling a bit out of control 2.

Dunham: I'd like to be feeling you right now.

Should she invite him over? She glanced at the clock, which now read 12:02 AM. She'd already engaged in a wanton sexual encounter with a strange man she met hours earlier. It shouldn't come as much of a surprise that a booty call was around the corner. Images of Mike leaving the bar with a random girl at the end of the night flashed through her mind. No. This wasn't her.

Caroline: Are you always like this?

Dunham: I want what I want and I take what I want. Right now I want U.

Holy hell, she thought, as she started to feel a throbbing down below.

Caroline: As enticing as that sounds, I do have an early meeting tomorrow.

Dunham: U R such a tease.

Caroline: I don't mean 2 B.

Dunham: You can make it up to me later.

Caroline: I'm sure I can find a way.

Her mind started racing, thinking of him and all of the things he could do to her... to her body. And what could she do to him? She frowned. She'd have to talk with Lydia or Kayle. *They would definitely be able to offer some thoughts on this topic,* she thought, chuckling to herself.

Dunham: Sounds fun. Speaking of fun, send me UR business plan. I'd like to look.

Caroline: OK. I'll email it over in the morning.

Dunham: Good. Call U when I'm back in LA.

Caroline: OK. Goodnight.

Dunham: PLEASANT dreams Caroline.

"PLEASANT" dreams, she thought. *How was she supposed to go to sleep now?* She lay back on the bed, her heart racing. She bolted upright and put herself into one of her calming yoga poses and took a few deep breaths. *Yes. This was better*, she thought as her breathing calmed. She quickly brushed her teeth, placed the room service tray outside of her door and climbed into bed ready for sleep.

But sleep didn't come. She looked at the clock. 1:52 AM. *Okay, if I fall asleep now, I'll have four and a half hours sleep*, she thought. She closed her eyes. Thoughts of Dunham invaded her senses. She glanced at the clock again. 2:36 AM. *Damn!* She thought. *Why won't sleep come?* And then she laughed to herself, knowing sleep wouldn't come until she did. Only relief would bring sleep. With a resigned sigh, she slowly lowered her hands down her tense body and began to stroke herself, letting her mind wander.

•　　•　　•

Upon her return to Los Angeles, Dunham and Caroline kept up their series of flirtatious texts.

Dunham: Hello gorgeous. How was Chicago?

Caroline: Meetings went well. Need 2 follow up in a few weeks. You?

Dunham: Still here. In meeting talking about golden handcuffs. Thinking of you...

Caroline: How do u make everyday business terms sound so... wanton?

Dunham: You mean like Open Kimono? Blowoff Top? Bottom Bounce? Shorting Against the Box?

Caroline: Oh my!

Dunham: Inverse Hammer? Kissing the Trendline? Spread Trading?

Caroline: Rolling a Forward Position?

Dunham: Oh you dirty, dirty girl. I just might fuck that dirty mouth of yours.

Caroline: I'm at work right now and you're making me...

Dunham: Hot? Wet?

Caroline: Yes!

Dunham: Good! CU soon!

Caroline: <gulp!>

Dunham: That's right baby... gotta run...

•　　•　　•

Dunham: Looking through ur biz plan now. Ideas to come. You will be soon too if I have anything to say about it.

Caroline: Oh my!

Dunham: Rest up. You're gonna get worked.

•　　•　　•

Caroline: Still on for Friday? The Last Drop in Brentwood? 7:30?

Dunham: Absolutely!

Caroline: Can't wait 2 see U.

Dunham: I can't wait 2 get you naked.

Caroline: Me 2!!!

•　　•　　•

Caroline sat at the bar, anxiously waiting for Dunham to arrive, her heart quickening at the thought of her evening adventures ahead. She hadn't seen him since their brief but memorable time in Chicago, although they had flirted via text and email for the past two weeks. She looked stunning in a silver halter top that showed off her tanned and toned shoulders. A small silver bag with a long chain strap hung off her knee to the floor.

Mike stood at the other end of the bar, mixing drinks for a couple that looked like they were meeting for the first time via Tindr. Morgan, in her waitress uniform of snug black pants and equally-fitted shirt with a white apron, passed by her.

"Hi, Morgan," Caroline said, giving a small wave. Morgan gave her a fake smile and walked by, approaching another waitress, Flora, a Hispanic beauty with long hair, long lashes, and long legs. Morgan glared at Caroline and then whispered something in Flora's ear.

"I don't think Morgan likes me very much," Caroline said to Mike, as he approached her from the other side of the bar.

"Why do you say that?"

"Steely-eyed glares," said Caroline, moving her head from side to side, bugging out her eyes and turning out her palms for emphasis. "Duh!"

"Oh, those. Yeah, well she gets a bit jealous."

"Of me? Puh-lease," she said, pushing her hand forward. "Doesn't she know we're just friends?"

"She sees a beautiful, smart, and talented woman and can't help but feel envious." Caroline's eyes glazed over and her head titled to the side.

"Why, Mike, that is just about the nicest thing you've ever said to me," she said, touching his arm gently with her hand.

"Plus I told her we did the nasty once," he shrugged.

"Biggest mistake of my life," she said, shaking her head with a grin. Mike smiled and raised his eyebrows at her.

"So when's this guy going to be here?"

"Soon. I think you'll like him. He's very smart and driven."

"So the opposite of that douchy artist Jason you dated a while back. Well, I'll be the judge of that."

"Be nice," she cautioned. "And give him a chance."

"What kind of a name is Dunham, anyway?" he asked with a hint of dislike already.

"He's from back east. It's a family name." And before she could even see him, she could sense he was there. "Here he is..." she said, inhaling sharply, as she stood up and hugged him. He kissed her cheek and swatted her behind. Meanwhile, Mike walked to the other end of the bar to address a pressing need of the Tindr couple.

"Hello gorgeous," said Dunham.

"Thank you," said Caroline, blushing and looking down into her lap. "So how was New York? Successful trip?"

"Awesome! I kicked some serious ass there. We're going to rake in an extra twenty to thirty million this year." Dunham snapped his fingers and motioned for Mike. "I need bourbon neat and none of that Johnny Walker crap." He turned back to Caroline, who bristled at his tone.

"That's fantastic. Sounds like a worthwhile trip."

"What about you? Did you get the notes I made on your expansion plan?" he asked. Mike, listening in, raised his eyebrows. He wasn't aware that Caroline was looking to expand her business. Caroline wasn't aware that she was looking to expand her business either. Dunham had sent her an extensive plan with options to branch into jewelry, belts, and sunglasses with the "Clutch" company name.

"It was good... interestin'... but perhaps a bit more aggressive than I would like to be..." she said, shifting around on her bar stool.

"Don't be foolish," he snapped at her. "No risk, no reward," he admonished. Caroline felt like an errant child. Mike placed the glass of bourbon in front of Dunham and was set to walk away when Caroline interrupted him.

"Dunham, I'd like you to–" she said as Dunham took a sip.

"This isn't Johnny Walker, is it? Tastes like shit," he said to Mike.

"No, it's Hirsch Reserve, the best I have. I'd be happy to get you something else if you would prefer," said Mike, being overly calm and congenial considering the circumstances.

"No, this will have to do," said Dunham. He turned to Caroline and continued, "What were you saying?" Caroline was starting to get a better handle on Dunham's intense personality and wasn't quite sure she liked it. But thinking back to her Chicago adventures and how her body responded – no, succumbed – to his touch, she was willing to give him a little latitude.

"I want to introduce you to Mike here, my very best friend," she said proudly, gesturing toward Mike with her hand.

"Very best friend, huh?" replied Dunham, giving Mike the once over. "Nice to meet you, Mike. So... how did you two hook up?" he asked, taking another sip.

"Mike and I went to business school together," she began. Turning to Mike she continued, "Dunham graduated a few years before us."

"Harvard Business School and you're working as a bartender?" Dunham scoffed.

"Oh, no, you don't understand. Mike is –" she began before Dunham cut her off.

"If you need a job, I'd be happy to see if we're hiring any entry level associates. Anything for the Crimson," he turned to Caroline, "and to help a friend of Caroline's, of course."

"That's a really nice offer. Thank you. But I think I'm happy where I am," said Mike, his hands balling into tight fists by his side.

"Suit yourself. But if you change your mind, just let me know. It's just unfortunate to see your degree going to waste."

"Thanks for your concern. I better get back to work. You two enjoy your drinks on me," said Mike, nodding and giving a smile that didn't reach his eyes. *What the hell*, thought Caroline. Dunham had clearly misinterpreted the situation and it was up to her to set him straight. She may not be able to stand up to him for her sake, but she certainly wasn't going to let him think ill of Mike.

"Dunham, I think you misunderstood. Mike isn't just the bartender here. He owns the bar."

"He owns a bar and you think that's a good thing," he jeered. "I'm sure the guy used to have ambitions beyond that. I mean, you don't go to Harvard to run a bar. Something must have happened to him." Caroline took a deep breath. Clearly, she wasn't articulating things properly.

"Trust me, if Mike wanted to be a wizard of Wall Street, he would be."

"I think you're letting your friendship cloud your judgment. The guy is happy owning a bar," he said condescendingly. "You don't get ahead in business without some drive."

"He *has* drive. He built this bar from nothin' and he turned it into a highly-successful business," she said firmly.

"That may be, but I would think most people who go to business school at Harvard want to do something more with their degree and their lives. It's competitive out there and maybe he just couldn't cut it."

"Mike is heir to the Barnsworth Brokerage firm. Believe me, he was born and raised with that world. If he wanted to be in it, he would be in it. He just chooses to do somethin' he loves," she huffed. That should shut Dunham up.

"What? He's a Barnsworth?"

"Yeah. Michael Frederick Barnsworth... the third," she sneered and rolled her eyes. "So listen when I say, it's just not what he wants."

"Oh man. His family is worth billions. Their firm is the top in the world." Dunham's mouth gaped open and his heart beat increased.

"I know. And he walked away from it all because it's not what he wanted to do, not because he couldn't hack it. So, can we talk about somethin'–"

"Shit! I offered to get the guy a job interview for an entry level position. Why didn't you tell me who he was?" he snapped at her, his intense eyes narrowing in anger.

"I did. I told you he was my very best friend and that's who he is," she said firmly, placing her hand on her hip. "Believe me, he doesn't want anythin' to do with his family or their work," she said in a softer tone.

"Shit!" said Dunham under his breath. He ran his fingers through his hair and motioned Mike to come over. "Hey, Mike!" Mike took a deep breath, plastered a fake smile on his face – for Caroline's sake only – and walked over.

"Another bourbon?" he asked.

"Listen, man, I'm sorry about what I said. This is a great bar and I can see what a great job you're doing with it. Really. Really like the place," he said obsequiously.

"Thanks," said Mike, unsure why Dunham had a sudden change of heart. "Uh, I appreciate that." Caroline watched the exchange, grateful that Dunham was finally befriending Mike in an appropriate manner.

"So… maybe we could go grab a drink sometime," Dunham said. Mike raised his eyebrows quizzically, looked up and down the bar and then looked back at an expectant Dunham. "I mean maybe we can hang out sometime – you know – catch a game or have dinner. I would love to talk with you more about business."

"I keep pretty busy here. But thanks anyway," Mike replied before turning around and walking away.

Dunham ran his fingers through his hair again. "Shit! Um… talk to him. Let's try to all have dinner sometime," he said anxiously. Caroline couldn't believe what a sycophantic asshole he was.

"You know, I don't think I want to have dinner with you either," she said, placing her hands on her hips and staring at him haughtily.

"What are you saying?"

"I don't really like the way you just treated my friend. I think you should leave," she said, her head bobbling back and forth and her eyes glaring at him.

"What?" Dunham said, looking contrite. "I'm just trying to get to know him better. He's your best friend, which means I should give the guy a chance."

"You only wanted to give the guy a chance when you found out who his family is. Like I said, I think you should leave."

"Caroline, don't be foolish!"

"Goodbye, Dunham," she said, before turning around on her bar stool, not looking at him again. Dunham took a last sip of his bourbon, threw $100 on the counter, and skulked out. Mike watched him leave and then turned his attention to a brooding Caroline. He walked to her place at the bar and refilled her wine glass.

"So..." he said, waiting for her to fill in the blanks.

"So he turned out to be quite the jerk, didn't he," she said – more as a statement than a question.

"What happened?"

"He was so rude to you, and then when I told him who you were..." she began.

Mike completed her sentence. "He all of a sudden wanted to get to know me better."

"Yeah," she said indignantly.

"I've grown up my whole life with assholes like that guy. I could have easily been that guy, making deals and trading favors with powerful people. But I chose not to be him. I'm quite happy just the way I am. And you deserve to be happy too."

"Well, I couldn't let him treat you that way," she said, looking at Mike with a grin.

"You shouldn't let him treat *you* that way," stated Mike. "I know you have a hard time standing up for yourself, but you're an amazing woman, Caroline Johnson. Don't let anyone tell you differently," he said, looking into her eyes, ensuring she heard what he was saying.

"Well, good riddance then," she said, shaking her head and placing her hands firmly on her hips.

Mike clasped his hands together over one shoulder and batted his eyelashes at Caroline. "Thank you for defending my honor. My hero," he said in a high-pitched, feminine voice. He winked at Caroline as she laughed. As she turned toward the other end of the bar, she noticed Morgan, who had overhead their conversation, rolling her eyes. Mike walked over to check on the Tindr couple. Buoyed by her recent, successful, and non-premeditated assertive experience, Caroline moved off of her bar stool and walked over to Morgan in an attempt to mend fences.

"Morgan, have I done somethin' to offend you? I feel like maybe I did or said somethin'," she began.

"No," responded Morgan, her stare once again like sharp daggers aimed at Caroline. Morgan walked away.

Loren, another waitress, looked at Caroline sympathetically. "She just really likes Mike," she said to Caroline.

"Well she shouldn't go off all half-cocked. I can assure you – and her – that he and I are just friends," said Caroline firmly.

"She thinks Mike's in love with you," Loren continued.

"No," said Caroline incredulously, pushing her head back and to the side.

"Yes," said Loren with an affirming nod of her head.

"That's just crazy. If anythin', Mike thinks the sun comes up just to hear him crow." Loren looked at Caroline, confused. "He's in love with himself and his freedom," she clarified.

"You may think so, but she sees things differently," Loren said, before turning to take drink orders at a nearby table.

Well, I think I know Mike a bit better than she does, Caroline thought. *He is definitely not in love with anyone, except himself.* Caroline shrugged and went back to her seat at the bar.

Wallet

*K*ayle puffed on the contraband Cuban cigar and let out a smoky round "o" before her lips curled up in a big smile.

"Will you excuse me a moment," said Caroline, dressed in a short powder blue mini dress that hugged all of her curves and made her eyes pop. Complementing the look was a small ivory clutch that matched her ivory-colored sandals. She walked through the haze of smoke that hung over the dark leather couches and chairs, accented by small round mahogany tables. She passed a mid-sized room with a glass door that resembled a bank vault. Gold numbered drawers with small locks lined the walls like safety deposit boxes. This was the temperature-controlled humidor where L.A.'s rich, powerful, and elite stored their cigars at the exclusive, member's-only Grand Havana Room cigar club.

It was kind of Kayle's brother to host her and the girls that night. He'd been a member for several years, as it was a perfect place to schmooze his entertainment industry clients. While she had been invited many times before, Caroline had never wanted to come. Smoking and cigars weren't her thing. But Kayle was insistent she get out of the house and set her mind on something other than her new line of bucket bags and Dunham Carter.

She walked into the bathroom, happy to have escaped the stagnant, dingy air. Glancing in the mirror, she dabbed a tissue under her eyes to remove some errant eyeliner. She stood back, taking in her reflection, using her fingers to comb through her long blonde hair.

Removing a nude lip gloss from her small bag, she applied a dab, rubbing her lips back and forth to make sure it was evenly distributed. Finally, she took a long, last deep breath, enjoying the relatively smoke-free atmosphere.

As she walked out of the unisex restroom and down the hall back to the main room, a handsome man with flopping blond hair and a strong cleft in his chin walked toward her and smiled, dimples puckering on both cheeks.

"Did you know that's the bathroom where Mel Gibson and Britney Spears supposedly had sex?" he said to her.

"Oh my. I feel a little dirty now," said Caroline, slightly aghast, clutching her hand to her chest.

"Just a little? I wanted to bathe in a vat of Purell after I found out," he said, smiling. "I'm Marcus." Caroline reached out to shake his hand.

"Speakin' of Purell, I washed 'em," she said. Marcus reached out his hand to greet hers and she let hers linger in his for a moment longer than necessary. "I'm Caroline."

"Good," said Marcus. "I like a girl who's clean. And maybe a little dirty." He cocked his head to the side and flashed her a panty-melting smile.

"You're in luck. I'm just the right amount of wrong," she said as she turned her head to the side and gave him a sly smile in return.

"Could I buy you a drink?" he asked, gesturing with his hand toward the bar.

"Actually, I was just leavin'. I don't really like all of this smoke," she replied as she waved her hand back and forth in front of her face and scrunched up her nose.

"Kind of a hazard when you come to a cigar bar." He furrowed his brow and nodded with his lips pulled together in a line.

"I know. I got dragged here by some friends," she said, looking up toward the ceiling and shaking her head.

"I know a place that makes a great dirty martini. It too is just the right amount of wrong."

"That's temptin'. But I don't even know you," she replied. *Tell me to come get to know you*, she thought as she lowered her head slightly and looked up at him, her long lashes casting shadows on her cheeks.

"Come get to know me," he said, echoing her thoughts. "The bar isn't too far. Just an hour flight on my private jet."

"Private jet?" said Caroline with skepticism.

"Did I forget to mention the bar's in San Francisco?" said a smiling Marcus, his dimples causing her heart to beat faster and her panties to become moist. Caroline gave a small girlish laugh.

"Oh, that's quite an offer, but I think I need to decline. It's a bit late for me to be jauntin' off up the coast with a man I hardly know."

"I can respect that. Maybe I could call you sometime and we could get a drink around here."

"Sure. Why don't I give you my number?" Marcus handed Caroline his phone, a lighter-than-air model she hadn't seen before. She programmed in her number and handed it back to him, letting her fingers brush against his skin. Marcus looked at the contact information.

"All right Caroline Johnson, I'll call you."

"I hope you do," she said before walking past him, knowing his gaze would be watching her ass as she went back to say goodbye to her friends.

●　　●　　●

"You're wrong. They were just a bunch of pretty boys in matching suits. They were too pop. Too mainstream. Trust me. That's *not* rock 'n' roll," said Mike emphatically as he wiped down the bar absentmindedly. It was 5:00 on a Saturday night and the bar was practically empty.

"Oh and bein' scruffy and unkempt is? As I recall readin', Mick Jagger went on the Ed Sullivan show wearin' an everyday T-shirt. He didn't even give a crap what he looked like. *That's* rock 'n' roll?" asked Caroline in disbelief.

"Jagger was a bad ass. He didn't have to care what he looked like. And yes, that's rock 'n' roll. Paul was faithful to Linda for all of those years, and John was faithful to Yoko. Believe me, that's *not* rock 'n' roll."

"Oh, so you can't be a rock star and monogamous at the same time?"

"No. You can't," he stated simply.

"If the Stones were so much better than the Beatles, why did it take them longer to get inducted into the Rock 'n' Roll Hall of Fame? The Beatles were innovators. The Stones were just followin' their lead."

"I don't think anyone can argue that the time between 'Beggars Banquet' and 'Exile on Main Street' was the greatest era of rock music ever released," Mike said, his hands waving back and forth with emphasis.

"That may be the case, but whatever the Stones did, the Beatles did first."

"No way!" he scoffed.

"No way," she sneered. "Really? That's a cogent argument?" she asked with sass.

Mike looked at her and raised his eyebrow. "Don't get smart with me."

"You're the one not bein' smart. And anyway, their 'Satanic Majesties Request' was just a clone – and a weak one at that – of 'Sergeant Pepper's.'"

"For fuck's sake, the only reason people think the Beatles have a better legacy is because they broke up before they got even shittier."

"Yeah, and the Rollin' Stones have been shitty for the last forty years," Caroline said, shaking her head. Her phone rang and she put up a hand to silence Mike as he was about to speak up. He walked to the back room to grab some food for them to munch on.

"Hello, this is Caroline," she said, uncertain who was calling.

"Caroline, hi. This is Marcus Greenleaf. We met last week at the Grand Havana Room."

"Could you be a bit more specific? I gave my number out to a lot of men that night," she replied. Caroline waited a beat before continuing playfully, "See, I'm just the right amount of wrong." Mike walked over with a plate of nachos.

"Ha! That's a relief," said Marcus, exhaling. "I thought for a second you didn't remember me."

"It's not that often a girl gets invited on a private jet." Mike began to listen intently.

"The offer's still open," said Marcus with a sly smile.

"Maybe we start off with somethin' a bit more local?"

"Absolutely. Are you free on Thursday?"

"Thursday works just fine," she said, smiling.

"How about sushi? Are you a fan?"

"Sushi would be great." Mike frowned.

"Have you been to Urasawa?"

"No, I haven't. That would be lovely."

"Great. I'll pick you up at 7:00."

"I'll text you my address."

"I'll look forward to it," he said before hanging up his phone. Caroline put down her phone and smiled broadly. She was like a giddy school girl inside, thinking back to the handsome and charming man she had met last week. Suddenly, her thoughts were interrupted.

"Private jet?" Mike inquired, his eyebrow raised.

"So I was at the Havana Room last week with some of the girls..." she began.

Mike raised his eyebrow further. "Lydia?" he asked with interest.

Caroline took a deep sigh. "Yes, Lydia. But honestly, Mike. I think that ship has sailed."

"Because of Kayle?" he asked, considering his question and nodding his head as he guessed her response.

"Yeah, Kayle," she said with sarcasm.

"That's a shame," he said, his thoughts trailing off before turning his attention back to Caroline. "So, you were at the Havana Room..." he offered, giving her the go ahead to continue with her story.

"And I met a man there who invited me to take a ride on his private jet to San Francisco for a martini." Mike cocked his head to the side and widened his eyes. "I declined, naturally," she said, waving her hand in front of her, "but gave him my number. He called and we're havin' dinner this Thursday."

"Private jet, huh?"

"I know. Pretty cool. But I'm not ready to hop on his plane."

"Are we talking literally or sexually?" asked Mike with mock seduction.

Caroline shook her head and laughed. "Literally. Regardin' sexually..." She turned her head coquettishly to the side and continued, "We'll have to see."

"Okay. Okay," Mike quickly interjected, a knot in his stomach tightening. Although he brought up the topic, he wasn't so sure he wanted to hear about Caroline's potential sexual exploits after all. "So you're having dinner on Thursday night."

"He's takin' me for sushi."

"Sushi? I thought you didn't like sushi. You once told me that where you're from, sushi is just a fancy word for live bait."

"You remember that?" she asked, putting her hand to her heart and giving him a sincere grin.

"I always remember what you say."

She smiled and reached across the bar to touch his arm gently. "Well, I stick to the mainstream stuff. It's at some joint called Urasawa? Never heard of it."

"Urasawa?" Mike said in disbelief. He exhaled loudly and whistled through his teeth. "That place is like a grand, easy. He's going to definitely be expecting you to hop on his plane."

"For a thousand-dollar spider roll, he just might get it," she said, raising her eyebrows up and down like Mike usually did.

"Really? I never took you for the materialistic type."

"Oh, I can easily be bought," she said, winking. "Seriously, I'm open to bein' swept off my feet."

"Well, just keep your head about you," he warned.

"Thanks, Dad," she said, giving him a joking glare.

"So, what are your thoughts on the East Coast vs. West Coast Hip Hop rivalry?" he asked, changing the subject.

"Uh..." she spluttered.

"Notorious B.I.G. and P. Diddy vs. 2Pac?"

"Uh, I guess P. Diddy. At least I've heard of him. He has a fashion line called Sean."

"So, you're team East Coast. We'll tackle that pop culture debate next week, so study up!"

●　　●　　●

"Sorry it's no Urasawa, but I abandoned life in the fast lane for more noble pursuits," said Mike, popping a tuna roll into his mouth as he and Caroline sat under a striped umbrella in a business office park. Inside of the building, a neon sign flashed *"Atomic Sushi: Best in the West"* as a line of eclectic people snaked around the corner.

"Quickie crab rolls are fine with me," said Caroline, smiling appreciatively. "To be honest, I wasn't quite sure what I was eatin' the other night. It was good, but I don't know if it was five hundred dollars good."

"So what's his story? Trust fund baby?"

"No. He hit it big with a software company in the Bay area. We bumped into a friend of his who kept callin' him Number Twelve. Apparently, he was the twelfth person at the company. When they went public, he cashed out."

"And now he just jets around wooing women with expensive meals?"

"Actually, his pursuits are a bit more noble than that... and yours," she said smugly. "He volunteers in the computer lab at a junior high school in Compton. In fact, he donated new computers to the school."

"Well, he sounds like quite the philanthropist," he said with mild sarcasm.

"Do I detect a hint of jealousy?"

"Yeah, you do. I want a sugar mama to come down and take care of me."

"I'm not like that," she said, offended at his suggestion that she only liked Marcus for his wealth.

"What? You're not a gold digger?"

"Of course not!" she exclaimed, putting down her chopsticks and placing her hands on her hips. "I may not have come from money, but I want to earn it myself."

Realizing he may have taken the joke a bit too far, Mike changed the course of the conversation. "I come from money and I want to earn it myself too."

"I know," she said, calming down and realizing his admission was also an apology. "You're a good man, Michael Barnsworth. And so is Marcus."

"I hope for your sake that he is."

•   •   •

Mike laid in his bed, resting his head against the black lacquered head board, a heather grey comforter pulled up to his neck. The clock read 10:43 AM. He stared at the ceiling, lost in thoughts, when he was disturbed by a ringing cell phone.

"Hey there," Caroline said solemnly.

"Hey. What's up?" he asked, his voice laced with concern.

"I wanted to see how you were holdin' up since Morgan quit."

"I found another waitress, so we're all good," he said flatly, rubbing his face.

"No, I mean how are you doin' *emotionally*. I know she said some pretty harsh things when she left."

"Yeah, she's got a pretty dirty mouth on her, doesn't she? Believe me, if you only knew some of the dirty things she did with that mouth," he reminisced, both seduction and humor evident in his voice.

"Be serious," Caroline said, holding back a smile. "I'm tryin' to be a concerned friend."

"Well, most of the awful things she said were about you, so I should really be checking on you. I know you can't stand it when people don't like you," he said, trying to deflect the conversation away from himself.

True, thought Caroline. She had tried – on many occasions – to befriend Morgan. And when she realized friendship was out of the question, she thought they could at least maintain some sense of civility. But Morgan was vehemently against any type of congeniality toward Caroline, and that drove her nuts.

"Right now, I'm more concerned about you. Despite what you say – that you don't give a rat's behind what other people think – I know she was harsh," she said, also trying to deflect the attention away from herself.

"I'm okay. Really. Thanks for checking on me," he said as he rose out of bed and walked into the kitchen to start some coffee.

"I also have a favor to ask. Marcus is meetin' me at the bar tomorrow night."

"Great," Mike said with fake enthusiasm as he rolled his eyes and put an individual pod in the coffee machine. "Can't wait to meet him."

"Actually, I wasn't plannin' on introducin' you," she said tentatively.

"He's that embarrassing?" said Mike, laughing, as the machine made a whirring noise and started a slow drip.

"No!" she retorted.

"Well, I know it can't be me. I'm a delight."

Caroline laughed. "You are indeed a delight. I was just hopin' you could get a read on him for me. We've been datin' for two months and after that fiasco with Dunham, I would really love your thoughts."

"Sure," he said, trying to keep his voice even, despite his growing frustration at being Caroline's relationship sounding board. Caroline didn't seem to notice.

"Thanks. You're the best. I'll see you tomorrow."

"Great," said Mike under his breath as he took a sip of his fresh dark brew.

•   •   •

Marcus held the door open for Caroline and ushered her into the bar, taking the grey pea coat she peeled off her back as they entered the warmth of The Last Drop. Caroline gave Mike a knowing glance and guided Marcus over to a small low table in the corner. She sat down, placing her black distressed leather knapsack behind the chair. Mike nodded his head at her in acknowledgment and walked over to Loren.

"I got table twelve," he said. Loren looked over and noticed Caroline sitting with her new beau. She smiled to confirm. Mike sauntered over, looking Marcus over as he did. Marcus was dressed casually in a pair of dark jeans, a tan cashmere pullover sweater with a plain white T-shirt underneath, a brown sport coat, and a pair of two-toned, brown oxford-style saddle shoes. *He looks rather unassuming for a man with a private jet*, Mike thought.

"Hi there. Welcome to The Last Drop. What can I get you?" he asked.

Marcus turned attentively to Caroline. "What would you like, babe?"

"I'll have a glass of Chardonnay, please," she said to Marcus and then looked up at Mike and smiled.

"A glass of Chardonnay for the lovely lady and a glass of Cognac for me. Thanks, sir," he said to Mike.

"Sure thing. Be right back," Mike responded. Marcus put his arm around Caroline and looked at her adoringly. He leaned in and put his lips to her earlobe, whispering in her ear. Caroline giggled and batted her eyelashes at him. Marcus reached into his finely-tailored sports jacket and produced a small black jewelry box, embossed with silver letters reading "David Yurman" on top.

"What is this?" she gasped in surprise. She looked deep into Marcus' eyes and shook her head slowly.

"Just a little something for you," he said, leaning in to kiss her cheek.

"You are spoilin' me," she said, looking at him disapprovingly.

"I like spoiling you," he said, staring hungrily into her eyes. "Open it." Caroline's fingers trembled as she lifted the top. Inside, resting on a cushion of black velvet, was a white gold necklace with a pendant made of pave diamonds. Caroline's eyes widened, and she clutched her hand to her chest.

"Oh my word. This is gorgeous," she exhaled.

"I thought you would like it. Let me help you put it on." Marcus brushed Caroline's wavy blonde hair to the side and then reached his arm around her front, pulling the pendant together at the nape of her neck.

Mike walked over and placed the drinks and a leather bi-fold with the bill on the wood table. Caroline placed her hand over the pendant and pulled her eyes down to look at it. She then looked up and met Mike's eyes, giving him a "can you believe it" look. Mike smiled slightly at her.

"Here you go," Mike said.

"Thanks," said Marcus. He pulled a hundred-dollar bill from his wallet and placed it into the leather sleeve without looking at the bill. "Keep the change," he said, smiling.

"Thanks," said Mike, who took the portfolio and walked away slowly, paying attention to Caroline's conversation.

"Oh Marcus. This is just so beautiful. Thank you."

"Not as beautiful as you, babe," he said, nuzzling his nose in her hair. Caroline looked adoringly into his eyes and took a sip of her Chardonnay. After a few moments of conversation and provocative little touches, Marcus whispered in her ear.

"What do you say we head out?"

Caroline pulled back. "But we just got here," she said, searching his eyes.

"I know. But I just need to have you right now," he said, looking hungrily back at her. Caroline's breathing hitched.

"Okay. Let's go." They stood up and walked toward the door. Marcus walked out of the bar, holding the door open for Caroline.

"I left my purse," she said. "Be right back." Marcus waited outside while Caroline walked back to the table and pulled her knapsack from behind the chair. She then walked over to Mike who was standing at the bar, watching her the entire time.

"Well, what do you think?" she asked, clearly seeking Mike's approval.

"The necklace is really pretty," he said with a slight smile.

"No, not the necklace," she said, tapping his arm with her hand. "What do you think of Marcus?"

"He seems like a good guy."

A broad smile crossed Caroline's face and she clapped her hands like a giddy schoolgirl.

"He is. Well, he's waitin' for me. I'll call you tomorrow. Good night." She blew Mike a kiss and walked out.

● ● ●

Caroline strummed her fingers nervously on the dark wood bar. Mike put a plate of chicken strips in front of her, but she gently pushed them away and shook her head at him.

"How late is he?" Mike said, wiping down the bar with a towel.

"An hour. I've left three messages. I'm really worried," she said. She put her hand to her temple and rubbed it. Her phone rang and she answered it immediately. "Marcus! Is everything okay?" she exhaled. Muffled sounds of Marcus talking on the other end of the phone brought Mike to attention. "That's it? You stood me up because you got caught up in somethin'?" she shouted in disbelief. Mike looked impressed with Caroline's assertiveness. "No. I'm not overreactin'. You've been thoughtless," she continued. As she listened to Marcus on the other end, she shook her head and pursed her lips. "You shouldn't be sorry I feel that way. You should just be sorry," she said, before hanging up the phone.

Before she even placed the phone back on the bar, Mike erupted in applause.

"Well, I do declare," he said in a fake, exaggerated Southern accent, "that was a mighty fine sight to see."

"The nerve!" she expelled.

"Who me?" said Mike, fearful his playfulness had only further fanned the flames of her ire.

"No, him," she said, shaking her head in anger.

"That clearly wasn't a conversation you planned out in advance," said Mike, laughing slightly.

"And I won't be rehashin' it either. The only thing I want to repeat right now is this drink. Let him stew. I'll deal with him tomorrow," she said shaking her head

"Well done, young lady," said Mike. Caroline grabbed her glass of wine, finished the last gulp and thrust it toward Mike for a refill.

•   •   •

"You haven't said anythin' about my earrings," she said, pulling her wavy blonde hair back and up, accentuating the tear drop-shaped aquamarine stones dangling from platinum hoops.

Taking a bite of his burger while seated in a fifties era diner, Mike responded drolly, "A: I didn't notice them. B: I don't need to notice them because you will tell me all about them, and C: I don't care about them."

"C'mon now," she said, lowering her hair and pushing her hand forward toward him. "If I can't talk about my new boyfriend and all of his lavish gifts to my best friend, who can I talk to?"

"I don't recall signing up for confidant duties. Isn't that what," he made air quotes, "the *girls* are for?"

"The *girls* have listened, but they tend to get a bit jealous of how well this wonderful man is treatin' me. And anyway, you did sign up for confidant duty when you agreed to be my bestie. They're aquamarine. My birthstone," she said, jangling the stones with her manicured fingers.

"He sure seems to be dropping a lot of cash on you," said Mike, frowning slightly.

"I know. I'm not used to bein' treated so well," said Caroline, oblivious to Mike's disapproving tone.

"Don't confuse being treated well with being treated to lots of things."

"I'm not. He treats me great," she declared.

"Oh yeah? What about standing you up the other night?"

"He apologized and acknowledged he was bein' an ass. He assured me it won't happen again."

"I hope so," he said, pursing his lips.

• • •

"I miss you too. I'll be back in two days," she cooed into the phone as she walked down 5th Avenue, taking in all of the sights and sounds that New York had to offer: the smell of hot pretzels and hot dogs, the sounds of taxis honking, the rush of people pushing their way to their next appointment.

"I'm sorry I couldn't come with you. Between the restaurants and shops, I know I could have shown you a great time," said Marcus.

"You always do, Marcus," she replied, passing a street vendor hawking counterfeit designer bags – Fendi, Prada, Louis Vuitton. She secretly wondered (and hoped) if one day she'd see faux Clutch bags being sold to unsuspecting tourists and housewives from Long Island.

"Listen, I'm here," she said, slowing down. Her heart pumped as she stared up at the familiar cursive letters of Lord & Taylor calling her like a siren's song. *New York retail never gets old*, she thought to herself. "Let me call you later."

"Good luck, babe," Marcus responded. "I have every confidence you'll do great." She hung up her phone, pulled her shoulders back, and walked through the glass doors, ready to dazzle the new buyer.

•　　•　　•

A few patrons sat at the bar sipping beers while all of the tables and chairs were filled with small groups of friends, several sets of lovers, and three nerdy guys hotly debating Betty versus Veronica from the Archie comics.

Ironic, thought Mike, as he noticed a woman walk in that looked like a cartoon character or Kewpie doll. She was an attractive brunette with a round face, dark pixie haircut, pink cheeks, and oversized eyes. She had her arm wrapped around a man, and the two took seats at the bar.

"Welcome to The Last Drop," said Mike, grabbing a clean towel from under the bar before looking up.

"We'll have a bottle of champagne, please, sir," said a polite voice that Mike recognized. He looked up to find himself eye to eye with Marcus. Kewpie doll clung to him like a life preserver, and the bastard was loving every minute of it. *What the fuck*, thought Mike.

"Sure thing," said Mike, pursing his lips in a thin line and exhaling loudly. "Celebrating something?" he asked with a fake smile.

"It's our two-month date-iversary," she said, her voice high and squeaky like a little girl. *It matched her look,* thought Mike.

"Two months? Congratulations," Mike replied, the ire building in his chest. His mind raced. *Do I confront him? Do I tell Caroline? What the fuck am I supposed to do?* he thought as he popped the champagne and poured it into two glasses.

Marcus removed his nose and lips from snuggling into the woman's ear and reached into his pocket to produce a small black jewelry box. Bile started to rise in Mike's throat. Kewpie doll squealed and clapped her hands with glee. She tore the box top open and produced a pave diamond necklace, identical to the one Marcus had given Caroline a few weeks prior.

"Oh my God," she squeaked. "It's beautiful! Put it on! Put it on!" she chirped, again clapping her hands. Marcus deftly clasped the necklace around her neck. Mike wondered how often he had done that.

"Wow. That's a really nice necklace," Mike said, his lips pursed, slowly nodding his head.

"Isn't it beautiful?" she squawked, beaming.

"My girlfriend would love that. Can I get a picture of it?" Mike asked.

"Sure!" she exclaimed. She quickly grabbed Marcus and posed for a photo with him. Mike snapped a quick cell phone image and turned to another bartender.

"Hey, watch the bar for a few minutes, will ya?" The bartender nodded affirmatively and Mike walked swiftly to the back room of the bar.

Standing among cardboard boxes housing bottles of wine and spirits, he ran his fingers through his hair and bent over, putting his hands on his knees. *Fuck!* He paced for a moment, before grabbing his phone and dialing. His heart pounded as the phone rang on the other end.

Sitting in a pair of striped button-down pajamas reading emails on her laptop in her New York hotel room, Caroline grabbed her phone. Seeing the caller ID, she smiled.

"Well, this is a nice surprise," she said, taking a sip of the chocolate shake she'd ordered from room service.

"I didn't wake you, did I?"

"Oh no. I've been runnin' all over hell's half acre," she said. Sensing Mike's frustration over the phone, she quickly said, "No. I'm super busy with work, both Maxine's and mine," she said with annoyance. "How are you?" she added with sincerity.

"I'm okay," he said. Caroline knew him well enough to know he wasn't okay.

"You don't sound okay. What's wrong?" she said with genuine concern, taking a long sip of her chocolate shake. *Not Morgan again*, she thought. *Please don't let this be about Morgan.*

"Listen. I have something to tell you. I didn't know if I should wait until you got back or if I should call you," he said.

"You're scarin' me. What's wrong?"

"It's Marcus. He showed up here with another girl."

"What?" she spluttered. "Who is she?"

"I don't know. But they are definitely more than friends. And he gave her a necklace like the one he gave you."

Caroline dropped her glass and splattered the cold chocolate shake all over the duvet. "Shit!" she exclaimed as she picked up the tipped over glass.

"Yeah," Mike continued. "I took a picture. Here," he said and then moved the phone from his ear to send the picture to Caroline.

"What are you doin', Mike?"

"I'm being a good friend. I figured you would want to know," he said, raking his fingers through his hair.

"You sound quite pleased with yourself." Her words were laced with anger.

"Pleased with myself?" he repeated in disbelief. "You think I enjoy knowing that this is hurting you?"

"You always enjoy seein' my relationships implode."

"The guy's cheating on you and you're pissed at me?" he hissed incredulously.

"You just don't want me to be happy," she blurted.

"Are you fucking kidding me?" he shouted, unable to control his ire. "When have I ever done *anything* to make you think I don't want you to be happy? You pick these loser guys and then wonder why it never works out."

"So I'm bein' cheated on and now you're sayin' it's my fault?" she challenged.

"That's not what I'm saying. Is that what you're paying a therapist for? To help you shift the blame when you're upset?"

"My therapist is teachin' me to stand up for myself. And I'm standin' up right now..." she said, standing up and pulling her shoulders back, "askin' you to clarify that if I picked a better guy, this wouldn't have happened, right?"

"Yeah, you never seem to have trouble standing up to me. But why are you picking a fight with me?"

"Just because you're fine hoppin' from bed to bed with waitresses and slutty bar girls doesn't mean that's what I want. I want a real relationship. I want someone who is gonna love me."

"Well, this ain't the guy. And if you want to be mad at me because he turned out to be a douche, then so be it." Mike hung up the phone and took a deep breath. He sat down in his leather desk chair and leaned back, running his hands through his hair.

Caroline sat in her hotel room, sobbing, as she cleaned up the spilled shake with hotel towels.

•   •   •

At 4:00 in the afternoon the next day, after returning from an early morning flight, Caroline walked in the bar sheepishly, wearing loose fitting jeans and an oversized hoodie. Her hair was piled up into a messy bun and her eyelids were heavy and red-rimmed. She didn't even have a purse with her, instead carrying her phone, wallet, and keys in her hand. She hesitantly approached Mike, unsure how he would feel about her being there, given her unforgiveable behavior the previous night.

"I'm sorry," she said, starting to cry. "I know you were..." her voice trailed off.

"Shh. Me too," said Mike. He pulled her into his chest and put his arm around her.

"I didn't mean what I said," she sobbed.

"I know," he confirmed. "Have you been up all night agonizing over all of this in your head?" Caroline pulled herself from his chest and nodded her head yes.

"Don't you give him another thought. Karma will take care of him."

"I know. The sun don't shine on the same dog's tail all the time," she said, sniffling. Mike pulled away from her and feigned confusion. "It's what you said," she explained.

"Oh," he said with a soft laugh.

"What's wrong with me? Why doesn't anyone want to be with me?" she sobbed. "Am I askin' for too much? Am I not givin' enough?"

"There's nothing wrong with you. You're perfect."

"So perfect that I'm gonna die alone," she scoffed, rubbing the back of her hand up her nose.

"You're not going to die alone. There's someone out there for you," he said soothingly, while gently stroking the back of her head.

"How do you know? This isn't like in the movies when the girl and the guy find each other and live happily ever after. This is real life. And in real life, I will die alone." Her shoulders sagged and she leaned into him.

"Why *can't* this be like the movies?"

"It just isn't."

"I promise you, you will not end up alone."

"You're right. I'm gonna end up here with *you*. You'll be alone because you can't commit and I'll be alone because nobody wants me and we'll end up bein' alone together."

"Is that so bad?" he asked, pulling away from her and looking into her eyes.

"Yes," she replied. Mike gave her an exaggerated aghast look, pretending to be insulted. Caroline laughed slightly. "You know what I mean."

"I think I do, missy," he said, again feigning insult. "Believe me, you could do a lot worse than end up with me."

"Oh really?" she asked, curious to hear his response.

"Yeah, really. You *could* die alone. At least I let you drink for free." Caroline burst into laughter and leaned into Mike again, who placed his arms around her in a consoling bear hug.

Cosmetic Bag

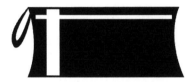

*I*t didn't take much for Lydia to convince Caroline to check out Prize, a new restaurant in Silverlake, an area of Los Angeles known for being "cool" and "hip." She wore a form fitting black blouse and polka dotted mini skirt, complemented by a black leather wristlet and matching lace up knee-high boots. It was the perfect mix of saucy and sweet, which she hoped would be like the menu at the restaurant.

From the outside, the restaurant was nothing to write home about. The inside was equally unimpressive. Wood tables and chairs dotted the middle and lined the walls, save for one wall that boasted a small stage and curtain. Caroline surmised they had live entertainment on occasion although there was no indication there would be someone there that evening.

Simple white tablecloths and candles sat in each table's center. The only thing that wasn't nondescript about Prize was the food. Caroline's mouth watered as she looked around the tables and saw beautifully-plated, colorful and delicious looking dishes.

Upon some good personal selling by their waitress, she, Lydia and Kayle decided to splurge on the chef's special tasting menu consisting of five courses with one key ingredient – radishes. While she wasn't quite convinced that radishes could be altered and enhanced in that many spectacular ways, she was willing to give it a try. At $135 per person, it was the most expensive meal she'd ever ordered, but if the food on the plates around her were even a fraction as delicious as they looked, it would be well worth the cost.

And the meal didn't disappoint. While she had been a fan of the radish as a garnish, she had a few – or to be honest, more than a few – doubts about it as a main ingredient. But it was quite possibly the best meal she'd ever had, the one exception being Aunt Mimi's biscuits and gravy, which she would walk across hot coals of fire to get.

The sautéed root in brown butter with toasted sesame seeds appetizer was her favorite of the five courses with the main dish of prawns with a carrot and radish slaw coming in at a close second.

As she finished up the final course of chocolate cake with a velvety radish sauce, she saw a handsome man in a white chef's coat walking around the restaurant. His eye caught Caroline's and she smiled at him. He made his way across various tables, shaking hands and speaking with guests. Finally, he approached Caroline's table.

"Good evening ladies. I hope everything has been to your liking," he said.

"Yes. Our dinner was amazing," offered Kayle, with a bat of her eyelashes.

"Yes, thank you," added Caroline.

"I'm glad to hear that. I'm Daniel, the chef here. And you are..." he began, reaching out to shake Lydia's hand.

"Lydia," she breathed, clearly enthralled by the handsome man in front of her.

"Lydia, nice to meet you. And you?" he said, turning to Kayle.

"Hi. I'm Kayle," said Kayle with the perfect combination of flirtation and bravado. He shook her hand, clasping his other hand on top of their two entwined ones.

"Thank you for coming in tonight, Kayle." He turned to Caroline who could not stop staring at his beautiful face and impeccable cheekbones.

"I'm Caroline," she said with a smile.

"It's my pleasure Caroline," he said, raising his hand to his lips and brushing them across her knuckles. Caroline felt a shock of electricity from his touch and, if she wasn't mistaken, heard Lydia sigh.

"I hope you'll return," he said.

Kayle looked between Caroline and Daniel, who appeared to be equally smitten with each other and said, "Oh we'll be back." Daniel tore his eyes away from Caroline and wished the three ladies a nice evening.

"What was that?" exclaimed Lydia, giving Caroline a playful tap on the arm.

"*That* was foreplay," said Kayle, seductively raising her eyebrows up and down. Caroline just laughed it off, but couldn't keep her eyes off of Daniel as he returned to the kitchen. The waitress came by with the check and started to explain about the Sunday themed brunches that the restaurant offered.

"So this Sunday is our gospel brunch. We'll feature gospel singers from the Silverlake Methodist Church along with free champagne." The three women all withdrew a credit card from their wallets and put them in the billfold while the waitress continued to talk. "Next weekend is really wild. It's our monthly..."

But Caroline had stopped listening. She couldn't stop thinking about Daniel and his talented hands turning such a boring root vegetable into such a culinary masterpiece. She wondered what else his magical hands could do.

She started to feel flush and took a sip of ice water as she heard Kayle say, "Thanks. Those sound like a ton of fun. We'll check them out."

"In the meantime, please just split the bill three ways," Lydia added.

When the waitress returned and as they each signed their credit card slips the waitress said, "Chef Daniel invited you ladies back into the kitchen for a quick tour if you're interested."

Caroline was more than interested, but didn't want to seem too eager. Kayle on the other hand had no qualms about speaking up for the three of them. She stood quickly and asked the waitress to lead the way.

Caroline was immediately impressed and overwhelmed by the cacophony of sounds and smells. Chef Daniel was placing small amounts of a bright green sauce around the rim of two plates while the sous chefs plated dishes, pulled items from the refrigerator and rattled heavy industrial pans on the stovetop creating plumes of steam and sizzling sounds.

"Welcome to my kitchen, ladies," he said, but kept his eyes on Caroline.

"Thanks for inviting us back," said Lydia, who was watching one of the sous chefs pull a steak from the stainless-steel broiler.

"Here you can see we have a small space, but are able to use it with great efficiency. We spend a few hours prepping for the evening including making all of our sauces from scratch daily." He handed Caroline a tasting spoon and encouraged her to try a blue cheese sauce that was used over the fresh-from-the-broiler steak.

"Mmm. Delicious," she said, pulling the spoon from her mouth.

"I'm glad you think so," he said, looking at Caroline as if he wanted to spoon the sauce all over her body and lick it off. Caroline didn't think she'd mind that at all.

As the brief tour concluded, he shook each of their hands and slipped Caroline a note. Her eyes widened in surprise. She pursed her lips together and slid the note into her jacket pocket. She didn't dare look at it as they walked out and planned to wait until she was home alone in her own apartment before taking a peek.

● ● ●

As Caroline walked into her apartment after dinner at Prize she let out a loud exhale. She placed the folded note on her kitchen counter and walked to her bedroom. She changed into a comfy pair of pajamas and then scrubbed her face free of makeup.

She placed a glob of toothpaste on her brush and started to rub the bristles across her teeth. While the toothpaste foamed up in her mouth, she wondered why they never showed that in toothpaste commercials. Wasn't that the best part – knowing that you were getting a good cleansing lather.

As she pondered this, she walked down the hall toward the kitchen, the folded note staring at her, begging to be opened. When she finally finished getting ready for bed, she scooped up the note and took a deep breath. She wasn't sure why she was so nervous to open it but she felt butterflies in her stomach.

She unfolded the note and in neat writing, all capital letters, it read:

I NEVER DO THIS BUT I WAS COMPLETELY CAPTIVATED BY YOUR EYES. PLEASE CONSIDER CALLING ME SO I CAN LEARN MORE ABOUT THE WOMAN BEHIND THEM. 626 555 2823

Caroline bit her lip and smiled to herself. She would definitely be giving Chef Daniel a call.

• • •

Caroline waited three days – three painfully long days – before reaching out to Daniel. During that time, however, she did Google him. She read six magazine and newspaper interviews and stared at ten different images that she could find online. She learned that Daniel was thirty-two years old and originally from a small farming town in Kansas. He knew he wanted to be a chef from the age of six and would spend hours in the kitchen with his grandmother cooking while his three siblings were helping on the farm.

Caroline couldn't help but think of happy times cooking with her mom and Aunt Mimi in her own small-town childhood kitchen.

Upon graduating high school with honors, Daniel had moved to New York to attend the Culinary Institute of America where, according to one of the articles, he distinguished himself as "one of the most innovative young chefs in years." After nearly a decade of working his way up through the ranks of kitchen staff and cooking alongside some of the nation's master chefs, he opened Prize which had been heralded as a restaurant to watch, which in the culinary world was apparently a huge compliment.

After her three-day, self-imposed waiting period, which she believed was enough time to indicate interest without any hint of desperation, Caroline picked up her phone and texted Daniel.

Caroline: I can't stop thinking about that amazing risotto with radish cream sauce.

Daniel: I can't stop thinking about your eyes.

Daniel: This is Caroline, right?

Caroline: Yes. It's Caroline.

Daniel: Thank goodness. Your number is surprisingly similar to my meat supplier but George is not nearly as cute as you are.

Caroline: Glad to hear that.

Daniel: Are you free Monday night? The restaurant is closed and I would love to cook you dinner.

Caroline: Wow. Like a chef house call. Sounds great.

Daniel: Why don't you come to my place in Silverlake since I have all of the equipment here.

Caroline: That would be great. My idea of a fancy cooking item is an automatic salt grinder.

Daniel: I'll text you my address later. Right now I've got to get back to the kitchen. Looking forward to Monday.

Caroline: Me too.

• • •

The week dragged out as Caroline anticipated what yummy things Daniel might conjure up and she wasn't just thinking about the food.

Caroline arrived at Daniel's loft which was in a warehouse district that had been converted into high-end condos. The place was sparsely furnished, but the kitchen was incredible with restaurant-grade stainless steel appliances and a large hanging rack with every shape and size pot and pan imaginable.

"This space is incredible," said Caroline, her mouth agape as she admired the kitchen.

"Thanks. We're just renting now but I hope the owners will sell it to me now that the restaurant is doing well."

"We?" Caroline asked, suddenly concerned.

"I have a roommate. Kendra. She's an actress slash waitress," Daniel said, rolling his eyes. "The good news is she's never here," he said, smiling at Caroline in a way to assure her they wouldn't be interrupted. "The bad news is she's always late with the rent. But we make it work," he added with a shrug.

"Oh," she said, turning away from him to hide her lingering concern that maybe Daniel wasn't as unattached as he purported to be.

"I hope you're hungry," he said, walking around to her and opening the refrigerator to pull out a load of fresh vegetables. "And I hope you like salmon."

"Sounds wonderful," she responded, deciding to focus on the moment. "Can I help?" she offered. Daniel pulled a cutting board and knife from a drawer and laid them on the stainless-steel counter.

"That would be great. Do you mind trimming the edges off of these green beans?"

"Not at all," she said, admiring Daniel's trim physique as he walked past her to pull the salmon out of the fridge. She methodically cut the edges off of the green beans while Daniel made a lemon tarragon sauce for the fish.

"This reminds me of my childhood, cooking in the kitchen with my mom and Aunt Mimi," she said. "While I wasn't the best cook, I can bake a pie from scratch that would knock your socks off."

"You'd be surprised how I might react to a good pie," he said flirtatiously and Caroline let out a little giggle. Daniel walked up behind her and wrapped his two arms around her. He placed one hand on top of hers, holding the green beans. He placed the other atop her hand with the knife.

"Here," he said, raising their hands together and running the blade through the beans. "Let me show you the proper technique." Together they eased the knife in and out of the green beans. His breath tickled her ear as his body crushed against her back and she could feel the intense chemistry between them.

"Do you feel this too?" he whispered.

"Yes," she exhaled.

She turned her head and his lips swept across hers. She turned her entire body so it was flush against his as their lips and tongues danced around each other. His thumb brushed her cheek and she could feel him grow harder against her body. It was, hands down, the best first kiss Caroline had ever experienced. The spell was broken by the dinging of a bell.

Daniel pulled back and breathed, "The oven's pre-heated."

"Mmm," Caroline moaned, feeling a bit light headed. Daniel brushed his thumb across her cheek again.

"I'm feeling pre-heated too," he whispered in her ear. Caroline let out a nervous giggle and then glanced at the floor as Daniel gracefully moved across the kitchen to place the fish under the broiler.

"Where would I find the ladies room?" She hoped to splash a little cold water on herself to cool off.

"It's down the hall, second door on the right." Daniel pointed in the right direction, his hand covered in a silicone oven mitt.

Caroline listened to her black heels click clack on the dark wood floor of the stylish loft. When she opened the door to the bathroom, her eyes widened in surprise. The counters were cluttered with cosmetics – from blushes and eye shadows to jars of make-up remover and moisturizing creams. It looked like the Stila counter at Sephora. Caroline absent-mindedly picked up a bright red lipstick and secretly wondered what Daniel's roommate Kendra looked like. She washed her hands and then used one of the baby wipes on the counter to cool down behind her neck before returning to help Daniel with meal preparations.

Over the incredible dinner, Daniel and Caroline bonded over shared experiences as big dreamers in small towns. She told him about her passion for handbags and her slowly growing company Clutch while he regaled her with stories about crazy and demanding chefs.

"I was working at a fancy steakhouse with a well-known chef," he started.

"Anyone I would know?"

"Believe it or not, I signed a confidentiality agreement when I started there, which should have been my first tip off that this guy was nuts. So yes, you probably have heard of him but I can't say who he is."

"Now you've really piqued my interest," she said. "Go on."

"It was a busy night and I had just sent out a filet to one of the tables. The server returned and said the woman had wanted the bones. Chef came over and placed several bones on the plate, decorating them with a drizzle of au jus. The server took the plate back and we thought that would be the end of it."

"Clearly it wasn't," Caroline said to which Daniel started to chuckle.

"No. Most definitely not," he responded. "So this lady started telling the server she wanted a *bone-in* filet. She was pretty rude and loud enough that Chef heard her complaining."

"Oh no. What did he do?" she asked, contemplating all of the possibilities.

"He opened the kitchen door and started throwing bones at her screaming 'Here's your fucking bones!' It took three of us to calm him down and drag him back into the kitchen."

"You're makin' that up," she laughed.

"Hand to god, it's the truth," he said, holding his hand over his heart and shaking his head slightly. "If you Google 'crazy chef throws bones,' you might be able to find the video on YouTube, but you didn't hear that from me," he added with a wink. Caroline laughed and made a mental note to log on when she got home.

After clearing the table, Caroline helped Daniel hand-wash select dishes and load the dishwasher.

"Thanks for helping to clean up," he said, rubbing his thumb across her cheek.

"My pleasure. Thank you for the amazin' meal."

"*You're* amazing," he said, moving toward her for a kiss. Their lips met and Caroline quickly wrapped her arms around Daniel's neck. His tongue darted out of his mouth, requesting entry. Caroline gladly complied. Daniel lifted Caroline up and sat her on the stainless-steel counter. She parted her legs, giving him room to stand close to her.

She wasn't sure how much time had passed as Daniel took his kiss deeper and then pulled back, building Caroline up, teasing her. She rubbed her hands across his back, enjoying his trim build and taut muscles. She could feel his growing erection pressing into her and relished the friction it was creating. But she knew she didn't want to take things that far this evening. She started to pull back and Daniel could sense it. He eased up on his kiss and, panting, rested his forehead on hers.

"You don't need to stop," she breathed.

"I do," he said. "I don't want to. But I do for tonight." Caroline nodded in agreement but didn't move, still holding her hands around his neck, running her fingers through his hair.

Daniel swept his hands down her back and then across one of her breasts, feeling her erect nipple straining against the fabric of her red sweater and red lace bra.

"Just want to see what I have to look forward to for date number two," he said. Caroline let out a little moan.

"That feels so good."

"You are so fucking sexy," he said, licking his lips. He let out a small exhale and stepped back, giving Caroline room to step down.

"I should probably get going."

"I'm glad you were here."

"Me too. Thank you for dinner."

"Thank you for joining me," he said as he walked her to her car and gave her a long, lingering kiss goodbye.

●　　●　　●

The next day, Caroline met Mike for a quick snack at a local frozen yogurt shop. While she loaded her paper bowl with tart yogurt, Mike filled a paper taster cup with a sample of each of the dozen or so flavors of the day. "Someone's in an indecisive mood today," she commented.

"Why commit to just one flavor when there are so many choices."

"Ah yes, and there it is. Mike's philosophy on life...and women," she said with a playful sneer. Mike slugged her in the arm before deciding on chocolate.

As they moved up in line, Caroline placed a spoonful of fresh blueberries on her yogurt. She continued to tell Mike about her date with Daniel. Initially she was unsure if she should confess her insecurities about Daniel having a female roommate, concerned Mike would be judgmental. But then she realized that was never the case with Mike. He never judged. Rather, he just had a way of saying all the things that needed to be said even if she didn't want to hear them.

"So after the shit that went down with Marcus, you're afraid he's a lying cheat too and is doing the nasty with his roommate?" he asked, shaking a container of chocolate sprinkles out.

"Doing the nasty?" she said, turning her nose up at his vulgar choice of words.

"Yeah, you know, the horizontal mambo."

"Where do you come up with these?" she said, shaking her head, a disgusted look on her face.

"I've got a million of them," he shrugged as he put two spoonfuls of chocolate chips in his bowl.

"A million?" she said, calling him out on his exaggeration.

"Okay, maybe dozens."

"Dozens? Dozens of gross ways to describe people having sex?"

"Yep. I bet I can name twenty in under a minute. Loser pays for yogurt," he suggested, giving the chocolate syrup two quick pumps atop of his frozen treat. Caroline looked at him with humor in her eyes.

"I think I'll just say yogurt is my treat and forego listening to your...list."

"Suit yourself," he said, reaching for an extra shot of chocolate syrup before giving her wink and placing his yogurt bowl on the scale.

● ● ●

Over the next few days, another series of texts were exchanged between Caroline and Daniel.

Caroline: Thank you again for dinner Monday. It was lovely, as are you.

Daniel: Thank you for dining with me. My only regret is that I don't have an evening free this week to see you again.

Caroline: Me too.

Daniel: Monday night again? This time, I'll take you to one of my favorite spots.

Caroline: It's a date!

• • •

Daniel: Don't want to wait until Monday to see you. We had a cancellation for our Sunday brunch. Table of six. Bring some friends at 10:30 my treat.

Caroline: Will there be French toast?

Daniel: With powdered sugar, vanilla custard, caramelized apples and a homemade vanilla maple syrup.

Caroline: You had me at powdered sugar. We'll be there.

Daniel: I'll look forward to it.

• • •

Caroline was surprised when she walked into Prize and the hostess welcomed her and her friends to their monthly "Drag Brunch." The wait staff were dressed in their normal attire, but a few drag queens roamed around the tables, welcoming guests, posing for photos and seeking out the most uncomfortable-looking men to make them squirm further.

"This is gonna be fun," she said, giving Kayle's arm a squeeze.

Mike chuckled and shook his head, while Kayle and Lydia huddled together and giggled. Two other friends – Steve and Devin – rounded out the group of six. Not long after they were seated in a corner table, the hostess came to the small stage that was set up along one of the restaurant walls.

"Ladies. Gentlemen. And everything in between. Welcome to our monthly Drag Brunch at Prize." She paused as the patrons applauded. "Chef Daniel has some amazing items prepared for you this morning and of course, we have some incredible entertainment. Our show will get started in a few moments."

Devin and Steve mumbled something to each other and then switched seats with Kayle and Lydia, placing themselves into the corner spaces, distancing themselves from the stage as much as possible. Caroline shook her head and laughed.

Their waiter approached the table and handed out menus with a range of brunch items from eggs and bacon to fresh fruit and juices.

"We also have a chef's special this morning – the Caroline. It's French toast with powdered sugar, topped with caramelized Georgian peaches," the waiter explained. Kayle gasped and reached her hand across the table to tap Caroline's arm. Caroline blushed and just shrugged her shoulders. Mike looked both impressed and annoyed. As the waiter took the table's order, the hostess returned to the stage.

"You're all familiar with a blowhard real estate mogul who recently got heavily involved in politics. Well, let me introduce you to our version. Put your hands together for Ivana Hump. She's guaranteed to blow hard too."

Caroline covered her mouth in surprise at the outrageous comment while Devin and Steve gave each other high fives.

A flamboyantly-dressed woman – or was it? – dressed in a sequined gown, boasting a short pink bob and matching pink glitter false eyelashes came out onto the small stage.

"Yellow diamonds in the light," she spoke, her deep and sultry voice carrying across the room. She circulated the room, strategically placing her well-manicured hand on the shoulders of the men in the restaurant.

An instrumental introduction to the song began to play as she spoke again, surveying the room. A boisterous group of ladies seated in the corner began to clap loudly and Caroline guessed they had attended one of these before.

"We found love in a hopeless place," Ivana said zeroing in on Mike who was trying to avoid eye contact. She gracefully sauntered over, her hips sexily swaying to the music.

Her long fingers wrapped around Mike's chin, stroking his skin as he chuckled loudly. Caroline couldn't tell if he was enjoying the attention or found it embarrassing. The song introduction having concluded, Ivana pulled the microphone closer to her mouth and began to sing about yellow diamonds in the sky.

Ivana grasped Mike's hands in hers and tried lifting him from his seat to join her on stage. Mike shook his head no and stayed firmly planted in his seat.

Kayle, Lydia, Steve and Devin all started to chant, "Mike! Mike! Mike!" while Caroline sat and giggled. Ivana stroked Mike's cheek with her pink-tipped fingers while the bass-bumping track continued to play.

Mike looked at Caroline with narrowed eyes, as if she had planned this all along. She shrugged her shoulders.

"I didn't know this was a drag brunch," she said between laughs. Soon the rest of the restaurant patrons joined in chanting Mike's name, as Ivana continued to coax Mike onto the stage with her. Finally, Mike stood, his hands up in mock surrender. The entire restaurant erupted in applause while Caroline pulled out her phone to capture the moment for posterity.

Mike followed Ivana onto the stage and sat on a stool while she continued to sing, accompanied by the applause of the crowd.

Once the song was complete, Ivana hugged Mike and leaned in to kiss his cheek. He pulled back, wagging his finger back and forth. "No, no," he said before grasping her hand and giving it a quick peck. The audience burst forward with thunderous applause, which only died down after Mike returned to his seat. Caroline gave Mike an enormous hug while Steve and Devin shared more high fives.

"You two make a cute couple," Caroline said with a smirk.

"Yeah, yeah, yeah," Mike said drolly.

"Seriously. Did you get her number?" she teased.

"To repeat something I've heard you and Kayle say when you see a lame guy, 'Fight for him. You win!'"

Caroline leaned back and laughed a body shaking laugh recalling a little game she and Kayle had developed over the years. When an unsuitable suitor approached, they would both, as quickly as possible say, 'FightForHimYouWin!' with the words all running together. The loser would be forced to endure the suitor's advances and give him a subtle brush off.

"I'm perfectly happy with my current beau," she said, craning her neck around to see if she could catch a glimpse of Daniel either in the kitchen or making the rounds among the restaurant patrons. She noticed the waitress had refilled her champagne flute and took a swig of the bubbly liquid.

The emcee returned to announce the next performer. "Gentlemen. Ladies. And even ladies of the night," she said, earning a laugh from the audience, "put your hands together for our next performer – coming all of the way from America's heartland – Dani May, as in Dani, May I Please Have Another."

From behind the small curtain a pair of red Mary-Jane high heels revealed themselves followed by the most flawless legs Caroline had ever seen. Not even in an airbrushed magazine ad or beauty layout had she seen such a set of stems - toned, slender, tanned. They seemed to go on for miles, ending at a pair of Daisy Duke cut-off jeans. The denim was complemented by a red and white gingham blouse, tied at a perfectly-round innie belly button and accentuating trim abs. Long blond hair flowed around Dani's shoulders. If not for the heavy make-up and tinsel-like false eyelashes, Dani looked like your stereotypical Midwestern farm girl.

"Come on," Caroline said, pushing Mike's shoulder and pointing at Dani. "Fess up. If you didn't know that was a dude, you'd be all over that."

"Pshaw," he said, shaking his head, not being remotely interested in fueling a discussion on that topic with her or anyone else at the table for that matter.

"What do I and every gay man in this restaurant have in common?" Caroline asked.

"No clue," Mike said, looking at her with skepticism.

"We all want his body," she replied, laughing. Mike leaned his head back and let out a loud howl, his body trembling with laughter.

Dani grabbed the microphone and in a deep, sultry voice said, "This is one of my favorite songs made famous by one of my favorite icons who was born and raised right here in Los Angeles." Channeling her inner Marilyn Monroe with a dash of Betty Boop thrown in, she sang about wanting to be loved by one special person and nobody else but that special someone.

Dani walked down from the stage, her long legs giving dramatic, well-timed kicks as she did. The audience started to shout out little cat calls, which egged Dani on further. She playfully touched a few of the patrons, making her way over to Caroline's table, punctuating each line with a "boop-boop-a-doop" as the song dictated.

Mike, sensing Dani coming near him, put his hands in the air and waved them in front of himself, indicating he'd had enough with Ivana Hump. Dani placed a hand on Caroline's shoulder and leaned in to her.

Caroline looked at her friends and gave a broad smile before turning her attention back to Dani who stroked her cheek with her thumb.

Something about Dani's touch felt familiar to Caroline but she couldn't quite place it. Before she could explore her nagging feelings further, Dani kicked one long leg up in the air and placed the red Mary Jane onto the chair next to Caroline's leg. The audience went wild and Caroline put her hands together in small, girlish applause.

The song complete, the audience applauded wildly, including Caroline. She winked at Mike and leaned over to give Dani a kiss on the cheek.

Dani leaned in to whisper in Caroline's ear, the false eyelashes tickling her cheek and earlobe. "I do wanna be loved by you," a voice said – a voice deeper than Dani's – a voice familiar to Caroline. Daniel's voice. Caroline gasped and raised her hand to her mouth.

"What's wrong?" Mike asked in concern. Kayle leaned over Devin and placed her hand on Caroline's knee.

"You all right?" she said. Daniel gave Caroline a sheepish look and shrugged his shoulders in. Caroline waved everyone off indicating she was fine, but chugged the rest of her champagne.

Daniel was still standing next to her. He leaned in and whispered in her ear, "Please stay after your friends go. We can talk and I'll drive you home if you want." He gave her a hopeful look and she just nodded yes, unable to speak.

Dani pulled the microphone to her lips and said, "Another satisfied customer" and everyone erupted in laughter. Mike looked at Caroline, his brow furrowed.

"You sure you're all right?"

"I'm fine," she said, downing half of his glass of champagne. Mike raised his eyebrow at her, but didn't say anything.

As they were set to leave, the waitress handed Caroline a note. Caroline told her friends that Daniel had been busy in the kitchen, which was why he hadn't come out to meet them but wanted her to stay around, making sure she got home. She was given the customary hugs and kisses goodbye and promised to call both Kayle and Mike later.

Caroline sat silently while the wait staff cleared the tables and the kitchen staff completed their clean-up for the day. Daniel, now returned to his masculine chef state, approached Caroline.

"Hey," he said, his voice full of hope and humor.

"Hey," replied Caroline, pulling her lips into a firm line.

"Thanks for waiting around." He leaned in to kiss her cheek but she pulled back.

"I...uh..." she started.

"Let me guess," he interrupted. "You have questions."

"No. I mean, well, yes, I do have questions, but I just don't even know what to say," she spluttered.

"Well, to answer the most obvious ones – One, I only dress like this when I perform as Dani May, which is once a month here at the restaurant and maybe once or twice a week around town at various events. Two, I don't make it a habit of wearing ladies underwear, unless that's something that turns you on," he said, giving her a hopeful look. Caroline's eyes just widened.

"Three, I started doing this as a goof with some friends and enjoyed being someone so different from myself. It's a real high having people applaud and laugh and be thoroughly entertained. Four, I like women, not men. And five, I really like you. A lot." Daniel reached for Caroline's hand. She let him hold it for a moment as she took a deep breath and pulled it away slowly.

Her eyes were filled with regret as she said, "I just don't think this can work out."

"You don't want to see me anymore," he said nodding his head up and down. "It's okay. I get it. You're not the first," he said, hanging his head down. "I usually wait a few months before Dani makes an appearance, but I thought you might be ready to meet her."

"Uh…" she started before he interrupted her.

"C'mon. I'll drive you home." He pulled Caroline out of her chair and walked her to his car, opening the passenger door for her. The forty-five-minute drive from Silverlake to Brentwood was awkward, the silence only punctuated as they neared Caroline's neighborhood and she gave Daniel directions to her building.

He pulled the car into a red zone near a fire hydrant and placed it in neutral. He walked around to open the passenger door for Caroline. *He's such a gentleman*, she thought and shook her head at the irony. She exited the car and leaned in to give him a brief hug.

"Goodbye Daniel," she whispered in his ear. He pulled her close, taking a deep breath.

"Goodbye Caroline," he said, his voice full of regret. She patted his shoulder and walked silently into her apartment.

• • •

Three days later, Mike knocked on Caroline's door. She was hesitant to answer, but he had been persistent and she feared her neighbors would call the police.

"What's up?" she answered as Mike took in her disheveled appearance. Caroline wore an oversized sweatshirt boasting a snowboarding brand Mike had never heard of, thick socks with neon colored stripes and a pair of sweatpants which bore stains of which he was less than curious of the origins. Without a stitch of makeup and her hair pulled into a messy bun, she was a walking disaster.

"You haven't returned my calls all week and I was getting worried," he said, holding up a bag with fresh bagels and orange juice. You pulled this crap after Frenchie. I didn't like it then and I don't like it now."

Mike walked to the kitchen and grabbed two plates, putting a bagel and cream cheese sandwich on each. He handed a plate to Caroline along with a glass of juice. She pushed the plate away only to find Mike pushing it back to her. "Eat!" he commanded. She reluctantly picked up the bagel, picking small bits off and sticking them in her mouth.

"You remember the drag queen, Dani May?" she asked.

"Uh, you'll have to be more specific," said Mike, taking a sip of his juice, being sure to put the condensation-laden plastic cup on a coaster.

"At Prize on Sunday? The singer with the farmer's daughter outfit who sang to me?"

"Yeah. What about him, er, her?" he said, unsure of the proper etiquette.

"That was Daniel," she said, matter of fact. Mike almost did a spit take.

"I..." he stammered. "So. Many. Jokes. Can't. Get. Them. Out." He rubbed his temples and exaggerated the pause between each word.

"Yeah, so that happened," said Caroline, shaking her head and tossing the quarter-eaten bagel onto the table.

"C'mon, Caroline. You've got to find the humor in this situation."

"I'm not in the mood for your silly puns and gross-out humor today, Mike."

"I've been duly warned," he replied. "Okay, I'm going to try my best to be serious here. Bear with me." Caroline gave a little grin.

"See, you're smiling already." He gave her a reassuring pat on the head. He pulled his hand away and wiped it on his chest in disgust. "When was the last time you washed your hair?" Caroline burst into laughter.

"So is he..." he started.

"He's not gay...or bi. He just enjoys dressin' up like a woman and performin'," she explained.

"Okay," said Mike, trying to wrap his head around the situation and trying desperately not to come across as an asshole. Caroline seemed to be in a rather fragile state. "Now don't take this the wrong way, but I assume that's a deal breaker."

Caroline shot him a deathly glare. "You know that expression that assumin' makes an ass of you and me."

"Okay. So I'm an ass," he said. "But seriously, nobody's perfect and everyone has their thing. This isn't something you can...I don't know," he said, rubbing his hand behind his neck, "work with."

"No," she said flatly. "I can't be with someone who's prettier than me. And Dani is prettier than me."

"There have got to be some benefits to dating a drag queen," he offered. "You practically double your wardrobe."

"Sadly, I think her waist is trimmer than mine. Another reason to hate her," she said with a sneer.

"Make-up tips?"

"Oh god," Caroline gasped. "The make-up. I was at his place and saw a big spread of make-up. I just assumed it belonged to his roommate. It was probably his," she said, dropping her head into her hands. Her body started to shake. Mike put his arms around her in a consoling manner. But Caroline wasn't crying. She was laughing – a full on, body shaking laugh. Mike joined her and said, "You're gonna be just fine."

Backpack

*c*aroline exhaled deeply as she tried to keep up with Lydia at Runyon Canyon, a three and a half mile looping hiking and running trail. The relatively easy trail should have been a snap for Caroline, but she had been foregoing her normally-scheduled workouts the past few weeks for chocolate-induced stress relievers and overtime at the office double checking orders Maxine was handling and subsequently screwing up.

"So tell me more about this guy," Caroline huffed, hoping Lydia would slow down if she got to talking about her new beau, an investment banking analyst that she met at a wine auction. Despite knowing little about wine, Lydia knew enough to know there would be a lot of eligible men at the event.

"He's perfect. Absolutely perfect," she sighed. "He's funny and smart and so sweet." Caroline smiled, both in happiness for her dear friend and for herself, as her prediction was correct and Lydia slowed her brisk walking pace. "Oh, and the sex. It'll make your toes curl."

Oooh. Curling toe sex, thought Caroline. *That's what I need. Someone that just sets off fireworks and is funny, smart and sweet at the same time. And doesn't wear ladies' clothes.*

"I can't wait to meet him," Caroline said with a little giggle. She unscrewed the cap of her plastic water bottle and took the last sip, letting the last few drops fall to her lips. Internally she cursed herself for not bringing more water with her.

Her internal scolding was interrupted by a handsome man walking a dark chocolate Labrador. He wore a white Nike tank top that showed off toned biceps. Her mouth started to water – a welcome relief from the thirst that was building in her.

"Here," he said, handing Caroline a stainless-steel water bottle. "Don't worry," he continued. "I don't have cooties." Caroline took the bottle from him, but otherwise stood motionless, daydreaming about his seriously strong arms. Lydia nudged her shoulder pulling Caroline out of her reverie.

"Thank you," Caroline said, shaking her head from her daze and offering him a wide smile. "You're very kind."

"Always happy to help a fellow hiker," he said smiling down at her. "Do you guys come out on this trail often?" Caroline took a sip of the water and licked her lips.

"I do," said Lydia. "But Caroline hasn't been out here for a while."

"Probably why I didn't bring enough water," she admitted. She handed back the water bottle, but he pushed it back into her hand.

"Keep it," he offered. His dog started to pull on the leash, eager to continue along the trail. The handsome stranger took that as a sign to move along. "Well hopefully I'll see you around here more often...so you can return the bottle to me," he said, looking Caroline in the eye.

"Perhaps."

"Maybe you could repay me by buying me a water while I buy you lunch sometime," he offered.

"She would love to," chimed Lydia, not giving Caroline a chance to respond. He patted down his shorts and said, "I left my phone in the car."

"Me too," said Caroline with a little shrug.

"Her company website is Clutch Bags LA dot com," said Lydia. "Email her."

"I will," he responded. He waved and started to walk away.

"Wait," Caroline called after him. "What's your name?"

"Jessie Collins," he said, reaching out to shake her hand.

"I'm Caroline Johnson and this is Lydia," she said.

"Nice to meet you Caroline...and Lydia" he added, turning toward Lydia who had a mischievous smirk on her face.

"She'll be looking for your email Jessie," Lydia said. Jessie smiled and walked away, his dog leading him down the path. Caroline just looked at Lydia and smiled.

• • •

After the first few days of disappointment from not receiving an email from Jessie, Caroline tried to put him out of her mind. But the image of his strong arms would invade her dreams at night.

Once a few weeks had passed, Caroline resigned herself to the fact that he wouldn't be contacting her. Rather than get mired in disappointment, she tried to focus on work and getting back into a routine of working out. And she eagerly awaited her upcoming trip to Philadelphia, with Mike, for the wedding of two of their friends who met and fell in love at business school.

•   •   •

Mike and Caroline walked up to the front desk of the modest Philadelphia hotel. "Good afternoon," said Caroline with a friendly smile. "Room under the name Caroline Johnson." The hotel clerk click clacked away on the computer, a concerned expression crossing his face as he did.

"I'm sorry Ma'am, but we don't seem to have a reservation under that name. Could it be under something else?" *Ma'am* thought Caroline. *When did I become a 'ma'am?'* Then the situation hit her. Maxine forgot to make the reservation. She gave Mike an exasperated look and shook her head.

"I'm going to have to fire Maxine," she resigned.

"Yep," said Mike. Caroline turned back to the hotel clerk.

"No, my assistant must have forgotten to make a reservation. I'll take whatever room you have available," she said smiling through gritted teeth.

"I'm sorry, Ma'am, but we're completely sold out," he said. "I'm happy to provide you the names of a few hotels in the area, but they are likely sold out too. We have a big conference happening this weekend at the convention center."

Caroline let out a loud exhale as Mike put a soothing hand on her shoulder. He turned to the hotel clerk and said, "Room under Barnsworth." The clerk easily found the reservation.

"Yes Sir. I have you checking into a king room today and checking out on Sunday morning," he said. "I'll just need a credit card for incidentals." Mike reached into his wallet and pulled out his American Express card.

"Do you have a room with two queens?" he asked.

"I'm sorry, Sir, but as I explained to your companion here, we're sold out." He ran Mike's credit card through the card reader and pulled out some paperwork for Mike to sign. Mike turned to Caroline.

"It's okay. You'll stay with me." She raised her eyebrow at him and he just laughed.

• • •

After dancing for hours including being the lead of a twenty-person long conga line, Caroline kicked off her heels and sat down. She rubbed her sore feet and smiled over at her friends who were sharing a kiss on the dance floor. Mike walked over, sitting down next to her. He looked over at their friends and grinned.

"You ready to head up?" he asked. Caroline let out a loud sigh.

"Sounds good. Thanks for letting me crash in your room with you."

"I'm thinking that maybe this whole 'Maxine screwed up the reservation' thing was just a ruse to get into my bed," he said, giving her a lascivious look. Caroline exhaled sharply.

"Oh yes, Mike. I've hired an incompetent and irresponsible woman and given her access to screw up all manner of things in both my personal and professional life, all as part of my master plan to seduce you," she mocked.

"I knew it!" he exclaimed, pointing his finger high in the air in triumph. "C'mon," he said, putting a friendly arm around her and guiding her to the bride and groom so they could say their goodbyes.

Once in the room, Mike let Caroline have the bathroom first to change and get ready for bed. *Thank goodness I brought pajamas*, thought Caroline as she threw on a light blue tank top and pair of cotton pajama bottoms. She exited the bathroom and alerted Mike that he was free to go in and take care of his business.

"So that's what you wear to bed to seduce me?" he said, giving her less-than-sexy nightwear a once over.

"Ha! Ha!" she replied with a roll of her eyes. "Clearly I was thinkin' I had my own room."

"Clearly," he said. "Well when you do plan to seduce me, just know I prefer red lace," he said with humor in his eyes.

"I'll keep that in mind," she sneered.

"Please do."

"What side of the bed do you want?" she called out as Mike prepared for bed. He leaned on the doorway between the bathroom and main room, holding his toothbrush out in front of him.

"Oh, I don't care. You pick," he said. Caroline chose the left side and settled herself in. Mike returned from the bathroom and climbed into bed on the right side, being sure to leave space between the two of them. He leaned over and kissed her forehead.

"'Night doll," he said before leaning away from her and flipping off the light.

"Goodnight Mike."

●   ●   ●

A small ray of morning light streamed through a crack where the hotel curtains didn't quite meet. "Mmm. That feels good," Caroline moaned. Someone was gently caressing her breast – a skilled thumb rubbing across her nipple. At the same time, she could feel a growing hardness against her back. "Mmm" she groaned, realizing there was a virile man pressed up behind her. It had been a long time – entirely too long a time – since she had been touched like that and she missed it. Caroline slowly opened her eyes and realized she was in a hotel bed...with Mike.

"Mike?" she asked sleepily.

"Hmm," he quietly grunted, as he spooned her from behind.

"Mike. You're touching my boob," she said, wanting to inform Mike what he was unlikely aware he was doing.

"Hmm." Mike groggily opened one eye but kept his hand firmly but sexily on Caroline's breast, rubbing back and forth across her taut nipple.

"Mike. You seem rather happy to be here in bed with me this morning," she mumbled, still half asleep and not eager for Mike to awaken and stop touching her. She noted again to herself that it had been way too long.

"It's nothing personal."

"Feels pretty personal to me," said Caroline, with a small chuckle, as Mike's talented fingers continued to brush across her chest. Even though she wore a thin blue tank top, she could feel the heat of his skin against hers.

202

"Just a guy thing. In the morning."

"So you have this reaction to everyone?" she asked sleepily but skeptically.

"Not everyone. But I will admit you feel good pressed against my body." He reached his hand underneath her tank top, fingers strumming against her skin.

"Mmm," she moaned lightly.

"Do you want me to stop?"

"Honestly? No."

"You saucy minx. Been a while?"

"Mmm hmm," she exhaled, as his fingers on her breast started to make her feel warm all over.

"I could help with that," he offered, his thumb and finger lightly squeezing her nipple, sending a jolt further south.

"Mmm. Not a good idea," she said, squirming slightly as his touch continued to arouse her. "You'll never let me forget it."

"True. I am pretty memorable."

"What I mean is that you will keep throwing it in my face that I slept with you again," she explained, making no effort to stop Mike's digits from lightly drawing circles across her heaving breast.

"I promise not to throw anything in your face – literally or figuratively." Caroline chuckled slightly. "I promise to never bring this up."

"You won't bring this *up*," she laughed.

"It's too early for me to be that clever," he said, giving her shoulder a little nudge.

"I've noticed," she retorted playfully. "But seriously, you would do that for me?" she asked.

"I would do that for *me*," he moaned as he grew harder against her backside.

"Okay," she said with little enthusiasm despite being excited at the prospect of being touched. It had been much, much too long. "Let me just go brush my teeth," she said. Caroline slipped out of bed and immediately missed the feel of Mike's skilled fingers on her body.

As she brushed her teeth, Mike walked up behind her, grabbing his toothbrush as well. As he brushed, a light blue and white foam covered his mouth. In between brushing and spitting, he turned to Caroline.

"Why don't they ever show people's mouths foaming up with toothpaste in the commercials?" he posed. Caroline swatted his arm.

"I can't believe you just said that!"

"Uh, okay," he said, unsure why she was having such an intense reaction to his musing.

"I was thinkin' the same thing a few months ago," she laughed. "I mean, really. Isn't that the best part? Knowin' you're getting' a good scrubbin' in."

"My sentiments exactly," he said, tipping his toothbrush toward her.

Mike grabbed a condom from his leather dopp kit and walked back to the bedroom. He lay down and waited for Caroline to return. She walked in and pulled her arms inward. She pointed her left toe and traced a pattern back and forth over the hotel carpet. Mike beckoned her over but sensed her uneasiness.

"Change your mind?" he asked, hoping she hadn't.

"No," she said, looking down at her feet. "You?"

"Not a chance." He reached his arm out for her and pulled her over to the bed. She smiled at him.

"It's just sex, right?" she clarified.

"Yeah. Just sex. Really, really great sex. But just sex."

"And we won't be bringing it up again?" she asked, wanting his assurance that he would keep to his word.

"Can't promise I won't bring it up again," he said waggling his eyebrows up and down. "But we won't talk about it again."

"You're making clever comments. Looks like you've woken up."

"I'm not the only one awake," Mike said, shifting his eyes down to the tented sheet and then lifting and lowering his eyebrows in mock seduction again. Caroline laughed a nervous laugh and lay down next to Mike.

"Perfect," she said.

"It has really been a long time for you."

"You have no idea," she responded with a mild huff. Mike flipped Caroline onto her back and started to trail gentle kisses across her neck. When he sucked her earlobe into his mouth, she let out a low moan, her hips rising up off the bed. Mike removed her tank top pulling her nipple into his mouth. *Entirely. Too. Long.* thought Caroline.

Mike pulled down Caroline's pajama bottoms and panties in one quick motion. His fingers started to explore her below and her body began to move in rhythm matching his movements.

Mike removed his boxer briefs and rolled the condom on. He eased into Caroline and let out a loud exhale, relishing in how soft and wet she was.

"Take me hard," she said, begging him to bring her the release she craved. Mike lifted her legs over his shoulders, moving in and out of her as she panted.

"Your tits are so fucking perfect," he said, watching her body move as he pounded into her.

"You're so romantic," she said, rolling her eyes and giving a little chuckle.

"Comes from the woman who just said 'take me hard,'" he said, playfully tweaking her nipple. Caroline let out a little yelp.

"Oh Mike, please make love to me like no man ever has," she moaned sarcastically. "Better?" she asked as her body climbed higher.

"Better. Now that wasn't so hard," he panted.

"Feels hard to me," she said laughing.

"Saucy minx!" he laughed and continued to press into her.

No one has ever been this deep inside me, she thought. *I'm afraid he's going to bore a hole inside me and come poking out the other end.* It was incredible.

"You okay?"

"Yes," she panted. "Don't you dare stop."

Mike chuckled while Caroline's red manicured toes pushed into his ears and cheeks. He pushed her knees forward, taking him even deeper into her warmth and her eyes rolled into the back of her head.

Mike could feel Caroline's body tensing up, her movements echoing her small whimpers. It took all of his concentration not to come right there. *Don't blow your wad yet jackass,* he thought.

"Let go," he said. And Caroline did. All of the stress and pent up frustration cleared from her mind. All she could think was how amazing her body felt. She was all sensation.

As the shudders of Caroline's body slowed, she realized that Mike was still – still inside of her, still hard, but still, allowing her body to come down from its climax. Once she calmed, he lifted her into his lap and began to kiss her, his hands running over her back and sides, up into her messy blonde hair.

Caroline tugged Mike's t-shirt over his head, her hands clutching onto his skin as he pistoned in and out of her while she straddled his lap.

Drilling. Nailing. Hammering, Caroline thought. *I get why they have all of the euphemisms for sex because something is definitely building up again in me right now.*

Mike could feel Caroline was ready to let go again and moved his hands to her hips. He used his impressive strength to move her body up and down on top of him. Within seconds, they were both quivering, pleasure rolling through them. He gently laid Caroline on her back and eased out of her, rolling to her side and giving her a quick peck on the side of her forehead.

"I needed that," she said. "Thanks."

"Anytime," he grinned. It took all of the strength she could muster at the moment but she swatted his arm.

"I think it was just a one-time thing," she chided.

"I'm pretty sure that this morning was two times for you," he said, raising his eyebrow.

"So it was," Caroline giggled. Mike stood up and walked toward the bathroom.

"I'm going to take a shower," he informed her.

"Okay," said Caroline, still in a euphoric state. "I'll take one after you."

"You can join me."

"No," she said, shaking her head. Mike walked back toward her.

"Can't blame a guy for trying," he winked. He leaned over and kissed the top of Caroline's head. Sensing her mind racing over what they had just done he added, "Don't overthink this."

"Okay," she shrugged as Mike walked into the bathroom.

•   •   •

After returning from Philadelphia, Caroline walked into her modest offices which were situated above a restaurant in Venice. She took a few calming breaths, having practiced what she was going to say to Maxine. *Maxine. We need to talk. You know that I think you're lovely and so much fun, but having you as my assistant just isn't working out. I think we'd both be better off if we just focus on a friendship instead of a working relationship.*

"Maxine," she started. "We need to talk."

"Welcome back, boss. How was Florida?"

"It was Philadelphia, not Florida and it was fine," she started. And as much as she had the scenario rehearsed in her head, something in Caroline just...snapped. "No, it wasn't fine," she said, standing tall. "You screwed up my hotel reservations," she said in a blunt and accusatory way.

"No way. I have the confirmation right here," Maxine said, clicking the computer mouse a few times and calling up an email. Caroline leaned over her and looked at the computer monitor. Staring back at her was a hotel confirmation for this past weekend at the Lowe's Hotel in Florida – Miami Beach to be more precise. "See?" Maxine huffed.

"That's for Florida," Caroline said through gritted teeth. "I was in Philadelphia – without a hotel room!" she yelled. Tears began to well in Maxine's eyes and her lower lip began to quiver at the harshness of Caroline's tone. Caroline looked at the confirmation in more detail and said, "great" under her breath.

"What's great?" asked Maxine, her demeanor brightening up, hopeful that the "great" was in response to something wonderful and helpful she had done.

"Because we didn't cancel the reservation 24 hours prior, I've been charged for the two-night stay." Caroline rubbed her temples.

"That doesn't sound great at all," said Maxine, totally confused.

"It's not, Maxine. That's called sarcasm. Believe me, nothing about this situation is great."

"Sorry. I'll do better next time," she said with a shrug. "Can I get you some coffee?"

"I don't think there's going to be a next time, Maxine. It's not just this hotel mess up. You have failed to pay invoices on time causing me a loss of my reputation and late fees. You've made two errors in ordering supplies and weren't able to get a sample order out on time, resulting in my losing an order, albeit a small one."

"I'm trying my best," said Maxine.

"I just don't think this is going to work out. You should clear out your desk," said Caroline. Maxine stood up and started gathering her personal belongings.

"Can I at least use you as a reference?" she asked. Caroline just shook her head in frustration.

●　　●　　●

It took Caroline two weeks to clean up the mess that Maxine had left behind – disorganized computer files, late invoices both incoming and outgoing and unreturned emails. It was while going through deleted and unopened messages that she spied one from Backpacker219. Her heart skipped a beat as she clicked open the message.

From: Backpacker219
Subject: Ready to collect

You owe me a water and I was hoping to collect this weekend. LMK – Jessie

Of course the message was dated two days after she had first met Jessie on the hiking trail. Even if she emailed him now, she wasn't certain he would be interested in seeing her.

From: CarolineClutch
Subject: Re: Ready to collect – PLEASE READ

My apologies for taking so long to respond to you. Your message was misplaced by my – now former –

assistant and I'm just seeing it now. If you're still up for that water, I would be happy to repay you. If we freeze it, we could even add some margarita mix and tequila to it. I hope to hear back from you.

Jessie's response was almost immediate.

From: Backpacker219
Subject: Re: Ready to collect – PLEASE READ

Great to hear from you. I thought perhaps you didn't remember me or were the kind of girl to renege on a deal. Glad that neither are the case. I'm out of town this weekend for work. Are you free Wednesday night?

Caroline bit her lip. She had a date!

From: CarolineClutch
Subject: Re: Ready to collect – PLEASE READ

Wednesday night sounds great. Why don't I meet you somewhere.

From: Backpacker219
Subject: Re: Ready to collect – PLEASE READ

There's a great restaurant on Melrose called Nude Food. The food's organic. The guests wear clothes. How about 7:00?

From: CarolineClutch
Subject: Re: Ready to collect – PLEASE READ

I love a good pun. See you then.

•   •   •

Caroline arrived at the restaurant a few minutes before 7:00. Jessie was already there, waiting for her, with a bouquet of yellow wildflowers in his hand. He leaned in and gave her a small kiss on the cheek before handing her the brown paper-wrapped blooms.

"Thank you. They're beautiful," she said with a smile.

"They reminded me of the flowers you see along the trail where we met," he offered.

"You're so thoughtful." He placed a hand on the small of her back and led her to the hostess desk where he informed the woman behind the podium that their party was complete and ready to be seated.

He kept his hand gently on her back as the two of them traversed the crowded tables to a cozy spot in the back of the restaurant. Jessie held out Caroline's chair and she gracefully sat down.

As she glanced around, soaking in the simple ambience, she said, "I've never been here before. Perhaps you can make a suggestion."

"I've been here a few times," he explained. "They have a great bison burger if you eat meat. Otherwise, the kale and quinoa salad is really good."

"I'm definitely a carnivore, but won't discriminate against a vegetable or two. Are you a vegetarian?"

"I eat meat too, but just try to make sure it's organic and grass fed."

"I'm guessing between the organic food and hiking, you're into pretty clean livin'."

"I wasn't always," he started. "But when I was in college, I met this girl who got on my case for not caring about the environment as much as she thought I should."

"Hmm," said Caroline wondering where he was heading with this story.

"Trying to impress her, I changed my diet, started exploring nature and basically doing things to protect the Earth. The girl didn't stick, but the habits did," he said smiling at her.

"I see," said Caroline, relieved to hear that there wasn't another girl in the picture.

"So what do you do now, aside from saving damsels in distress from severe dehydration on the hiking trail?"

"Believe it or not, that's not a full-time job," he started. Caroline gave a flirtatious giggle. "I work for REI running adventure classes for individuals and groups."

"That sounds very...adventurous."

"We get a lot of corporate organizations that want to do outdoor team building and trust building programs for their teams. I take the groups out into nature and put them through their paces."

"That sounds like a perfect fit for your love of the outdoors. And I imagine you meet a lot of interesting people that way."

"Not as interesting as with my second job," he smiled back at her.

"Your second job?" she questioned.

"Yeah. Rescuing damsels in distress from severe dehydration."

"Oh," Caroline blushed, recognition flickering within her.

"So tell me more about you and your clutch bags," he prompted.

For the next two hours, over a delicious and wholesome organic dinner of spaghetti squash casserole and braised grass-fed beef short ribs, Jessie and Caroline talked and flirted.

Caroline was pleased to learn that Jessie was not only handsome and interesting, but kind and fun. He volunteered at an animal shelter once a month, was a die-hard Chicago Bulls fan and, despite his pledge for healthy and clean living, wasn't averse to sneaking a handful of peanut M&M's every day.

After dinner, Jessie walked Caroline to her car and opened the driver door for her. Before she sunk into the seat, she leaned up and gave him a sweet, open-mouthed kiss on the cheek and whispered "thank you" in his ear.

Jessie returned the favor, giving Caroline an equally sweet and lingering kiss on the cheek before whispering "you're welcome" into hers.

Caroline drove away with a huge smile on her face, congratulating herself on having the best first date ever.

• • •

From: Backpacker219
Subject: Amazing Time

Just got home from an amazing first date. I hope my saying that and not waiting three days to email you isn't freaking you out. I also hope it won't freak you out if I invite you to join me and a group of friends at the beach on July 4th. We do a big BBQ/bonfire every year. LMK – Jessie

From: CarolineClutch
Subject: Re: Amazing Time

Thank you so much for your sweet email and for a wonderful time last night. I'm not freaked out at all and find it rather refreshing to have a man not play games. I would love to join you on July 4th, too. Let me know what I can bring.

From: Backpacker219
Subject: Re: Amazing Time

I realize as I'm typing this that I don't have your phone number. Give me a call at 310.555.4345 so we can make a plan.

• • •

Jessie grabbed the large throw-away storage containers from Caroline's grasp as the two of them walked down the steps of the pier to the warm sand.

"You didn't need to bring anything but yourself," he said.

"I know, but my momma and Aunt Mimi taught me to never attend a party empty handed."

"Well I'm sure everyone will enjoy these watermelon slices. Thank you." As they walked up to the large crowd gathered around a few pop up tents set up with tables covered in food, Jessie placed a gentle hand on Caroline's elbow.

Caroline let out a loud exhale, a bit nervous about meeting Jessie's friends. He smiled at her and said, "There's no pressure, Caroline. Just relax and enjoy yourself. Everyone here is really cool."

"I will," she nodded.

"Jessie, my man," said a short and stocky, freckle-faced red headed man, who reached out to bump knuckles with Jessie.

"Hey Joseph," Jessie said, giving a solid fist bump. "Let me introduce you to Caroline," he added. Joseph reached his hand out to shake Caroline's hand.

"Nice to meet you, Caroline," he said. "Let's find you guys a place to put your stuff and get you a hot dog," he added.

Jessie guided Caroline over to an empty patch of sand and laid out a blanket and two towels. Caroline put her striped beach bag down and kicked off her flip flops.

"Hot dog?" he asked. Caroline nodded. "Beer?"

"I'll pass on the beer."

"Okay. C'mon," he said, gesturing for her hand. Caroline grasped his in return and allowed him to guide her over to the food and to meet more of his friends.

Once their plates were loaded with hot dogs, chips, and potato salad, Jessie and Caroline took a seat on the towels he had placed down earlier. Jessie grabbed the back of his shirt and pulled it up over his head. Caroline nearly choked on a bite of watermelon as she checked out Jessie's incredibly toned torso. He looked like a model for a Men's Health workout spread, complete with an eight-pack set of abs and a sexy line of muscle creating a "v" down to his swim trunks.

Caroline's mouth went dry and she tore her glance away, not wanting Jessie to catch her checking out his impressive physique.

After lunch, Caroline contemplated removing her bright yellow sundress to reveal the cornflower blue tankini she wore underneath. She initially felt a bit self-conscious but then decided she was who she was. If Jessie didn't think she was pretty enough, skinny enough or toned enough, better to find out now.

She eased forward onto her knees and pulled the dress over her head. She placed it atop her beach bag and then stretched her legs out in front of her. Jessie looked over at her, his eyes roaming up from her painted toenails, to her big blue eyes.

"You're even more beautiful than I imagined you would be," he said. Caroline blushed.

"Thank you."

"No, thank you for joining me today." The private, unspoken moment between the two of them was broken when several of Jessie's friends plopped down on the blanket and started talking about sports, work and even the weather.

Caroline and Jessie spent the next few hours alternating between the blazing sun and respites in the shade.

Caroline was enjoying her time with Jessie and his friends. Everyone was friendly and fun. Several of the girls were impressed with her business and promised to check out her line of bags either online or in local stores.

As the sun dipped into the ocean, Jessie ran back to his car to get some more blankets and sweatshirts. He helped Caroline pull an oversized surf shirt over her head and brushed some hair off of her forehead as her head poked through.

Kiss me, thought Caroline. It was a perfect moment and she longed to feel his lips on hers. Jessie, picking up on the beckoning look she was providing, leaned in to kiss her, but his attempt was thwarted by a friend who slapped him on the back and asked about work. Jessie responded to his friend good naturedly while giving Caroline a little shrug. She smiled and glanced down at her feet.

An hour later, Caroline found herself snuggled up in a blanket, next to Jessie and sitting around a bon fire with thirty others. Wire hangers were being passed around so they could roast marshmallows for s'mores.

"Want one?" Jessie asked, holding a wire hanger and preparing to spear a marshmallow on its pointed end.

"Yes, please," she said. Caroline absolutely loved s'mores. She reached her arm out from under the blanket to grab the hanger, but Jessie pulled it back.

"I've got it," he said. "Do you like your marshmallow soft and gooey or a bit burnt?"

"Soft and gooey, please." Caroline was feeling soft and gooey herself. Jessie pulled the warm marshmallow off the hanger, sliding it between two graham crackers and two squares from an oversized Hershey bar. He handed Caroline the treat and started to make one for himself.

Caroline took a bite and let out a little moan.

"Good?" he asked, holding his marshmallow in front of him, letting the fire brown the outside.

"Mmm. So good," she said with a smile.

"Good," he responded, blowing on his marshmallow. He pulled it off with his fingers and stuck it in his mouth. He licked his lips and the small strands of melted marshmallow that stuck to his fingers.

Caroline's pupils dilated and her breathing hitched. She wanted to be the one to lick that marshmallow off his fingers and anywhere else on his delicious body he desired. Jessie leaned in to Caroline. "Want to go for a walk?" he asked.

"Love to," she said, rising from her seat. She dropped her blanket next to his and took his hand. They walked hand in hand under the cloudless sky, down toward the water, her feet squishing in the cold, wet sand as the last remnants of waves tickled her toes.

Jessie stopped walking and turned Caroline to face him. He leaned closer to her and whispered, "I'm going to kiss you now."

"About time," she said with a smile. He leaned in even farther and Caroline pushed herself up on her toes. His lips gently brushed across hers as she drew in his tongue, still sweet from the sugary dessert. And then...fireworks burst. Unfortunately, Caroline could only sense them from overhead. As Jessie gently placed his hand around the back of her head and drew her in closer to him, licking and taunting her with his lips and tongue, she felt nothing. No spark. No electricity. No heat. *Damn!*

On paper, Jessie was quite possibly, the perfect man. He was sweet and kind, funny and smart, thoughtful and athletic. And his gorgeous body was something she would normally be aching for. But as she stood under the moon, with her body pressed up next to his, his arms wrapped around her, his lips nibbling the side of her mouth, she felt nothing. She pulled away slightly and Jessie, left panting, placed his head on her forehead.

"We should probably head back," she said, not wanting to give anything away yet and make things awkward.

"Okay." He pulled her to his side and slid his arm around her. Once back at the fire pit, he nestled Caroline close to him. With each squeeze and gentle rub of her back, Caroline felt pangs of guilt and remorse for not feeling about Jessie the way he apparently felt for her.

●　　●　　●

From: CarolineClutch
Subject: Thank you

Thank you for such a wonderful time last night. Your friends are lovely, as are you. And as amazing a guy as I think you are, I just don't think you're the right guy for me. I'm sorry. So so sorry. I would really like for us to be friends, but I'll understand if that's not something you're interested in.

From: Backpacker219
Subject: Re: Thank you

I've read and re-read your email over and over and I've gone over last night in my head a dozen times. I'm not sure what I did wrong. But I'd like the chance for a do-over. There's something special about you Caroline and I really think we would be great together.

From: CarolineClutch
Subject: Re: Thank you

*You did nothing wrong, Jessie. Truly, nothing wrong.
You're an incredible guy. And on paper, you're perfect
– not just for me, but absolutely perfect. I don't really
know how to explain it except to say that I just don't
think we're right for each other.*

From: Backpacker219
Subject: Re: Thank you

*I'm not sure how you can say that after that kiss we
shared. But I'll respect you enough to leave you alone.*

Caroline sat down at her office desk and cried. If she
couldn't make things work with a perfect guy like Jessie, what
chance did she have with anyone else.

Clutch

*a*www. She's so cute," said Caroline, noticing a little girl dressed in a Snow White gown walking through the mall with her mother and a toddler stroller in tow. She and Mike were sitting outside enjoying a quick lunch before she planned to check out the new display of her bags in the nearby Bloomingdales.

"Don't tell me you like all that princess shit," he said, his mouth twisting to the side as he shook his head.

"Of course I do," she said, placing her hand over her heart. "I'm from the South where every girl wanted to grow up bein' a princess."

"Well, those Disney princesses are nothing to aspire to."

"I'm sure you'll enlighten me," she said with a huff, rolling her eyes heavenward.

"Let's start off with Ariel."

"Oh, I love her," Caroline cooed.

"She changed everything about herself – and gave up her one tremendous gift – for a man. A man," he added for emphasis.

"Mulan changed her appearance for a man – her dad – and she kicked some serious ass," she responded as a challenge.

"Point well taken, Ms. Johnson," he said, pursing his lips and holding up his index finger as he nodded his head. Caroline smiled smugly. "Okay, but what about," he pointed in the direction they saw the little princess walking through the mall, "your Snow White."

"What about her?"

"Didn't her parents tell her not to take food from strangers?" Caroline tilted her head back and laughed. "And an apple? Seriously. It's not like those don't just grow on trees," he said. "Am I right?"

Caroline laughed further. "Okay. Okay. I get your point," she said, holding her hands up in surrender.

"Oh, and then there's Belle – the *thinking* woman's princess," he sneered as his nostrils flared in mock anger.

"What's wrong with Belle?" she gasped. "She reads. And she wants more than that misogynistic lunk Gaston."

"She's the worst offender," he nearly shouted. "She meets this guy – this beast of a guy! – and basically changes him into a loveable prince."

"And that's bad because..." Caroline started, tilting her head to the side and shaking it slightly.

"She gives hope to every woman out there that they can change a man, when you and I know that can't be done." Before Caroline could respond, Mike looked down at the caller ID on his ringing phone and ran his fingers through his hair. He punched the green button and waited.

"Michael?" said a feminine and cultured voice on the other end.

"Hello, Mother," he said flatly. Caroline's mouth fell open and she mouthed "your mom" to him. He nodded.

"Please don't call me mother."

"Please don't call me Michael."

An audible sigh was heard on the other end of the phone. "Okay, Hello *Mike*. How are you, darling?"

"I'm fine, Mom," he said, more relaxed. "But what's wrong? You calling during Fashion Week isn't a good sign."

"It's your grandfather, Michael. I mean Mike," she said, correcting herself. "He passed last night in his sleep."

"I'm sorry. How's dad taking it?" he asked, his face impassive. Caroline, curious as ever, mouthed *"What?"* Mike gestured with his finger for her to hold a moment.

"He's doing as well as can be expected. The funeral is planned for Thursday. We're expecting you here. I'm arranging for Carina to send you a plane ticket."

"Make it two."

"Two? Is there someone special you want us to meet?" She sounded hopeful.

"A friend."

"Okay. Should I have Carina call you?"

"No. I'll call her later."

"Okay. I'm sorry this is the reason for you to come home, but it will be wonderful to see you."

"Yeah. You too, Mom. Okay, I gotta run. I'll see you soon." Mike hung up the phone and placed it on the table.

"Everythin' okay?" asked a worried Caroline, her brow furrowed.

"My grandfather passed away last night," he said without emotion.

"Oh, I'm so sorry," she gasped, clutching her hand to her heart. "Were you two close?"

"Not at all. He was a very cold and very stern man. When I decided to move out here and open a bar instead of going into the family business, he pretty much wrote me off. I haven't seen or talked to him in years."

"I'm sorry. I can't imagine not havin' my family's encouragement."

"Yeah. He was no Aunt Mimi, that's for sure."

"And this was your dad's dad?" she asked, clarifying the relationship.

"Yeah, and that's why my dad is probably the way he is. At least he still talks to me. But I haven't seen him in over a year."

"That's awful. Well, perhaps this is what y'all need to bring you back together."

"Maybe," he shrugged. "Will you come with me?"

"To New York?" she asked, surprised.

"Yeah. I could use a friendly face," he pleaded.

"Of course," she responded immediately. "When?"

"We'll leave tomorrow and be back on Saturday? I know Brianna can handle the bar. Can you get away?"

"Of course. I can rearrange a few things."

"Thanks. I'll call my mom's secretary, Carina, to make the arrangements."

"Okay. Is there anythin' else I can do?"

"You're doing plenty. Thanks." Caroline reached across the table and placed her hand on Mike's arm, rubbing it gently, her brow furrowed.

•   •   •

The black town car pulled up to a large circular drive. Mike stepped out and held out his hand to help Caroline from the backseat. Her eyes widened as she took in the site before her: a 9,500 square-foot shingle-style Victorian home, which sat on two acres of beautifully-landscaped grounds featuring mature trees, sprawling lawns, and lush gardens. Mike had told her it had been originally built in 1895 and completely renovated just three years ago.

"Whoa. Talk about livin' in high cotton," she said in awe as her eyes trailed up and around.

"You might as well have just said two plus two equals orange," he said, looking at her, confused. "I have no idea what that means. When are you going to drop the whole Southern act, huh?" He motioned his hand over her body before she tapped his arm playfully.

"It means, you weren't jokin' when you said you came from money."

"No. I wasn't," he said grimly. Suddenly his eyes lit up as a small grey woman in an equally grey maid's uniform came down the front walkway. She wiped her wrinkled hands on a white apron as her white orthopedic shoes skipped every other brick.

"Mike! So wonderful to see you," she exclaimed. Mike gave her a warm embrace and then turned to his side, keeping his arm around her.

"Hi, Rose," he said warmly. "It's great to see you too. Rose," he gestured toward Caroline, "this is Caroline."

"So nice to meet you, Rose," Caroline said politely. "Mike has told me so many lovely things about you."

"Rose here is the best," Mike said, giving her a squeeze.

"It's nice to meet you too, Caroline," said Rose. Turning to Mike, she added, "Your mother didn't tell me you were bringing your *girlfriend*."

"We're just friends. Old friends from school," he responded.

"Oh, okay. Well there's plenty of room here, even with your cousins coming in tomorrow from Chicago."

The three walked up the brick walkway toward the oversized wooden front door, through a large foyer, and into a formal living room.

The room was sumptuously appointed, with two large couches sitting opposite one another, covered in dark green and burgundy striped fabric. Four armchairs, two on each side, sat perpendicular to the couches and a large walnut table sat in the middle. The walls were adorned with original works of art and Caroline could only speculate on their value. Light from the setting sun shone on a shiny black grand piano that sat in the corner. Although there was no dust covering the instrument, Caroline wondered if anyone actually played.

As she craned her neck to see the formal dining room just beyond the doorway, an elegant and impeccably-dressed woman with jet black hair and green eyes – Mike's eyes – that perfectly matched her cashmere sweater set walked in. Oversized solitaire diamond stones were set into each ear and were dwarfed only by the large stone she wore on her wedding finger.

"Michael," she said, reaching out to hug him. Mike cocked his head to the side and gave her an exasperated look. "Mike," she corrected herself. Mike smiled and leaned in to give her a hug and kiss on the cheek.

"Hi, Mom. Sorry about Grandfather," he shrugged.

"It's okay. He was…" she started.

"An asshole?" suggested Mike, raising an eyebrow. Mrs. Barnsworth laughed and then leaned in to hug him again.

"I've missed you." She reached to grab his hand and gave it a squeeze. While doing so, she noticed Caroline, who was standing off to the side, trying not to get in the way. "Oh, you must be Mike's girlfriend."

"Girl and friend, but just a friend," Mike corrected her. "Mom, this is Caroline Johnson." Mrs. Barnsworth held out her soft, well-manicured hand and gave Caroline's a graceful shake. She glanced down and took in Caroline's appearance – navy and cream t-strap pumps, navy pants, cream blouse and matching saddle bag.

"Nice to meet you, Caroline," she said.

"Nice to meet you too, Mrs. Barnsworth. I'm sorry for your loss."

"Thank you, dear. Well, you two must be tired from your long trip. Come in and sit down," she said, gesturing toward a couch. Just as they sat down, they stood up again, as Mike's father, Michael Barnsworth Junior, entered the room.

He was tall, formal, and formidable. He had the same face shape as Mike, but the similarities ended there. Caroline picked at some nail polish on one of her nails nervously as Mr. Barnsworth reached out to give his son a business-like handshake.

"Michael. I'm glad you're here."

"Hello, Dad," he said, shaking hands. "This is Caroline Johnson," he said, gesturing toward Caroline with his hand. Caroline tentatively walked forward. Mr. Barnsworth looked her up and down quickly, sizing her up and determining that she was a blonde bimbo that Mike knew from the bar.

"Nice to meet you," he said coolly.

"Likewise, Mr. Barnsworth. I'm sorry for your loss. I can't imagine how hard this must be."

"Thank you," he said dismissively. "So Caroline, how do you and Mike know each other? From the bar?" he said, a hint of disdain in his voice.

"We met on the first day of class at Harvard," she said, lifting her head high and pulling her shoulders back.

Mr. Barnsworth's demeanor toward her shifted immediately. "Really? You went to business school at my alma mater?" he asked enthusiastically.

"Not only did Caroline attend, but she graduated *magna cum laude*, which as you know is a hell of a lot better than I did," said Mike with pride.

"That's very impressive," Mr. Barnsworth replied. "So tell me, how are you putting that Harvard degree to use today?" He gestured for them all to sit.

"She owns and runs her own business," chimed Mike.

"Let the girl speak for herself, Michael," Mr. Barnsworth scolded. He turned back to Caroline. "Go on, Caroline."

"As Mike said, I own and run a handbag design company. I fell in love with handbags when I was a little girl thanks to my Aunt Mimi. I studied fashion design in Los Angeles and then started my own company after graduate school."

"And you make a nice living doing this?" Mr. Barnsworth asked.

"I do," she said nodding. She turned to Mike's mom and continued, "I would love to show you some of my designs if you're interested. I noticed your beautiful Burberry bowler bag when we walked in and have somethin' similar in my new line."

"I would love to look at them. Thank you," said Mrs. Barnsworth.

"Your parents must be very proud of you," commented Mr. Barnsworth.

"Real discreet, Dad," said Mike, rising from his seat and shaking his head. He started to walk away when Caroline grabbed his arm to stop him.

"What I mean is that Caroline sounds as if she has really become a success and naturally her parents would be proud of her accomplishments," said Mr. Barnsworth.

"Well thank you. My family is very proud. And you should be proud of Mike too. He has become a highly-successful entrepreneur," said Caroline.

"I'm sure he has," replied Mr. Barnsworth coolly.

"He really has," she said proudly. "Inventory control. People management. Government relations. Promotions and marketin'. He does them all and really well," she said with emphasis.

"Young lady, I think I'm in the best position to judge whether my son is living up to his potential," he snapped. "And I think you should best mind your tone–"

"With all due respect, Mr. Barnsworth–" she started before Rose entered the room.

"Sorry to interrupt, Mr. Barnsworth. The funeral home is on the line for you." Mr. Barnsworth glared at Caroline, rose from his seat, and walked out of the room. Mrs. Barnsworth followed him. Caroline stood and turned to Mike.

"Thanks. But I don't need you to defend me," he snapped. "And you don't want to start an argument with my father," he said to her after drawing in a deep breath and in a more measured tone.

"I'm not defendin' you and I don't believe you need to defend yourself," she stated. "I'm just..." she drew a deep, calming breath, "articulatin' what I see as bein' the truth. And I don't care if your parents like me. I'm just bein' honest, consequences..."

"Be damned?" he completed.

"Exactly," she said, smiling, a twinkle in her eyes. Mike leaned over and pulled Caroline into a hug, kissing the top of her head. Mrs. Barnsworth, who had walked back to the living room, stood in the doorway, looking at them, and smiled.

•　　•　　•

Dinner with the Barnsworths was like a scene out of a movie, thought Caroline – a snooty English period drama where the rich couple sat on opposite ends of an impossibly-long mahogany dining table while silent, uniformed servants catered to their dining needs. In this case, Mr. and Mrs. Barnsworth sat across from one another – along the length of the table – while she and Mike sat opposite each other across the width. Even though they dined on fine China with heavy silver flatware, Caroline mused that they were using the everyday dishes.

"So, Caroline. Tell us a bit more about yourself," said Mr. Barnsworth, his deep eyes boring into her while he took a bite of his Cornish game hen.

"Well, I was born in a small town in South Georgia, but left when I was eighteen to go to design school in Los Angeles," she began. "After a few years of workin' in my field, my Aunt Mimi, bless her heart," she continued, holding her hand gently over her heart, "encouraged me to get my MBA and start my own business."

"She was an amazing lady," offered Mike, giving Caroline a smile before sipping the vintage Pinot Noir from the family's private wine collection.

"Was?" asked Mrs. Barnsworth.

"She passed about two years ago. We were very close, so I can surely sympathize with what y'all are goin' through," Caroline responded.

"It's nice you can be here to support Michael," Mr. Barnsworth replied.

"I couldn't imagine bein' anywhere else," she said, looking directly into Mr. Barnsworth's eyes before turning to Mike with a smile. Mike winked back at her and then took another sip of wine when he noticed his mom smiling at him.

"Oh, she only hangs out with me for the free wine," Mike said flatly. Caroline's eyes bugged out and she let out a small gasp, embarrassed at the thought his parents would think she was using Mike. Despite her protestations that she didn't care what they thought of her, Caroline really did want to impress them only because she knew they were Mike's parents and he was an important fixture in her life. And despite his protestations that *he* didn't care what his parents thought of him, Caroline knew their admiration and respect were something Mike missed and desired. Mike let out a low chuckle, letting everyone know he was only joking.

"Has he always been like this?" said Caroline, turning to Mrs. Barnsworth.

"Afraid so," she replied.

"True," said Mike, considering the question and response and happily acknowledging that he was the way he was.

• • •

The large Catholic church was filled to capacity with men in dark suits and women in conservative black dresses. Caroline wondered if the original Michael Barnsworth had this many friends or whether they were merely business associates paying their respects. Based on what Mike had told her about his grandfather, it was likely the latter.

The priest, Reverend Carmichael, was a frail, old man whose hands trembled as he clutched his worn Bible. According to Mike, he had presided over Barnsworth family ceremonies – baptisms, weddings, and funerals – for what was likely the past seventy years. Dressed in traditional black vestments, he read prayers and said comforting words intended to console those in attendance.

As Caroline held Mike's hand, she glanced over and noticed that he looked wholly impassive throughout the service. Over the course of an hour, they sat and stood, sat and stood.

The priest offered the option of kneeling and Caroline noticed that Mike's parents reverentially bowed onto the padded wooden kneelers. Mike's choice to remain standing didn't go unnoticed by his father. But Mike continued to stare straight ahead with an unreadable expression on his face.

When it came time for the eulogy, Mike's father stood and walked toward the podium. Caroline squeezed Mike's hand. He looked over at her and she gave him a slight grin. He grinned back, lifting her hand to his lips and gently kissing her knuckles.

Mr. Barnsworth spoke of a highly successful man – a philanthropic man – but didn't shed a tear nor did his voice waver with any sense of emotion. It was like he was reading an obituary from *The Economist*, if they ran those types of stories. It was sterile and dispassionate.

When Mr. Barnsworth finished the eulogy, Reverend Carmichael returned to the podium and offered one last closing prayer. "That concludes our morning service. The family invites you to attend a reception at the home of Michael and Gwen Barnsworth. Ushers will provide you with directions as you leave," said the priest.

Mike continued to hold Caroline's hand as she brushed her thumb back and forth in a comforting manner. "I have to go over to the funeral procession. Wait for me?"

"Of course," she said. "I'll just be over there," she continued, pointing to a small alcove to the right of the altar.

Mike gave her hand a squeeze and smiled at her before walking over to his parents and taking his place next to his dad. Caroline noticed they were both dressed in tailored black suits, white dress shirts, and subdued ties. She couldn't help but think how easy it would have been for Mike to become a man just like his father. Mrs. Barnsworth stood on the other side of her husband wearing a classy black suit adorned by a simple, single strand of cultured pearls, matching jewels in each ear.

A steady stream of guests walked through the procession line, each taking their turn to offer Mike and his parents sympathetic platitudes and trite words of comfort.

"Thank you. Thank you for coming," Mike mumbled as each hand was raised to shake his. Caroline glanced over and gave Mike a kindly look and small smile. He winked back at her. As she watched the scene unfold, a man, mid-thirties, in a sharp business suit and highly-polished loafers walked over to her.

"Charles Barnsworth, from Chicago," he said, reaching out his hand to shake hers.

"Caroline Johnson," she said, giving him a small smile. "Sorry for your loss," she added.

"Oh, thank you. Yes, Uncle Michael was quite a man. We were... very close," he said, looking down and shaking his head, as if trying to elicit sympathy from Caroline.

"So, how long have you and Michael been dating?" he asked.

"Oh, we're just friends...from business school," she said distractedly, watching Mike.

"The Crimson? Me too. Class of 2004," he said, now looking at her with hungry eyes. "I bet you'd turn *crimson* right now if I told you what I was thinking." Caroline let out a nervous giggle, made uncomfortable by Charles' inappropriate overture. "Maybe I could tell you this weekend... on my yacht. She's a forty-footer," he said, moving so close to Caroline she could feel the heat emanating from his body.

If he says it's not the size of the boat but the motion in the ocean, I think I'm gonna hurl, she thought, her lips turning downward and her shoulders drawing in.

"Why, that's a mighty kind offer, but Mike and I are headin' back this weekend," she said politely. "Will you please excuse me," she said as she walked away, a disgusted chill running through her.

When the last of the banal memorial greetings was uttered, Mike shook his dad's hand formally and gave his mom a warm hug. Caroline walked over to meet him.

"Hey there. How are you holdin' up?" she said, giving him a small reassuring smile and grabbing his hand.

"Holding up? Does this refer to my grandfather's death or being forced to endure three days with these people?" he replied dryly.

"Maybe a little of both," she shrugged.

"I'm holding up," he said. "I saw you talking to my cousin Charlie." He nodded his head in Charlie's direction and noticed him eyeing Caroline lustfully.

"Oh, yes. Charles is quite the character. After I told him we were just friends, he started tellin' me how successful he was."

"That doesn't surprise me," he said, pursing his lips and slowly nodding his head. "He's just about that classy to hit on you at a funeral."

"Well lucky for me, I've sworn off men for the time bein', so I'm immune to that sort of stuff," she said, patting his chest with her hand.

"If you knew what a douche Charlie was, you *really* would know how lucky you are."

"So where to now?" she asked.

"Back to my parents' house. Is that okay?"

"Of course. Whatever you need. I'm here." Mike put his arm around Caroline and pulled her to his side, kissing the top of her head. They walked with their arms around each other to the waiting town car.

•　　•　　•

Their visit complete, the black town car to take Caroline and Mike back to the airport waited patiently in the oversized circle drive. Mike, Caroline, and Mr. and Mrs. Barnsworth stood on the brick pathway leading away from the front door. Mike had a gentle hand placed on the small of Caroline's back, guiding her forward. Mrs. Barnsworth took note. To begin the goodbyes, Mike approached his father first, out of respect for the new family patriarch.

"Bye, Dad," he said.

"Sure I can't convince you to come home?" Mr. Barnsworth said to Mike.

"Nope," said Mike flatly. Mr. Barnsworth shook his head, as if that was what he expected to hear. He reached his hand out and shook Mike's hand. Mr. Barnsworth turned to Caroline and began to reach his hand out. She bounded forward and hugged him.

"It was so nice to meet you. Obviously not under these circumstances. But nice nonetheless," she said. Mr. Barnsworth couldn't help but smile at her genuine warmth, feeling glad that Mike had someone of her temerity and quality in his life.

"Nice to meet you too, young lady." Meanwhile, Mike walked over to his mom and wrapped an arm around her.

"Are you happy?" she asked him.

"Yeah, I am," he said, nodding his head slowly as if truly considering the question.

"Does she make you happy?" she asked.

"I told you. We're just friends," he corrected her.

"I know what you said. But I also know what I see. Does she make you happy?"

"Yeah, she does," he said, giving her a small smile through pursed lips.

"Good. I like this girl," she said, giving Mike's waist a squeeze. She pulled away from him and then met his body straight on. Reaching her arms around him, she gave him a hug and a small kiss on the cheek. As she pulled away, she turned to Caroline, who had just joined them. She leaned in to Caroline for a swift hug.

"Lovely to meet you, dear," she said with genuine affection.

"It was so nice to meet you too. And I'm gonna send you my new catalog when it's ready. You pick out anythin' you'd like. My treat," responded Caroline.

"I'll look forward to it." Mike walked toward the town car and placed his leather satchel and Caroline's messenger bag into the back seat. Mrs. Barnsworth, making sure Mike was out of earshot, continued, "Hold onto him." She looked into Caroline's eyes and smiled.

"What?" said Caroline, taken aback by her choice of words.

"Just hold onto him," she repeated. Caroline nodded and proceeded to enter the town car.

•   •   •

Mike's head rested on Caroline's shoulder as they entered their third hour of the five-hour trip back to Los Angeles. A first-class flight attendant clad in navy blue brought two blankets to Caroline and gently placed one over Mike as Caroline grabbed the end and pulled it up toward his neck. Mike let out a contented sigh and adjusted himself on Caroline.

"Just hold onto him." She heard Mrs. Barnsworth's words over and over in her head. "Just hold onto him." And then she thought back to Mimi's words: "Find something you love and just hold onto it." Her mind flashed to Mike and all of the moments they'd shared:

Mike flashing his dazzling smile at her on the first day of Harvard classes, Starbucks latte in hand.

His boyish exuberance during their Nerf gun fight as he raised his arms in victory.

How he knew what she needed – someone to make her laugh, put her at ease, and push the envelope. How he knew she wanted someone that "gets" her.

The myriad of kind and encouraging words: "Don't let Caroline here undersell herself. She's quite remarkable," and, "You're an amazing woman, Caroline Johnson. Don't let anyone tell you differently," among others.

When Sam dumped her, Mike's admission that there's never anything wrong with being with someone that makes you happy.

His advice that being able to talk honestly and openly with your partner was the cornerstone to any solid relationship.

The afterglow of their passionate trysts and how he had made her body feel. How sated she felt in his arms.

Did she love Mike? Could she love Mike? She wondered. *Promiscuous Mike? Scoundrel Mike?* A small "v" formed between her eyes. *No. Inconceivable.* Her mind continued to think. *Bawdy Mike? Hilarious Mike? Fun-to-argue-with Mike?* She smiled, considering the possibility. *Easy-to-talk-to Mike? Thoughtful Mike? Kind-hearted Mike? Holy hell*, she thought, her heart pounding. *I'm in love with Mike! It was a revelation. How had she not seen it before?*

She couldn't help but run through all of the scenarios in her head. *Does he feel the same way about me? Should I tell him how I feel? What if he doesn't feel the same? How will my unrequited love alter our friendship?* Then she laughed a quiet laugh to herself as she realized the person she would ask for advice in this situation was Mike. What would he say?

I've never held back my feelings from him before. Never cared how he would react, she thought. *He would tell me to do what feels right – consequences be damned.*

She let out a deep sigh. She shifted her body slightly to the left, jostling Mike, who lifted his head. She looked at him intently.

"I'm sorry," she said. Mike, groggy from being awoken mid-sleep, readjusted himself on her shoulder.

"It's okay," he muttered.

"No, not for wakin' you," Caroline said. She moved her shoulder to jostle Mike again and placed her hand on his cheek. "I'm sorry for not seein' what's in front of me." Mike blinked, adjusting to open eyes.

"What?" he said.

"I don't know why I didn't see it before. It's always been you. There's no one else that makes me feel so comfortable and safe. I never have to think about what I'm gonna say or how you're gonna react. I can totally be myself. There's no one that makes me laugh – full-on belly laughs – every day like you do. And there's no one that I have more fun hangin' out with or arguin' with."

Mike blinked rapidly a few more times and then stared at her. Caroline wrung her hands in her lap and wondered what was going through his mind.

"You're saying that you want to be with me, after all of this time?" he questioned, his chin down, squinting his green eyes at her.

"Yes." She pulled her shoulders back and straightened herself up. "I'm sorry," she repeated, biting her lip nervously, staring longingly into his eyes, tears beginning to well.

"I forgive you," he said, smiling and nodding his head. His thumb brushed a falling tear away from her cheek.

Caroline exhaled, not realizing she had been holding her breath. She leaned in and kissed him on the lips before pulling back, searching his eyes for a reaction. He reached his hand up and gently grasped her chin, lifting her head up. He returned her kiss with an intensity and force that resonated deep within her.

"You don't know how long I've waited to hear you say that. I'm the best version of myself when I'm with you," he said, stroking her cheek with his fingers.

"This is your best version?" asked Caroline, cocking her head to the side and grinning at him. Mike laughed a low growl.

"Sad, but true," he responded, nodding his head up and down before flashing her a dimpled smile. "I've said it before, Caroline. You're amazing. And I'm one lucky SOB if I get to be the one who makes you laugh and makes you smile every day," he said, still stroking her cheek gently with his fingers.

"I love you. It's always been you," she sighed.

"I know," he said smugly. She laughed and shook her head. "Incorrigible."

"I know," he repeated, scrunching up his face and nodding his head knowingly. Then he leaned in and kissed her again.

And that's pretty much how it happened. How she found her clutch. The one Aunt Mimi had told her about. The one she loved and needed to just... hold onto.

Epilogue

*I*t's 3 a.m. and I can't sleep. I'm lying here in bed watching Caroline's chest rise and fall and her perfect, pink lips open and close slightly as she sleeps. Fuck, she's beautiful. It was only a few hours since I was buried deep inside her and I'm already hard just thinking about being there again.

But now's not the time for that. It's been six months since that plane ride where she finally told me she loved me. And they've been the best six fucking months of my life. She's it for me and always has been. Just been a helluva time waiting for her to catch up.

I reach over to my nightstand, open the drawer and pull out the small silk pouch. Rubbing my fingers over it, I can't help but think back to that phone call I got nearly three years ago.

"Hello. I'm trying to reach Michael Barnsworth."

"I'm Mike. What can I do for you?"

"Mr. Barnsworth. My name is Fred Jenkins and I'm the estate executor for Mimi Johnson."

"Is this about Caroline? Is she okay?"

I remember a crippling fear overcoming me as I thought something might have happened to her.

"No. Caroline is just fine, all things considered. As I'm sure you're aware, Mimi was very dear to her."

"Absolutely. I know all about their special relationship. So, if this isn't about Caroline, what is this concerning?"

"Mimi left something for you with strict instructions that I contact you directly, outside the knowledge of the rest of the family."

Came as a big shock to know that Mimi left me something in her will. And that she didn't want any of the Johnsons to know about it. Hell, I had only met her two times – briefly at Harvard graduation and then again that time she came to Los Angeles for a week to visit Caroline. But I fell in love with her right away. She was the perfect combination of sassy and sweet. I could tell that back in her day she was quite the hell raiser and had no doubt she was still a woman who always got what she wanted.

I pull the letter out of the little bag and read it again. I've read it dozens of times over these last few months, but today is different. Today is going to be special.

My dearest Mike:

If you are reading this letter, which I had typed because Caroline is always complaining that she can't read my handwriting, I've gone on to greener pastures. And that means Caroline is now going to need you more than ever.

I know you've been a good friend to her for a long time, but I also know that you want more. Don't sit there trying to deny it. I may be an old lady, but with age comes wisdom and the right to say whatever I damn well want to. I know love when I see it. And I could see it in your eyes last year when I spent time with you. And I can see it in Caroline's eyes even if she hasn't figured it out yet. So be patient with her. Stay by her side and give her time to realize you're two peas in a pod.

When you come to the time she's ready to hold onto you, I want you to have this. Caroline's Uncle Danny gave me this ring and promised his undying love to me. We were happily married for 39 years before he passed into the next world. I have no doubt we are together now as if no time has passed at all.

I can tell you're a special young man, just like my Danny was. I want you and Caroline to be as happy as we were. Take care of my sweet girl.

Much love,
Mimi

And dammit if this spitfire of a woman wasn't right. It took some time for Caroline to come to her senses and being patient was starting to wear on my, well patience. But she finally came around and I've spent the better part of six months making sure she doesn't regret it. And now I've got a plan to make sure she'll spend the rest of her life letting me prove to her I was the best decision she ever made.

• • •

It's Monday and the bar is closed. So this evening, I settle Caroline on the couch to watch a movie. She's sitting in a plain white T-shirt and pair of pink polka dotted pajama pants. Her face is scrubbed free of make-up and her hair is pulled up into a messy ponytail. She takes my breath away and I still can't believe she's mine.

I ordered in her favorite dinner from the Thai place around the corner and settle her onto the couch, hitting play on the DVD player to start the movie I compiled. I head into the kitchen to get her a glass of wine while she starts to watch.

"Hey, where's the remote?" she calls out. "There seems to be some sort of preview on." I walk back into the room and see her watching Billy Crystal tell Meg Ryan that he's figured out he wants to spend the rest of her life with her in *When Harry Met Sally*.

"Yeah, I think it's a montage of movie scenes. Don't know where the remote is. Just sit back and relax," I tell her, sitting down next to her and handing her some Chardonnay.

After Harry confesses his love, the DVD transitions to Adam Sandler's Robbie serenading the love of his life on an airplane in *The Wedding Singer*. Caroline just sits and watches with a smile on her face. After Colin Firth learns Portuguese to propose to his beautiful housekeeper in *Love Actually*, Caroline's mouth gapes open.

It's not until a scene from *Pride and Prejudice* appears, where Mr. Darcy tells Elizabeth, "You have bewitched me, body and soul, and I love, I love, I love you. I never wish to be parted from you from this day on," does she grab my hand. She doesn't look at me but continues to stare at the TV, my hand sitting in hers. After proposal scenes from *Gone with the Wind, Walk the*

Line, While You Were Sleeping and *Love Story*, my ugly mug appears on the screen.

"Caroline. I can't imagine my life without you in it and I'm asking you to marry me. Share my life with me. Have fun with me. Roll your eyes at me. Drink wine with me. Excite me. Use your fake southern accent with me. Watch Tom Cruise movies with me. Laugh with me. Fight with me. Make up with me. Sing off key in the car with me. Have babies with me. Grow old with me. Be with me always."

I'm not sure if she even noticed that I had moved from her side and was down on bended knee. Finally, her eyes shift from the TV screen to my expectant face.

If being proposed to wasn't enough to bring her to tears, seeing me holding Mimi's diamond and sapphire ring in my hand has her blubbering. And seeing her cry is always like a punch in the gut to me.

"Aww. Don't cry," I start, putting my arms around her.

"H-h-h how?" she breathes.

"Mimi left it to me after she passed, so when you finally got your head on straight, I could give it to you." Channeling my inner Julia Roberts from a scene from *Notting Hill*, which we watched last week, I continue, "Caroline, I'm just a boy, standing in front of a girl, asking her to marry him." She finally lets out a laugh.

"Yes. Yes, I will marry you," she says, sobbing and smiling at the same time. "Mimi always told me to find something you love and just hold onto it. And that something I want to clutch is you," she says, holding onto my cheeks.

"That's not the only thing you want to clutch," I tell her, raising one eyebrow.

"You're incorrigible," she huffs.

"Yup. And I'm all yours," I answer smugly.

"And I wouldn't want it any other way."

The End

Keep reading for an exclusive sneak peek of

Starfish

A new, standalone romantic comedy from Lisa Becker

Coming 2019

(This is an uncorrected copy and may differ from the final
published novel)

Chapter One: Marin

"Dress for the job you want." Mom always used to say that. I remember watching her get ready for work when I was a little girl. She always took great care to select classic, elegant pieces she could mix and match together for a sleek professional look. She was a secretary for a rich, investment banker at a high-end brokerage firm in our hometown of Roseville, just outside Sacramento. Little did I know she was dressing for the job she really wanted – *wife* to a rich, investment banker at a high-end brokerage firm.

It's been fifteen years since she left me, then nine, and my dad for her boss. It's also been fifteen years since I've taken much stock in anything she has to say, but "dress for the job you want," stuck with me and has served me well, as I prepare for my orientation for a summer internship with Carla V PR, the most prestigious boutique public relations firm on the west coast. Everyone from major tech brands to television shows wants to work with her agency, which specializes in branding, media relations, social marketing and promotion.

While Carla runs a rather casual office, I'm dressed smartly (in black pants, a pink silk blouse and structured grey jacket) for the job *I* want – the four-month stint at Zamon, a tech company in Seattle. Carla hires four new graduates every summer and gives them a four-month position. If you can survive, you either get offered a full-time job with her or one of her clients. Alternatively, if she likes you, you can basically write a ticket to a job anywhere, as a recommendation from her opens doors. It's that prestigious and rigorous and I'm absolutely up for the challenge. Carla seems to think so too, having recruited me right out of my master's program in communications from USC.

I arrive early to the El Segundo offices, which are only an eight-minute drive from the apartment in Manhattan Beach I share with my college roommate, Claire. Our dwelling is a one-bedroom place above a larger family home located right off the strand. It's kind of small for the two of us and the rent is pretty expensive given the size, but you just can't beat the location. Plus it comes with two parking spaces, so we don't ever have to worry about finding a spot by the beach. It's also walking distance to a fantastic dive bar with dollar beer specials on weekdays. So there's that.

As I arrive at the offices, I find myself in the elevator with an attractive woman. She's really my exact opposite in many ways. She's tall, thin and leggy, where I'm lucky to break 5'5" in my highest heels and have a curvy ass and thighs. She's got long blonde hair in stark contrast to my shoulder-length brown bob. She is heavily made up, with perfectly-blended eye shadow, blush-covered cheekbones and pouty, pink-coated lips. I'm more comfortable with a quick swipe of lip gloss and a basic coat of mascara. She's wearing tight, dark-wash jeans, chunky, high-heeled boots and a clingy taupe-colored top, in contrast to my more conservative attire. Not to mention her clingy top sure shows off something quite different from my physique. She's got boobs – big ones. Maybe even fake ones given their size in relation to her skinny legs. Thanks to some padding from the geniuses at Victoria's Secret, I can pass for a B cup.

She looks young and when she pushes the third-floor button – despite the fact I've already pushed it and it's lit up – I figure she works for Carla.

"Do you work at Carla V?" I ask, as the elevator takes us up to the third floor.

"Yeah. I start a summer internship today," she says, turning to look at me. "I'm Brynn."

"Marin," I say, holding out my hand for a shake. Dad always said you can tell a lot from someone's handshake. (Too bad he couldn't tell what a sleazeball cheater mom's boss was.) Given Brynn's long bony fingers, bubblegum pink fingernails and loose grip, I'd say she's little competition for me and prospects for a long-term position with Carla V.

We make small talk while we wait for the other interns to arrive and I learn Brynn grew up in Beverly Hills and her father is a famed plastic surgeon. Explains the boobs. She studied communications and music at UCLA. Despite my earlier impressions, she's not a complete ding dong. Just looks the blonde bimbo part. She's surprisingly smart and nice. Too bad I'll be off to Seattle in a few days and won't get the chance to know her better.

We're soon joined by two guys – Rich and Pete who both graduated with MBAs from Wharton and University of Texas, respectively. Rich is a pretty intense guy. You can tell he's eager to work in financing. Pete comes across as pretty laid back. He's got spiky blond hair and a slight southern drawl. He talks slow, but animatedly and has a rather gross habit of biting his nails. He doesn't seem to have a particular niche, but I'm sure Carla's got the perfect spot for him.

The four of us spend the day going through human resource issues including payroll and tax forms, technology tutorials and a review of the Carla V Company Code of Ethics. We also meet all of the senior account executives at the agency we'll be reporting to one way or another. Before I know it, its 6:15 and we're dismissed for the day. As I'm walking out, I see Carla who calls me into her office.

"Take a seat, Marin," she says, gesturing to a white leather couch. I dutifully obey. One thing I've learned about Carla in the short time I've known her, you dutifully obey. Even at the young age of forty-two, she's already a legend in the industry. We read various case studies in grad school about projects she and her company worked on from the launch of the first virtual reality headsets for consumer use to the passage of Proposition 22, a controversial piece of state legislation. She's savvy and shrewd and very successful. I want to be just like her.

"Thanks," I say, as I watch her take a seat on the couch and wait for her to take control of the conversation.

"I trust you had a good first day and are getting situated okay?"

"Absolutely. I really enjoyed meeting the other summer interns. While I realize we won't all be working on the same accounts or perhaps even in the same city, it's great to be surrounded by smart people." I'm sure that came across sounding like a total suck up. But I did not intend it to.

247

"Yes, well that's a good point. I know we spoke about this before you came on, but I just wanted to confirm you are okay relocating and traveling."

"Yes," I reply, my heart racing. This is it. She's going to offer me the temp job in Seattle. I feel like jumping out of my chair and doing a happy dance, but I remain cool and calm.

"Good. Assignments will be made tomorrow, but I hope you don't mind rain," she says with a wink before standing up and walking around to her desk. "I'll see you tomorrow." Dismissed, I get up and walk away, turning back to say thanks before exiting the door. When I get home, I tell Claire the good news and we head over to our local bar for a few cheap beers.

"I'm going to miss you," Claire whines.

"I know, but you'll have the whole apartment to yourself. Just think of all the fun you can have without having to share a bedroom for four months," I offer, raising my eyebrows up and down. Claire and I have been roommates (and I mean literally sharing a room) since junior year of college, when we moved out of the dorms into our first apartment. We've both had boyfriends during that time which always made for some awkward encounters and tedious coordination. We've both been single for a while now and honestly that's just easier.

"Ah yes. All of the crazy sex I'm going to have...by myself," she finishes. I practically do a spit take before choking. "You okay?" she asks, hitting me between my shoulder blades.

"I'm fine," I say, raising my hand to ward off any more pounding on my back.

"Seriously. It's not like their lining up on my doorstep and without my wing woman..." her voice trails off.

"I'm sorry," I explain.

"You don't need to be sorry. It's only for a few months and then you'll be back, right?"

"Right," I say, but the truth is, I don't know what will happen. If things work out, I could stay in Seattle for good. If they don't, I'll be back here in LA.

In case I return to LA, Claire is saving my room for the next four months until I know for certain what the future holds. My dad, despite the fact he doesn't make a ton of money as an insurance salesman, offered to cover my rent while I take this mostly-unpaid internship for the next few months. I hate to rely on him. He's already done so much for me. That's why I've got to make the most of this job opportunity. My future starts tomorrow, so after a few beers, we head home.

Chapter Two: Brad

I don't even know why I'm here and I mean that on so many levels. First off, why the fuck do I have to be in an office to meet some intern we're hiring to do promotions and marketing while we're on our summer tour? Why can't Damon just handle this crap on his own? He's the manager. That's what we pay him for and believe me, he gets paid a lot.

Not that I'm complaining. I've made a shit ton of money these past few years. After toiling away in crap bars and small venues, Damon landed us a small label deal, which led to opening for Maroon 5 a few years ago, which led to a three-album deal with Atlantic Records, which led to some Grammy nods and now headlining our own tour.

We're finally big enough to draw the crowds on our own. Sadly, we're not big enough to garner the private charter plane to take us from venue to venue. That's when you reach the Maroon 5 level. That's what's next – at least Damon says so – and that's why we're hiring someone to help us raise our profile.

At least we've graduated from the bus tour where you sleep in those little coffin-like pods, packed in like goddam sardines. We'll still travel by bus, but stay in hotels overnight. Until you've traversed the country in a crowded bus with a bunch of sweaty, horny guys with little privacy, women throwing their tits in your face, a steady stream of booze and drugs and hours and hours with nothing but landscape to stare at, you won't appreciate a private hotel room and real shower.

Over these past few years, I've mellowed out on the whole scene. The constant partying and spread legs just doesn't do it for me like it did in the beginning. Don't get me wrong. I'm enjoying the perks, but not going overboard like Jase or Johnny.

That being said, I know this next statement is going to make me sound like an ungrateful bastard, but every day I wonder why I'm even in this band. Yeah, sure, I can play guitar and I've written a few songs attracting the attention of some prominent people in the business, but music was never really my dream. That belonged to my older brother Craig. He was always the one who dreamed of being a rock star.

Growing up, both of our parents were busy as teachers at the local high school. Dad taught computer science and was pretty damn good at it, when he wasn't nursing a hangover. I probably got my love of computers from him. When he was in a good mood, I loved helping him build them and program them. When he was in a shitty mood, though, you'd want to be anywhere else. That's when I started to follow Craig around.

Mom was too busy to completely insulate us from Dad's issues. She taught music and took extra jobs playing the organ at weddings or giving piano lessons on the side to make money to supplement what dad spent on whiskey. Even though she had a lot on her plate, she did make sure Craig and I had an instrument in our hands by the time we could walk. We both learned piano first and then showed an aptitude for string instruments. I started with viola and quickly mastered the guitar, cello, violin and even the ukulele – pretty much any string instrument you can find.

Craig took to the bass guitar. He would listen to Metallica, Red Hot Chili Peppers, Led Zeppelin and the Who for hours, watch their videos on You Tube and had posters of John Entwistle and Flea on his walls. He was set on perfecting the craft and being a famous musician one day. To that end, when he was thirteen, he started a garage band and let me – at age nine – play along. It was the two of us, Oliver Eastland, who remains the band's keyboardist, and a hot chick named Tabitha who served as lead singer.

At the time, I had a serious case of hero worship. I would do anything to spend time with Craig and his friends. I thought they were so cool and it was nice to be accepted, even if they did make fun of me for messing around with my computers.

After a few months, we started making appearances at local events like the annual Strawberry Festival near our home in Camarillo, California – midway between Los Angeles and Santa Barbara. We started playing more gigs and when I graduated from high school, we all moved to Hollywood to make our dreams – or I should say their dreams – come true. For me, it was more about spending time with the guys than the music. Don't get me wrong. It was fun and I was good at it, but if I had my way, I would be rebuilding hard drives, coding and basically getting my full computer geek on.

Craig said, though, if we stick together, we could really make it far. We'd get away from our dad, the sleepy town where we're from, and one day boys would have posters of *him* on their walls. Once we hit the LA club scene, we refined our sound. We hooked up with our lead singer, Jase, and drummer, Johnny, and officially formed what is now Kings Quarters. Fast forward to today and we just wrapped up the first four months of our tour and have four more to go.

Craig couldn't be more psyched to get back on the road. He gets a major rush from the crowd each night when we play. Plus, his long-time girlfriend Cyndi is along on tour with us. Looks like he's got everything he's ever wanted all wrapped up in a neat little bow. If only it were that simple for me. Once again, I know I sound like a thankless prick. I've been blessed many times over. It's just not fulfilling me the way I want it to and I don't see any way out.

I'm flipping through emails on my phone when in walks this tall blonde, who I'm guessing is our summer intern. She's attractive in an obvious, Malibu Barbie kind of way. I'm not the only one who thinks so. Jase can't stop making eyes at her and by the way she's looking back at him, it seems to be mutual. What do I care? At least someone should be getting some.

Not that I should be complaining in that area too. Once again, I sound like an asshole. There's no shortage of available and willing participants for guys like me. After a while, the one-night stands and anonymous sex with girls who just want to bang a guy in a band – it gets old.

I answer an email from my buddy Scotty and look up to see Carla and Damon huddled together in a corner. Carla asks the blonde – I never even paid attention to her name – to leave and calls out for someone else to join us. Whatever. I go back to email and then it smells like vanilla in here. Like the air freshener Cyndi sprays on the bus to kill the stench of us guys. Or like someone lit one of those scented candles you light to get everything smelling sweet and clean. I look up and, fuck me, it's a brunette wearing a brown dress wrapping around her body, showing off a curvy ass begging for a squeeze.

"Marin, let me introduce you to Damon Grimes, Jase Conners, Oliver Eastland, Johnny Davidson and the Osterhauser brothers, Brad and Craig," says Carla, gesturing to us around the room.

"Nice to meet you all," she replies, shaking Damon's hand, as he's the only one who extended his to her. I would have gotten up, but I've sprouted a hard on at the sight of her.

I see Damon give her a good look up and down, which just pisses me the hell off. I don't know a thing about this girl, yet I'm already feeling protective and possessive. Perched atop her head is a pair of tortoise-shell frames. Dear Lord. She's like all of my hot geek girl fantasies come true. *Put them on*, I try to communicate telepathically. *Put them on.*

"I was hoping you could tell Damon a bit about your master's thesis," says Carla.

"Sure," she responds. She taps a few buttons on the iPad she's holding and reaches for the glasses. *That's it. Put them on. Put them on. Bingo!* "My thesis was on the impact of search engine optimization on social media metrics," she says, turning the screen to Damon. "I created an algorithm which enhances SEO metrics by .0003%, which may not sound like a lot but could result in millions of new impressions annually," she explains.

Fuck. She's smart. Like really smart and hot. This girl is a perfect ten in my book especially compared to the skinny blonde who was here earlier.

"She's perfect," says Damon, turning to Carla with a big smile.

Chapter Three: Marin

These must be the guys from Zamon and Damon – likely one of the founders and the "amon" in "Zamon" – said I was "perfect." Inside I'm jumping up and down, but on the outside, I try to maintain a sense of calm professionalism. Things move rapidly in the tech space and I don't want these guys to think I get rattled easily.

I look around the room and really inspect my client. They look familiar, likely from all of the research I did on the company ahead of time. Three of the guys look like typical, hipster tech dudes, wearing faded jeans, worn out sneakers and t-shirts. Johnny, I think his name was, must be one of the coders. His eyes are all bloodshot and he looks like he hasn't gotten much sleep. Must be burning the midnight oil on some new app.

The last guy, though, he's got my attention. He's cute. No, more than cute. He's pretty hot. He's kind of got a Clark Kent thing going with black-framed glasses and dark wavy hair just begging to be tugged. Hard. *Really, Marin? You know better than to get involved with someone you work with*, I think. *Don't want to end up a cliché like dear old Mom.*

"Well, Marin," let me introduce you to your new client. "This is Kings Quarters. Damon is the manager and these gentlemen are who *Rolling Stone* called the next big thing." Kings Quarters?

"Wait. What?" I ask.

"This is your assignment. For the next four months, you will be on the final leg of the band's tour." I'm in absolute shock.